Dear Reader,

Magicians fascinate me. Whenever I see one performing on television, I want to know how he did a particular trick.

In doing research for this book, I had some of my questions answered but not all. I'm not ready to start holding magic shows in my living room, but I am much more aware of things when I observe a magician. I've learned to watch his *other* hand and to notice anyone else who comes on stage or goes near the props.

Sometimes life is like magic: you have to look quickly or you'll miss something. In *Sleight of Hand*, things are disappearing, both on stage and off, and Sadie is trying to look past all of the distractions to see what is really happening.

I had a lot of fun researching and writing this story. I hope you enjoy it as much as I did.

Susan Page Davis
writing as Carole Jefferson

Mysteries of Silver Peak

A Mountain of Mystery

Nobody's Safe

Silver Surprise

Wildfire

A Lode of Secrets

Time Will Tell

A Code of Honor

Empty Saddle

Reunion Dance

The Counterfeit Caper

A Blessing and a Curse

The Restoration Project

Lights and Shadows

When Lightning Strikes

God Bless Us, Every One

Instrument of Peace

Flurries of Suspicion

Heated Accusations

Piece by Piece

Things Unseen

Dangerous Beauty

Sleight of Hand

MYSTERIES
of SILVER PEAK

Sleight of Hand

CAROLE JEFFERSON

Guideposts

New York

Mysteries of Silver Peak is a trademark of Guideposts

Published by Guideposts Books & Inspirational Media
110 William Street
New York, New York 10038
Guideposts.org

Acknowledgments

Every attempt has been made to credit the sources of copyrighted material used in this book. If any such acknowledgment has been inadvertently omitted or miscredited, receipt of such information would be appreciated.

Scripture quotations are taken from *The Holy Bible, New International Version*. Copyright © 1973, 1978, 1984, 2011 by Biblica, Inc. Used by permission of Zondervan. All rights reserved worldwide. www.zondervan.com

Cover and interior design by Müllerhaus
Cover art by Greg Copeland represented by Deborah Wolfe, Ltd.
Typeset by Aptara, Inc.

Printed and bound in the United States of America
10 9 8 7 6 5 4 3 2

Prologue

YOU THINK YOU'RE SUCH AN UPSTANDING CITIZEN, BUT YOU ARE a heartless, conniving man. When I get the chance, you will pay for this. Thanks to you, that will be a while, but when the time comes, watch out! I'll be there when you least expect me.

1

SADIE SPEERS SLID ON TO THE BENCH SEAT IN A BOOTH AT THE Depot, beside her best friend, Roz Putnam.

"Oh, good, you made it," Roz said.

"Julie just got back from lunch." Sadie placed her purse on the bench between them and smiled across the table at Edwin Marshall, the town's handsome mayor. "Hey."

"Glad you're here." His smile held a special touch of affection for Sadie, and it warmed her. "We were just talking about the fair program."

"That's right," Roz said. "I've got a lead on a possible headliner act to replace the singer who bowed out."

"Who is it?" Sadie asked.

"None other than the magnificent Ainsley Rodin."

Sadie stared at her. "You're kidding! One of the most famous magicians ever? How did you manage that?"

"Well, it's not final yet, but when I called the booking agency, they said he'd just become available for next week. Something about the weather in California."

"Wow! I've seen him on TV, but... can we afford him?" Sadie cast an anxious glance at Edwin.

"We're already stretching the fair committee's budget," Roz admitted. "But I explained to the booking agent how tight things are here—and also how thrilled we would be to host Mr. Rodin. He said he'd ask and get back to me. Pray hard."

"I will," Sadie said. "I'd love to see Rodin perform in person."

"Same here," Edwin said.

Sadie looked up as a waitress stopped beside their booth. "Hi. I'll have the spaghetti western."

"Me too," Roz said.

"I'll have a club sandwich," Edwin told her.

"Coffee all around," Sadie added, knowing her friends well. When the waitress left them, she turned back to Roz. "So the fair starts Friday. Can he be here that quick? In just four days?"

Roz shrugged, grimacing. "We hope so. I asked Jerry Remington, and he said we could have a couple of rooms at the B and B for him. Don't tell anyone I said this, but I'm glad we needed a replacement. Personally, I'd rather watch one of the best magicians in the country than a second-tier blues singer. Not that I'm glad she broke her leg," she hissed quickly, glancing around to see if any nearby diners had heard what she said.

"Of course not," Sadie said. "But I'm with you. I love magic shows."

"So do I," Edwin put in.

"Do you remember the magician who performed at the opera house when we were in junior high?" Roz asked.

"Oh yes!" Sadie wriggled in her seat. "He was terrific. What was his name?"

"I can't remember," Roz confessed, "but he was the first professional magician I ever saw."

"Me too."

Roz snapped her fingers. "Marvin the Marvel, wasn't it?"

"I think you're right." Sadie chuckled, remembering how happy she and Roz had been that day. "I remember he did some levitating tricks, and he pulled a ton of stuff out of his hat. I loved every minute of it."

"I must have missed it," Edwin said.

Sadie focused on him, not wanting him to feel left out. "All the more reason to look forward to seeing Rodin perform. Now, don't forget about the auction tonight."

"Are you kidding? I wouldn't miss it." His eagerness was back. Sadie loved the way his steel-blue eyes twinkled when he was happy. Edwin had moved away from Silver Peak for many years after high school and had recently come back to live in his family's old home. He and Sadie had been sweethearts long ago, but they had drifted apart and found other life mates. They were both widowed now, and their long-standing friendship had grown into something deeper.

"I hope you get the Arapaho pipe you want," Sadie said.

"What is that?" Roz asked with a frown. "An Indian artifact?"

"Yeah, there's a big auction in Denver tonight with quite a few Native American items from private collections. Edwin's driving in to the city for it."

"Are you sure you can't go?" Edwin asked, eyeing Sadie hopefully. "I know I'll be late getting back…"

"Sorry. I promised Sara I'd take her and Mia Garza to the movies. We've had this date scheduled for a week." Sadie would do just about anything for her grandchildren, Sara and Theo, but she usually managed to have fun herself while doing it.

"Next time," Edwin said.

She smiled at him. "For sure."

The waitress brought their plates, and they began to eat.

"So what is this pipe thing?" Roz asked after a few minutes.

Edwin's face lit as he launched into a description. "It's a ceremonial pipe in a beaded case—authentic Arapaho work, circa 1850. It was given to a man who had saved the life of the chief's son. The family's had it all these years, but they finally decided to auction it as part of an estate."

"For real?" Roz said, her dark eyes wide.

"The auctioneer says it's genuine, and the provenance is sound."

"He's a very reputable auctioneer," Sadie said. "I've dealt with him a lot." She often attended Ron Waverly's sales, or submitted online bids to his auction house, when buying stock for her store, the Antique Mine.

"I didn't know you were interested in Native American things, Edwin," Roz said.

He shrugged. "I like anything that's connected to Colorado history, and lately I've picked up a few tribal pieces. My collection's not very big yet, but I'd like to improve it."

Roz nodded. "Well, that pipe sounds really special."

"It is," Sadie assured her.

───────

The next morning, Sadie pointed her Tahoe toward Edwin's house before going to the store. With any luck, she would catch him at home and could see his new acquisition. He had called her the previous evening, while she was still at the theater with the girls.

When she came out after the show and turned on her phone, she had seen that she had a message from him.

"What are you smiling about, Grandma?" Sara had asked as Sadie listened to the message.

"Edwin. He won the bid on the Arapaho pipe he wanted."

"Awesome," Sara said.

Sadie figured that by that time, Edwin was driving home. She sent a quick text: "Can't wait to see it." Then she put her phone away and took out her car keys. "Okay, who wants pizza?"

She was tickled that he had gotten the piece he had his heart set on. At quarter to nine in the morning, she pulled into the driveway of his three-story white house with its turret and gingerbread trim. She loved the old Victorian that Edwin's parents had left him. The garage door was closed, however, and she couldn't tell whether or not he was home.

She opened her car door and hesitated. He wouldn't sleep in this late, would he, even after his late drive home? Maybe she ought to give him a call.

As she reached into her bag for her phone, she heard hammering. Curious, she got out of the Tahoe and listened. The pounding seemed to come from behind the house. She closed the door of her vehicle and took the path that led to the backyard.

On the back porch, a man with blond hair knelt and hammered industriously at the decking. As he reached for another nail from his apron, Sadie stepped forward.

"Hello. Is Mr. Marshall in?"

The young man jerked his head toward her with clear blue eyes in startled mode.

"Oh. Hello." He climbed awkwardly to his feet.

"Sorry," Sadie said. "I didn't mean to interrupt your work."

"That's all right."

"I'm Sadie Speers."

He nodded. "Skip Stewart. I'm just working on the porch for Mr. Marshall."

Sadie nodded. "Is he in?"

"No, he headed out a few minutes after I got here this morning. Said something about Arbuckle's, I think."

"Thanks," Sadie said, her mind outpacing her by miles. Edwin had probably gone to get coffee for them both and was no doubt waiting for her to open the door to the Antique Mine.

"You can go in and leave him a message if you want," Skip said, waving a hand vaguely toward the back door.

"Oh no, I'll catch him downtown, but thank you." She turned and walked quickly around to the driveway and pointed her Tahoe toward Main Street. She didn't see Edwin's car anywhere near Arbuckle's or her store, but that didn't matter. Edwin had probably walked the few blocks and she'd missed him.

Sure enough, when she entered Arbuckle's, he sat at a small table near the closed connecting door to the antique shop with a mug of coffee and half an oatmeal muffin on the table before him. He jumped up when he saw her.

"Hi! Figured you'd be in before long. Luz has a standing order to bring you a tall black coffee. In fact, here she comes."

Sadie glanced over her shoulder to see Luz Vidal, who owned the coffee shop with her husband, walking her way with a steaming mug. She grinned and sat down.

"I should have known you'd be here. I stopped by your house instead."

"Oh. Sorry. I guess I should have called you."

She brushed that aside. "It's fine. I was thinking I could see your prize from the auction. But the young fellow working out back told me you'd left early this morning."

"Oh, Skip. Yeah, he's doing some work for me."

Luz set the coffee mug on the table and smiled at Sadie. "Good morning, lady! Can I bring you something to go with that?"

"*Hmm*, that muffin looks awfully good."

"You've got it." Luz turned away, and Sadie took a sip of her coffee. As always, it was the best. "So it looked like he was replacing some boards."

"Yeah," Edwin said. "A couple of them were starting to rot near the steps. I'm going to have him repaint the floor of the deck when he's done, and the railing."

Sadie nodded. "He, uh, mentioned that I could go in if I wanted. Do you leave the door unlocked when he's there?"

Edwin shrugged. "I thought he might need the bathroom. I also told him he could use the microwave in the kitchen if he wanted."

Sadie thought about that. "Seems pretty trusting of you, with valuable antiques in the house. How well do you know him?"

Edwin's smile faded. "Not that well, but I knew his grandfather. And he was recommended to me by Clark Langdon. Skip did some work for him a few weeks ago."

"Oh well, if one of the town councillors vouches for him." That seemed to settle it. "So when can I see it?"

Edwin laughed. "How about tonight after you close up? I'll fix dinner for the two of us."

"I can't turn that offer down."

Roz bustled into the coffee shop.

"Sadie! Edwin! Just the people I wanted to see. We've snatched victory from the jaws of defeat."

"No! Don't tell me—Rodin is coming?" Sadie almost squealed, despite her sixty-two years.

Roz grinned and pushed back a lock of her becoming shoulder-length gray hair. "He sure is. He'll do one show every night of the fair, and for a ridiculously low fee."

Sadie slid over so Roz could sit beside her. "Wow. Congratulations! How did you pull that off?"

Roz blew on her fingernails and pretended to polish them on her shirt. "Your humble committee chairman has the touch."

"Does she ever," Edwin said. "I can hardly believe it, on such short notice. I mean—Ainsley Rodin!"

Roz laughed. "Seriously, it wasn't just me. We called him at just the right time. It seems he was scheduled to appear somewhere in California next week, but the theater there was flooded, and so his entire week's contract was canceled. He'll come here with only his prop man, so we'll get a scaled-back version of his usual show, but…"

"But I'm guessing that's good," Sadie said.

Roz nodded. "That's why he was able to give us such a good price. He usually takes about thirty people with him when he goes on the road. Since he's only going to bring one guy here, we don't have to compensate him for all the other people's wages, or book rooms for a crowd."

"Fantastic!" Sadie hugged her. "I can't wait to see the show."

Sadie, Roz, and Edwin met on Wednesday at the Silver Peak B and B. Jane Remington brought them coffee in the living room, where they awaited the arrival of the new star of the fair's stage show.

"We're tickled to have Mr. Rodin staying here," Jane said. "Jerry's as excited as I am. We're giving him and his stage manager the two best rooms upstairs and letting them use the lounge up there as a private sitting room."

"I'm a little nervous to meet him," Roz admitted. "That's why I asked Sadie to come—for moral support. Well, and because I knew she wanted to meet Mr. Rodin too."

"It doesn't hurt to have the mayor with you either." Jane chuckled. "I'll set the extra cups here and bring out a fresh pot of coffee when they arrive, in case they want some."

She went off toward the kitchen.

"You were lucky that Jane and Jerry had rooms open," Sadie said. "They're usually packed this time of year."

"Well, the singer had booked the whole place for her entourage," Roz explained. "I think it was a blow when she canceled. Jane told me they'd taken a few reservations since they learned about the cancellation, but they weren't full by any means."

"I'm sure they'll make the guests comfortable here," Edwin said. "It's better than having them stay in a hotel in Breckenridge."

Sadie nodded. "Mr. Rodin will only be a mile from the fairgrounds. And I'm sure it will be peaceful here, if he wants to rest."

"So how did you do at that auction, Edwin?" Roz asked. "I forgot to ask if you got the artifact you wanted."

"I sure did." Edwin's boyish smile belied his gray hair and eyebrows.

"I saw it last night." Sadie leaned toward Roz. "It is gorgeous, let me tell you. One of a kind."

"I'd love to see it sometime," Roz said.

"You're welcome to, anytime," Edwin replied.

"I've rarely seen better beadwork," Sadie added, lifting her mug for a sip.

Edwin, who was sitting near a front window, looked out. "Someone just drove in. Looks like a rental plate to me."

"That must be them." Roz set her mug on a coaster on the end table and stood. "Should I go out to meet them, or wait until they come in?"

Sadie smiled. "Just spread your magic wherever you like, Roz."

"Ha-ha."

Edwin stood. "I'll go alert Jane." He walked into the entry.

Sadie placed a hand on Roz's shoulder. "You're not usually nervous about meeting people."

"I know, but I feel as though the whole fair committee should be here with me." Roz frowned. "Everyone was working today but me."

"Well, you've got me and Edwin, and the Remingtons. That's probably plenty of people for a welcoming committee."

"I know. I just hope we don't lose a lot of money on the show, with the last-minute change. We advertised blues music, but we're delivering magic instead."

"How can you go wrong with magic?"

Roz nodded. "You're right, and we're actually paying Mr. Rodin a little less than we would have the singer, even though he's ten times as famous."

Edwin returned, carrying a coffee carafe. "Jerry's gone out to greet them and get their luggage. Jane's going to wait at the front desk." He set down the coffee, and they all waited.

They could see Jane at the check-in desk in the entry, and soon the front door opened. Jerry's strong voice said, "Straight ahead there. That's my wife, Jane."

Jane greeted the guests, and the two newcomers chatted with her for a moment.

"We have some folks in the living room who would like to meet you," Jane said. "The fair committee chairman is especially anxious to speak to you."

She walked into the room as she spoke, and two men followed her. First came a silver-haired man about five feet, ten inches tall, with a pleasant, open face. He wore a dark gray suit and a necktie with colored starbursts on it that put Sadie in mind of fireworks. Behind him was a slightly shorter man of about forty, with light brown hair that just brushed his collar. He looked muscular and competent in his khaki pants and blue polo shirt.

"Mr. Rodin," Jane said carefully, as though she had been practicing the introductions, "I'd like you to meet the fair committee's chairperson, Rosalind Putnam."

Roz stepped forward, smiling, and shook his hand. "It's such a pleasure to meet you. I can't tell you how much we all appreciate your making room for us in your schedule."

Rodin gazed up at her, holding her hand in both of his. "Thank you, dear lady." After a short pause, still holding her hand, he said, "Tall, aren't you?"

Roz laughed. She had long ago made peace with her six-foot frame. "Yes, I am."

"You carry yourself well," Rodin said.

Jane seemed more embarrassed by this exchange than Roz. She said quickly, "And this is Sadie Speers, a dear friend, and our town mayor, Edwin Marshall."

Rodin took Sadie's hand. "Pleased to meet you, Mrs. Speers."

"Hello," Sadie said. "I've seen you perform on television several times, and I'm looking forward to watching your show in person."

"Ah, thank you." The magician turned to Edwin. "Mr. Mayor."

"Welcome," Edwin said. "Silver Peak is very pleased to have you here."

"And I'm happy to be here. Your town seems charming. And so beautiful!" Rodin gestured toward his companion. "This is Steve Parrish. He's my right arm. Couldn't go anywhere without him, and he was kind enough to give up what would have been a week off to come here with me."

"It's a pleasure," Steve said. "If you'll excuse me, I'll go take Mr. Rodin's things upstairs."

"Oh, Jerry will get them," Jane said.

Steve smiled. "Not Mr. Rodin's luggage. I'm the only one allowed to handle that." He nodded and hurried out of the room.

Of course, Sadie thought. It would be strange if a magician *wasn't* protective of his props.

"We won't keep you, Mr. Rodin," Edwin said.

Roz smiled. "I'm sure you want to get settled. But I'd be happy to give you and Mr. Parrish a tour of the fairgrounds later."

"That would be most kind. Steve will be anxious to see the stage, so he can plan how he'll set up. I understand it's an outdoor show."

"Yes, we have an open stage, with the audience in the grandstand," Edwin said. "If there's heavy rain, we'll have to cancel or postpone. The stage itself is covered, but we wouldn't want people to sit through a deluge to watch the show. The forecast looks good so far though."

"Glad to hear it." Rodin looked at his watch. "Five o'clock, perhaps? That will give us time before dinner afterward."

"That's wonderful," Roz said.

"Good. And can you recommend a place close by for us to eat?"

"We have several restaurants on Main Street," Edwin said. "Sophia's is always good, and so is Los Pollitos."

"Don't forget the Depot," Sadie said.

Roz nodded. "And if you like pancakes, Flap Jack's serves an unbeatable breakfast."

"Well, it sounds as if we'll eat well during our stay." Rodin eyed the two women quizzically. "Since I gave most of my troupe the week off before I knew I'd be performing here, I will need an assistant."

Sadie blinked at him. "You mean, a personal assistant—like a secretary? I think we can arrange…"

"No, no. I meant someone to help me onstage with the act. Preferably a woman, and I will accept an amateur, provided we have time to rehearse." Rodin arched his shapely white eyebrows. "Perhaps you would be interested, Mrs. Speers?"

"Oh, call me Sadie, but I don't think I'd be the best person for that job." Sadie placed a hand on her best friend's shoulder. She could feel Roz's excitement, like static electricity in the air. "Now, Roz would be lovely. She has a wonderful stage presence, and she has a fair amount of experience in amateur theatricals. I know she loves magic, as well."

"I'd love to," Roz almost gushed. "That is, if I'm not too tall."

Rodin laughed. "Not at all. In fact, I was wondering if you were a fashion model. So statuesque, and with such a striking face."

Roz's cheeks took on a becoming rose color. "Thank you. And, of course, I'll be happy to work with you." She looked at Sadie. "Roscoe will go into shock."

Edwin laughed. "I'm sure your husband will take it in stride, Roz."

Sadie said, "May I ask one question, before we leave you?"

"Certainly," Rodin said.

"Roz told us you're doing a scaled-down show this week."

"That's right. Because I don't have all my entourage, we brought only as much equipment as Steve and I could fit into the SUV."

"I hope that doesn't mean you won't be able to perform your famous vanishing act," Sadie said.

Rodin smiled graciously. "I assure you, where Rodin goes, the disappearing cabinet goes, as well."

"Whew," Sadie said with a chuckle. "I can't wait to see it."

"Perhaps you will come to the rehearsal tomorrow with your friend."

"I'd love to, if you don't mind," Sadie said.

"Not at all." Rodin looked at Edwin. "You too, Mr. Mayor, if you wish. Maybe you will introduce the act for us during the fair?"

"I'd be glad to do that, and to attend your rehearsal."

"Good."

"Will I need a costume?" Roz asked.

"Ah, yes. Thank you for mentioning that. Do you have something flowing and feminine? And high heels, perhaps, or ballet slippers?"

"I think I can come up with something," Roz said, barely able to contain herself.

"Maybe Julie could help you," Sadie suggested.

"Yes, and Jenna Henderson. She's a good seamstress. I'll call them and see if they can come over tonight, after we show Mr. Rodin the fairgrounds."

2

_____

ON THURSDAY AFTERNOON, SADIE AND EDWIN SAT IN THE FRONT row of the fairgrounds' grandstand to watch Roz and Ainsley Rodin rehearse. The magician walked his new assistant through several opening tricks, during which Roz stalked about the stage, waved silk scarves, handed things to Rodin, and gestured toward the master magician while bowing, indicating that the audience should applaud. She took to the role naturally.

Then came the vanishing act. Sadie was determined to figure out how it was done, though Roz had already told her that Rodin had had her sign a nondisclosure agreement.

"So don't nag me about it. I am sworn to secrecy."

"I don't nag," Sadie said with as much dignity as she could muster.

"No, but you probe relentlessly," Roz replied.

Steve Parrish had already set up the disappearing cabinet onstage. Rodin took Roz over to the apparatus and opened the black curtain on the front. He spoke to her so quietly that Sadie and Edwin couldn't distinguish any of his words, but after a moment, Roz got into the cabinet. Rodin spoke again, and Roz nodded. He closed the curtain and turned the cabinet completely around on its casters and tapped the back with his short wand.

"You see, no wire, no trapdoors," he said to the audience of two. He pushed the cabinet around so that the curtained side again faced the front.

"And now…"

He tapped the top of the box sharply with his wand and threw open the curtain. The cabinet was empty.

Delighted, Sadie clapped her hands.

Beside her, Edwin shouted, "Bravo!"

Rodin bowed and turned back to the cabinet. They could hear him murmuring in low tones, and Sadie could only surmise that Roz was behind the cabinet, or perhaps behind the rear stage curtain, enabling her to hear the magician while she was concealed from the audience. Having performed in past ensembles and introduced shows at the fair, Sadie knew this stage well. There was no trapdoor in the floor. Those had been outlawed for safety's sake. After a moment, Rodin closed the cabinet's front curtain and turned to face the grandstand.

"And now, I am sure you would like to see your friend again, and so I will bring her back to you." He waved the wand over the cabinet, tapped it twice, and opened the curtain.

Roz took his hand and stepped out of the cabinet, grinning from ear to ear. She posed and took several bows as Edwin and Sadie applauded vigorously.

Rodin insisted they practice the trick several times, and then they moved on to other illusions he would perform during the show.

"Oh, Mr. Mayor," he called out at one point, "would you come up on the stage please?"

Edwin left Sadie's side and joined Rodin and Roz on the platform.

"I'm honored that you'll be introducing the act, Mr. Mayor."

"I'm happy to do it," Edwin said. "We have a musical group who will open the show—local boys called the Skylarks. When it's time for the main attraction, I'll come up and present you. How would you like me to do that?"

Rodin handed him a card. "This will do nicely, thank you. Would you like to practice coming in from the wings and reciting it? By tomorrow, I am sure you will have it memorized. And after you do your bit, we'll go right into our routine one more time, from start to finish." He patted Edwin on the back and sent him off to the side of the stage. Then he took Roz by the hand and led her into the wings on the other side.

Edwin walked out to the center front and grinned at Sadie. With a mere glance at the card, he said in stentorian tones, "And now, ladies and gentlemen, for your entertainment and amazement, Silver Peak is proud to present one of America's premier magicians. He is assisted tonight by our own Rosalind Putnam. I give you the Great Ainsley Rodin!"

As Rodin and Roz strode on to the stage hand in hand and bowed to an imaginary throng, Anne Hastings, the high school's principal and also a member of the fair committee, slid on to the bench beside Sadie.

"Well, hi," Sadie greeted her friend.

Anne joined her in applause and whispered, "Thought I'd pop over and see how it's going."

"Great! Just great, and Roz is having the time of her life."

Edwin discreetly left the stage and joined them.

"Hi, Edwin," Anne said. "Are you going to do that every night?"

"I suppose so. The fair's a big deal for the town, and it will only be nine performances. I don't mind."

"It's good of you," Anne said. "We were lucky to get Rodin at the last minute."

"We certainly were," Sadie said. "I'm looking forward to the show immensely."

————————

On Friday, the fair's opening night, the whole family drove together in Alice's Jeep Cherokee. Sara ran to meet Mia Garza and her family as soon as they had parked.

"I want to look at the food exhibits," Alice said, and they headed across the fairgrounds toward the exhibit hall. Theo soon veered off toward a cluster of his own friends on the midway.

"I'm thinking about entering the Colorado Wild Raspberry Baking Contest," Alice confided as they gazed at tables of plump vegetables and jars of preserves.

"When would you have to turn in your entry?" Sadie asked.

"Not until next Friday. The judging will be Saturday."

"The last day of the fair," Sadie said. "You've got plenty of time."

"Yes. Any chance you could find Grandma Wright's wild raspberry pie recipe for me? I'd love to use it."

"I'm sure I could dig it out."

She and Alice continued on to the arts and crafts exhibit hall, examining the fine needlework, handcrafts, and woodwork. When it was time for the stage show, they wended their way to the grandstand. Sara waved to them from her seat with the Garzas, but Theo, Roscoe, and Edwin joined them for a front-row view of the performance.

"Was Roz nervous tonight?" Alice asked Roscoe as they settled in on the bench.

"Not a bit. She's looking forward to it." Roscoe's eyes gleamed, his pride in his wife evident.

Edwin took center stage for a minute to introduce the opening act, Spike Harris and the Skylarks. Spike, a tall, lean man with haunted blue eyes, led the group. He owned a music store on Main Street and taught music lessons there. Sadie loved to listen to his smoky baritone, whether he was offering a solo at church or fronting the Skylarks, a country-bluegrass-roots band. The fact that he adored Alice usually was not mentioned, especially around Alice, who did not return his sentiments.

After the first song, Sadie smiled at her daughter. "They sound good tonight."

"Yeah, they usually do." Alice clapped with everyone else, but as Sadie had expected, she didn't seem enthralled.

Still, the Skylarks proved to be in rare form that evening. Sadie didn't think she imagined the way Spike homed in on Alice for a moment whenever the lyrics turned romantic. At the end of the set, the grandstand was packed, and the crowd cheered enthusiastically, including Alice.

She leaned toward Sadie. "Okay, you're right. They're even better than usual."

Sadie smiled and relaxed. It was time for Edwin to return to the stage and introduce the magic act.

He had donned a dark blazer and tie for the occasion. His powerful build, patrician nose, and attractive shock of steel-gray hair would have made him stand out anywhere, but tonight he looked splendid. Without even glancing at his crib card, Edwin gazed at the audience, seeming to make eye contact with everyone as he recited the introduction word-perfect.

"And now, ladies and gentlemen, for your entertainment and amazement, Silver Peak is proud to present one of America's premier magicians. He is assisted tonight by our own Rosalind Putnam. I give you the Great Ainsley Rodin!"

Deafening applause and cheering greeted Rodin and Roz as they strode onstage hand in hand. They separated a few yards, and Roz, in a swirling, diaphanous dress and four-inch heels, made a graceful curtsy. She then gestured toward the magician, who bowed low as the roar from the audience crescendoed. He wore a black suit, a fingertip-length cape, and a top hat, which he doffed as he bowed.

Edwin slipped into his spot beside Sadie. "Roz looks great."

Roscoe's broad grin indicated that he agreed.

"Rodin's pretty spiffy too," Sadie said. "This is going to be terrific."

Rodin began his spiel, and started off by producing a full bouquet of lilies from nowhere and presenting it to Roz. She acted amazed and overjoyed and set them aside. He did several more tricks, then handed his top hat to Roz, upside down. He proceeded to take several items from his pockets, including a chocolate bar and half of a sandwich in a Ziploc bag, then tossed them into the hat. He walked across the stage to meet Steve, who came from the wings dressed in a black shirt and pants. He met Rodin and handed him a bottle of a sparkling peach beverage.

"I love the things you people drink here in Colorado," Rodin said as he opened the bottle, and the audience laughed. Rodin took a sip. "*Mmm*. Peach." He waggled his eyebrows and tipped the bottle up, pouring the liquid into his hat as Roz held it steady.

"There we go. That should feed the rabbit." He looked at the crowd with a startled expression, as though someone had asked him a question. "What? You don't see the rabbit? Well, he went skydiving today, but he'll be back any minute, and he'll want his dinner."

He waved his wand over the hat and tapped it three times.

"All right, my dear, turn it over."

Roz eyed him doubtfully, which Sadie knew was part of the trick.

"It's all right," Rodin said. "Go ahead."

Roz turned the hat over, and nothing came out.

"Let me see." Rodin took the black top hat and peered inside. "What, already?" He reached into it and lifted out a stuffed bunny. "Guess he got home sooner than I expected. He's already polished off his supper."

The audience applauded, while Rodin made the bunny vanish behind the flutter of a sparkly scarf. Several more tricks followed, each one seeming more complex than the one before.

"And now, I'm going to make my lovely assistant disappear, although I hate to." Rodin smiled at Roz. "I'll miss her terribly when she's gone. But, after all, that's what you came here to see, isn't it?"

The crowd began clapping.

"All right," Rodin said, holding up his hands. "My dear, are you ready to vanish?"

"Yes, I am," Roz said confidently.

They walked over to the cabinet and pushed it forward, to the center of the stage.

"Observe the equipment carefully," Rodin said, turning it around and tapping it with his wand to demonstrate its solidity. "The fair committee can vouch for the stage—there are no trapdoors beneath us."

The magician held out his hand to Roz. She took it and walked slowly to the front of the cabinet. She stepped in, turned, and waved. Rodin slid the curtain into place to conceal her. He then rotated the cabinet and held out a hand, drawing the audience's attention to it.

"And now the fair lady will obey my command. When I count to three, she will vanish. One, two, three." He tapped the cabinet with his wand and opened the curtain. The dark recess was empty. The audience burst into a brief but hearty round of applause, till Rodin held up his hand.

"I see my hostess in the audience," Rodin said, pointing at Jane Remington in the second row. "Madam, would you please think of a number from one to ten? Don't say it out loud. I'd like you to write it down on the tablet my assistant will bring you."

Steve Parrish carried a tablet and pen out to Jane.

Rodin proceeded with the short mind-reading trick, while everyone wondered where Roz was. During the rehearsal, Sadie hadn't seen a delay like this. Finally, the magician revealed the number he insisted he had read from Jane's mind—four. She held up the tablet, proving that she had, indeed, written the same figure on the paper.

Rodin smiled and accepted the applause that followed.

"I see you are impatient to see whether the lovely Rosalind will rejoin us," he said. "Let us see if I can make her reappear."

He walked over to the cabinet and held out his wand. "On the count of three, Rosalind, reappear. One, two, three." He tapped the top of the cabinet with each number, and then pushed the curtain back.

Sadie had her hands ready to clap, but she stared at the inky interior of the disappearing cabinet. It was empty. Her throat went dry. Where was Roz? Something was wrong!

Rodin did a double take as he started to turn back to the audience. Sadie thought she heard him say something in a hushed tone. Quickly he drew the curtain.

"Well! Apparently she disappeared to a farther destination than we expected." He walked to the edge of the stage. "I've heard roses are high lately." From somewhere inside his cape, he produced another bouquet, roses this time. He let go of it and watched it as it floated, seemingly without support, into the air and then above his head. "Yes," he said confidently. "They're high, all right."

Everyone laughed.

The bouquet descended, and he took it in his hand. Looking down at Sadie, he said, "Ah! Another one of Silver Peak's fair ladies. May I present this humble offering to you, Miss Sadie?"

Sensing that she needed to play along, Sadie rose. "Why, thank you, sir." She walked to the edge of the stage, took the bunch of flowers, which seemed to be made of sturdy paper, waved them high to the audience, and then took her seat.

Roscoe leaned forward so he could talk to her across Alice. "You think Roz did something wrong?"

"It's probably just a minor glitch," Sadie said.

"Now," Rodin said with a smile. "Let us see if the lovely Rosalind has returned from her metaphysical journey." He walked back to the cabinet. "One, two, three." He tapped it and slid the curtain aside.

The audience roared as Roz stepped out, gripping Rodin's hand. He murmured something to her, and she nodded. She seemed a bit shaky to Sadie; maybe it was just the high heels. But as Roz smiled and lifted her free hand to wave to the crowd, Sadie saw a large bruise darkening high on her left cheek.

Sadie grasped Edwin's wrist. "Look. Roz has a black eye!"

3

SADIE, ROSCOE, AND EDWIN HURRIED BACKSTAGE AS SOON AS the magic show was over. Roz, Rodin, and Steve Parrish stood in a tight knot behind the closed stage curtain, talking earnestly.

Roscoe reached Roz's side first. "What happened? Are you hurt?"

Roz patted his arm. "I'm a little sore, but I'm okay. There was a man back here. When I got out of…" She glanced quickly at Rodin. Sadie remembered that the magician had made Roz promise not to reveal how his tricks were done. "That is, when I was doing the vanishing act, I saw a man with a knife."

"A knife!" Sadie turned to her friend so she could look closely at her face. "Roz, what in the world? Who was he?"

"I have no idea. But Ainsley thinks we should call the sheriff."

"I certainly do," Rodin said. "We can't have people assaulted right here onstage during the show! It's unthinkable."

"I'll call Mac if you like," Edwin said, taking out his phone. "I'm sure he's here on the fairgrounds tonight."

"Thank you," Rodin said.

Edwin stepped aside.

"Honey, you should come sit down," Sadie said, taking Roz's arm. "You did great during the show. I'm surprised you could carry on so well after what happened."

"She was magnificent," Rodin said. "The idea! Who would attack someone like Rosalind? It boggles the mind."

"I'll say." Roscoe guided Roz to a stool that Steve had brought from the wings.

"I'm okay, really." Roz sat down, but Sadie felt she did it more to please them than because she needed to. "And he didn't really attack me. I mean…" She broke off when Sheriff Mac Slattery strode in through the wings.

"What's going on?" Mac demanded, looking from one to another of the small group of people.

"Roz was hurt by a man backstage while she was doing the show with Mr. Rodin," Edwin said. "Sheriff Slattery, this is Ainsley Rodin, the magician, and his prop manager, Steve Parrish."

Mac nodded to them but turned his attention to Roz.

"That's quite the shiner, Roz. Do you need medical attention?"

"I don't think so," she said, touching her cheekbone gingerly with her fingertips.

"Are you hurt anywhere else?"

"Well, I fell when he pushed me. I landed on my face, obviously, and my arm is a little sore, but it's just bruised. I'm sure I'll be all right."

"Did you recognize this man?" Mac took out his notebook.

"No."

"What did he look like?"

Roz frowned and looked off toward the wings. "He was white. Not as tall as me, but stocky. Maybe forty or so. Fifty. I don't know—I'm not that good with ages."

"Hair?" Mac began writing in the notebook.

"Light brown, I think." Her face cleared suddenly. "Oh! He had a beard. Close-trimmed."

"Clothing?"

"Uh…I don't remember. Some sort of jacket. Olive drab, maybe? I'm sorry, Mac, I just don't recall. It happened so fast!"

"It's okay."

"I missed my cue. I was a little shocked, I guess. It took me a minute to pull myself together, but Ainsley did some extra tricks to fill in the gap."

Mac took his radio from his belt, turned away from them, and spoke into it. "Kyle, tell the people at the exit gates to be on the lookout for a Caucasian male, age forty or older, with a short beard and brown hair, under six feet tall, possibly wearing an olive green jacket. Stop anyone by that description from leaving the fairgrounds, and beware—he's armed with a knife."

"Copy," came Deputy Kyle Kenmore's voice over the radio.

Mac turned back to Roz. "Start from the beginning, please, and tell me exactly what happened."

Roz looked up at the magician. "Ainsley and I were doing the show. Mr. Rodin, that is. He told the audience he would make me disappear, and I got into the cabinet."

"What cabinet?"

"My disappearing cabinet." Rodin went to where the rear stage curtains met and pushed one half aside. He pointed to the upright box that still sat out front, center stage, before the black curtain he held. "You can examine it if you like."

Mac nodded and looked at Roz. "Go on."

"Well, I spend a short time backstage, behind the cabinet and the black curtain, while he shows the audience that I'm not in the cabinet anymore. And he does a short trick in between. While I got out of the apparatus back here, I immediately noticed a man with a knife."

"What kind of knife?" Mac wrote furiously in his notebook.

"Bigger than a pocketknife. Maybe a hunting knife? Not a kitchen knife. I'm sure of that."

"Okay, what did he do? Did he threaten you with the knife?"

"No," Roz said. "Not really. He just kind of froze when he saw me looking at him. I was only a couple of yards from him, and all of sudden, he dashed over and shoved me. I fell down and whacked my face on the stage floor. When I sat up, he was gone."

"Can you show me exactly where he was?"

Roz got up and led Mac to the wings, stage left.

"He was right here when I first saw him. I was over there, by the gap in the curtains, because I had to wait for my cue to get back in the cabinet."

"Okay. What was he doing?"

"I don't know. He had the knife up like this." Roz raised her right fist to shoulder height. "Maybe he was going to cut something? And then he saw me."

There was silence for a few moments as Mac wrote more notes, and then he and Roz came back to where the others stood.

"There are ropes over there that the stage managers use," Mac said.

Steve Parrish said, "Yes, those move flats and props when needed."

"*Hmm.*" Mac frowned and looked up toward the lights and equipment suspended from the ceiling over the stage. "Roz, do you remember anything else?"

She shook her head and winced. "I guess I was a little dazed."

"I think you should let Doc Conroy check you out," Sadie said.

Roscoe nodded emphatically. "Me too, sweetheart. People get concussions from less than that."

"And you don't have to do the show tomorrow if you don't feel like it," Rodin said with a bleak glance at Steve.

"Are you kidding?" Roz's face took on its usual animation. "I wouldn't miss the show for the world. Unless…" She looked at Sadie. "How bad does my face look?"

"I'm sure a good coat of pancake makeup will cover most of it." The tissue under Roz's eye had swollen by this time, however. "But really, you should get checked right away. Maybe get some ice on that."

"Come on," Roscoe said. "I don't want any arguments. I'll call Doc, and we'll go by his house if he's there."

"Mr. Rodin," Mac said as the Putnams walked away, "do you have anything pertinent to add?"

"I didn't see or hear a thing, Sheriff. I knew something wasn't right, and I kept the act going, like I always do when there's a glitch. But I knew Roz was an amateur. I had Steve help me with a small trick out front, but then I thought, no, I should have had him go back and check on Rosalind. I was a little on edge, I guess. I hope you find out who that fellow was." Rodin shook his head. "It's terrible."

"Mr. Parrish, how about you?" Mac asked.

"I was out front, helping with the trick Ainsley did as filler. I took a tablet and pen to Mrs. Remington and had her write a number on it. When that was done, I hurried back here to set up for the next trick, but I was over on the other side of the stage from where Roz saw the man." He pointed stage right.

"You came up those steps from the audience?"

"Yes. I heard a thud when I got up here, and I looked in and Roz was on the floor. I ran out to help her, and she told me someone had pushed her. I didn't know about the knife then. Ainsley was doing some fast talking, the kind of patter he uses to cover a slipup. It happens occasionally—some small glitch— so he's always prepared for that situation. I peeked between the curtains, and I could tell the one on the front of the cabinet was shut, so I helped Roz get in, and then I went around to watch from the left wings, to make sure she was steady when she came out."

Mac made some notes. "And you didn't see the intruder?"

"Afraid not. I wish I had."

As he spoke, Alice, Theo, and Sara approached timidly from the wings.

"Is everything all right, Mom?" Alice asked.

"Hi," Sadie said. "We're not really sure." She looked at Mac. "You don't need us, do you, Mac?"

"No, but thank you, Sadie. Edwin."

"What do you say we go over to the Depot for some ice cream?" Edwin said.

"Yay," Sara cried. "Can we, Mom?"

"That's a good idea," Sadie told Alice. "We can tell you all about it over there."

Edwin looked back. "Mr. Rodin, Steve—would you like to join us for ice cream?"

"Oh, no thanks," Rodin said. "It's been a long day, and I think I'll retire."

"Just let me make sure all the equipment is secure, and I'll drive you over to the B and B," Steve said.

Rodin nodded. "And Sadie, if you talk to Roz, tell her to let me know if she doesn't feel well in the morning."

"I will. And by the way, the show was great."

"It sure was," Theo said.

"We all loved it," Alice added.

Rodin gave a little bow from the waist. "Thank you. You're very kind."

Sadie and her family, along with Edwin, traipsed down the steps into the evening air. The colored lights and blaring music from the midway hit them. The Ferris wheel spun slowly against the sky. Sadie could smell cooking onion rings and fried dough. Spike and the other fellows from the band were carrying their instruments toward the parking lot. The fair was in full swing, and only a few people knew what had happened backstage.

On the way to the parking lot, Sadie gave Alice and the kids an abbreviated version of what had happened.

"I sure hope Roz is okay," Sara said.

"Yeah," Alice agreed. "We saw them heading out, and her eye looked awful."

"I'm afraid it will probably look even worse in the morning," Sadie admitted. "But she wants to do the show tomorrow night."

"I guess she can, if it's not too swollen," Alice said.

Sara skipped for a couple of steps. "Maybe I can be her understudy if she doesn't feel up to it. I could learn how to do the vanishing act."

"Now, there's a pleasant thought," Theo said, and Sara scowled at him.

"Do I need to separate you two?" Alice asked in a menacing tone.

"I'll ride with Grandma and Mr. Marshall," Sara offered.

Sadie laughed. "Climb in, kiddo. Alice, Theo, we'll see you at the Depot."

————

Alice joined Sadie at the Antique Mine on Saturday, as she often did, and Sara came along with her. Sadie hoped people would stop in that morning to browse before moving on to the fairgrounds.

Alice surveyed two boxes of dishes and knickknacks Sadie had picked up at an early morning yard sale.

"Want me to arrange these?"

"Just that white box. I haven't catalogued the others yet. And I have a special job for you, Sara," Sadie said. "There are three old table games on my workbench in the back room. I found them online and printed out a list of all the pieces that should be there. Want to go through and check to see if anything is missing?"

"Sounds like fun." Sara took the list from her. "Are you going to see the show at the fair every night?"

"I don't know," Sadie said. "I might. Last night was a little scary. I'll definitely go tonight just to make sure Roz is okay, but as for going all week long, I'll have to see how things go."

"I told the kids they can't go every day," Alice said. "I'm letting them go this afternoon and do the rides, but I don't think we want to be over there constantly. Of course, I'll be going on Friday to take my pie in."

"Oh, I forgot to look for the recipe you wanted. I'll do it this weekend, I promise," Sadie said.

"Thanks, Mom. Did you hear that *Colorado Mountain Life* magazine wants to do a feature on the contest?"

"No." Sadie leaned on the counter, excited to hear more about this development. "Troy told me there might be some reporters from out of town here to cover the fair and interview Rodin, but I hadn't heard about the magazine."

Alice nodded, and her smile grew. "They said they'll feature the winning recipes."

"Wouldn't that be something?" Sadie said.

Sara's eyes grew large. "Yeah! Great-Grandma Wright's raspberry pie recipe in a magazine!"

"I sure do have great memories of her pies," Alice said dreamily. "But she's actually Grandma Sadie's grandmother, so she's your great-great, not that it matters. And don't forget, Mom—we're going to pick berries Monday morning."

"I'll remember," Sadie said.

Alice opened the flaps of the box. "What do you think is the best place to pick them?"

"Maybe out at Milo's. Of course, Ben Trainer has a nice patch on his ranch. Maybe he'd let us pick there."

"Let's go to Milo's," Alice said. "It's closer."

"Yeah, maybe we can go horseback riding," Sara said.

Alice shook her head. "No, this will be a business trip. We want to get as many berries as we can after the dew goes off, but before it gets hot."

"You check with Milo," Sadie said. "I'll make sure Julie can open the store for me that morning."

"Mom." Sara touched Alice's arm. "Will you ask Milo if he'll haul Daisy over to the fairgrounds for me on Saturday?"

"What for?" Sadie said.

Alice rolled her eyes. "They're having a gymkhana on Saturday."

"It's all games," Sara said. "Barrel racing, pole bending, relay races. No equitation classes or anything like that."

"Sounds like fun." Sadie arched her eyebrows at Alice.

"We'll see," Alice said. "If Milo's too busy, you'll have to skip it."

The bell on the front door jangled, and Sara scurried toward Sadie's workroom with her list of game parts. Alice took her box of items to arrange in the proper display areas, and Sadie stepped out to meet the newcomer, a man of about forty-five with shaggy, dark hair. He wore jeans and an open, zippered gray sweatshirt over a navy T-shirt, but what interested Sadie the most was the item in his hands.

"Hello," she said. "Are those handcuffs?"

He grinned and held them up. "Yes, ma'am, they sure are. Are you the owner of this shop?"

"Yes, I'm Sadie Speers. Are you looking to sell those?" Usually when someone brought an old item into the shop, it was for that purpose.

"That's exactly what I'm hoping for. What'll you give me?"

"Well, let me look at them." Sadie took the set from him and carried it behind the counter, where her magnifiers and other tools were within easy reach. "What can you tell me about these?"

The old bracelets were more oval than round, and they had a chain less than a foot long between them. They didn't look exactly like the ones she had seen Mac Slattery use, but Sadie couldn't quite pinpoint the differences. The metal was a dull silver, with a hint of rust around the lock.

"Those are special."

She looked up at him keenly, and he winked at her.

"What do you mean?" Sadie asked.

"Houdini used 'em."

"Oh, really?" She didn't try to keep the skepticism from her voice. Wouldn't they be all rusty if they were as old as the master magician?

"Yes, ma'am. He used 'em right here in Silver Peak, when he performed here."

That claim tempted Sadie to end the interview at once. She was reasonably sure it was bogus, but she managed to keep calm. "Do you have any documentation of that?"

"Huh?"

"Can you prove it?"

"Well..."

Sadie sighed and reached for a pad of paper and pen. "What's your name?"

"Tulley Morse."

"I'll do some research, Tulley. Come back in a day or two, and I'll let you know what I think they're worth."

"Oh." He stood uncertainly, watching her write on the pad. "Pete Osborn told me that sometimes you buy old things from pickers."

"That's right, sometimes I do." Sadie straightened and met his gaze. Pete was a junk picker she dealt with fairly often.

"Well, I figured this item would be of particular interest, since they've got a great magician performing at the fairgrounds this week."

"*Hmm.*" Sadie took a pair of magnifying glasses from a drawer and put them on. She studied the latches on the handcuffs and the places where the chain was attached to them. "How old do you think these are?"

Tulley shrugged. "I dunno."

"Well, you said Houdini performed here. When was that?"

"Uh... Maybe in the thirties?"

She pulled off the glasses. "If my memory serves me right, Houdini was dead by then."

"Oh well, I guess it must have been earlier then. My grandpa saw him perform. Maybe it wasn't 1930. Maybe it was 1903."

"I see. Well, I'll look into it. Do you want to leave your phone number?"

Tulley frowned and patted various wrinkled pockets. Eventually he brought out a business card and handed to Sadie. One corner was bent, and the front had a smudge that looked like mustard.

"That's my cell phone, but it's one of those prepaid ones, and I ran out of minutes yesterday."

"Okay," Sadie said. "Then how will I reach you?"

"Maybe I should buy more minutes."

She smiled. "Do you think?"

He eyed the handcuffs. "Are you sure you can't just give me a lump sum?"

"What kind of lump were you thinking?"

"I don't know—maybe two hundred?"

Sadie chuckled. "I don't think so. Let me do a little research. Drop by in a couple of days, like I said."

Tulley sighed. "Got it."

He left, and Alice came slowly to the counter, where she stood gazing down at the old handcuffs.

"Houdini, huh?"

"So he says."

Alice shook her head. "I never heard that Houdini performed in Silver Peak, did you?"

"Nope." Sadie opened the cash register, tucked Tulley's card under the cash tray, and shut it firmly.

"What was that?"

"His so-called business card, with his useless phone number."

"I see." Alice's eyes met Sadie's, and they both laughed.

More customers came and went, and Sara finished ticking off all the pieces in the game boxes.

"The Candyland is missing a couple of cards, Grandma," she reported, "but it's okay. You got an extra thimble in the Monopoly."

"Oh well, I guess it all evens out, then," Sadie said.

Sara held up her left index finger with a dull metal thimble on it. "I don't think this one belongs with it."

"I should say not." Sadie leaned closer. "That looks really old."

Sara grinned. "It says *Colorado Centennial* on it."

Sadie let her jaw drop, exaggerating her surprise and pleasure. "Good job, sweetie! I'll give you half of whatever it sells for. And I know a woman who collects old thimbles who will probably snap it right up."

"Wow, thanks!"

The bell jingled and the front door opened, admitting Roz.

Sadie and Sara stared at the blue and purple bruising around her left eye.

"Ouch," Sara said.

"That looks painful," Sadie added.

"It really doesn't hurt that much," Roz said. "Only when I touch it, so I don't."

"Are you going through with the show tonight?" Sadie asked.

"Planning on it. Julie's going to come early and help me cover it with makeup."

"Better ice it first and see if that will take down the swelling."

"I know." Roz grimaced. "Doc looked at it again a few minutes ago. He says I'll be fine, and they don't use leeches anymore."

Sadie laughed.

"Seriously," Roz said, "I'm on my way to the fairgrounds now. Ainsley and I are going to rehearse again, just to make sure I'm not shaky."

"I wish you'd take a night off," Sadie said.

Roz shook her head and winced. "I'll be okay. He wants to make sure I'm safe though, so from now on, his prop man will be backstage every time we do the vanishing act."

"Well, that's comforting," Sadie said. "I'll feel better knowing Steve is back there and alert while you're performing."

"I admit I will too. Not to mention Roscoe." Roz let out a little sigh. "I came by to tell you that Mac called me this morning."

"Has he found out anything about the man who pushed you?" Sadie asked.

"Not really. He said he didn't find any clues backstage, and the gate tenders didn't see anyone matching his description trying to leave last night. Of course, it had been a few minutes before Mac alerted them."

"Yeah, he probably got away before then," Sara said soberly.

Sadie nodded. "It's too bad they weren't able to catch him right then and there."

"Well, I'd better get going." Roz waved cheerfully and went out the door.

"Do you really think she can hide that black eye?" Sara asked.

"I don't know. Theatrical makeup can cover a lot of secrets." Sadie smiled as a customer approached the counter. "Find something you like?"

She was tired by closing time, but Edwin had invited her over for supper, so she went directly to his house from the store.

"This is twice in one week, you know," she told him as she watched him hovering over the grill.

"Are you complaining? Is it my cooking?"

She laughed. "No. In fact, I was thinking I could get used to it. You'd better not invite me over for a while. You're spoiling me."

"Impossible." He came over and kissed her on the cheek. "I'll put you to work for your supper. How's that? You can toss the salad."

"I'd be happy to." Sadie headed for the kitchen, where she felt almost as at home as she did in her own house.

He cooked the steaks to perfection, and Sadie enjoyed the meal and the company, but Edwin caught her covering a yawn as he was pouring their coffee.

"Are you sure you want to go to the show tonight?" he asked anxiously. "You look tired."

"Well, thanks," she said sarcastically. "Seriously, I do want to go. I'm sure Roz will be all right, but I want to be there to support her."

"Yeah, I kind of want to see her get through it without a mishap this time too," Edwin said.

Sadie smiled up at him. "But before we go, I want to see that Arapaho pipe again."

"Sure," Edwin said. "I like looking at it too. Come on."

She followed him into the room he had claimed as a study, off the living room. Sadie loved the leather easy chairs and the old rolltop desk. Some of the Colorado artwork Edwin had collected graced the walls. Julie had helped him decorate, steering him toward comfortable but classy furnishings and ornaments, not too rustic, but with a western feel.

He walked toward a set of built-in display shelves that he had put in since returning to Silver Peak. He kept his small collection of tribal pottery there.

Edwin stopped a stride away from the shelves, then slowly moved closer.

"What—?" His head moved quickly back and forth, and he reached out to touch one of the shelves.

Sadie stepped closer. "What is it?"

"It was right here." He laid his index finger on the edge of a shelf that held a small Navajo pot on either end. Between them, the greater part of the shelf lay empty.

Edwin turned to her, his features blank, but his steel-blue eyes in turmoil. "Sadie, it's gone."

4

"ARE YOU SURE?" SADIE ASKED.

Edwin swung back to look at the empty shelf. "Yes. It was right there."

"Okay, think. Might you have moved it to another spot—say, somewhere more secure?" She didn't like to imply that leaving a valuable artifact in plain sight on an unlocked shelf was not the wisest thing Edwin had ever done, but in her mind, logic would dictate layers of protection for something like that Arapaho ceremonial pipe and its exquisitely beaded case.

"No, I–I'm sure. I wouldn't have moved it."

"Call Mac, then."

Edwin brushed a hand over his eyes. "You're right." He took out his phone and stepped toward the window to make the call.

Sadie leaned in to study the shelves, careful not to touch anything. There didn't seem to be any dust on the pottery or the shelf where the pipe case should have sat. The rest of Edwin's Native American collection seemed to be intact, however. She knew that some of the pottery and a hand-carved flute with beaded ornaments hanging from it, from the Ute tribe, were choice pieces.

"Mac will be here in ten minutes," Edwin said.

"Good. Now, it might be helpful if you look around and see if anything else is missing. But don't touch anything in this area."

Edwin sighed and stood gazing at his display for several seconds. "Everything's there but the pipe."

"Okay, what else in the house is valuable, that a thief might target?"

"That stuff is the cream of the crop." He waved a hand at the shelves. "There are a few other things, I guess."

"Paintings," Sadie prompted.

"Yes. And I usually leave my extra credit cards upstairs on my dresser."

"Check them."

"Okay." He hurried out of the room.

Sadie walked slowly around the edge of the study, trying to see anything out of place, paying special attention to the windows. When Edwin returned, she faced him.

"Everything's where it should be," he said.

She nodded. "Then I guess we just wait. Do you want more coffee?"

They waited for Mac in the kitchen, with Edwin alternately sitting down to take a sip of his coffee and jumping up to pace the tile floor. Twice Sadie started to say something but then thought better of it.

Mac was punctual, though the ten-minute wait seemed interminable. Edwin hurried out to meet him on the driveway. Sadie followed, but waited on the porch while Edwin explained what had happened.

"Well, let's take a look," Mac said, mounting the porch steps. "Evening, Sadie. Feels like we've been seeing a lot of each other these days," he said, half-joking.

Sadie chuckled. "I know. And as much as I like seeing you, I'm not as thrilled about all these strange incidents. But we're lucky to have you, Mac. Thanks for coming so quickly."

In the study, Mac looked the shelf over carefully. He took out his notebook and began asking questions. Edwin told him how he had purchased the pipe at the Denver auction on Monday, and how much he had paid for it.

"You got any pictures of it?" Mac asked.

"Yes."

"There are some excellent ones on the auctioneer's Web site," Sadie said. "I could pull them up for you."

"I'd appreciate that," Mac said.

Sadie took out her smartphone and went to the bookmarked site. "Here you go."

Mac looked at the first photo and grunted, then swiped the screen to go to the next. "Can you send me this link?"

"Sure." Sadie took the phone and sat down before the rolltop desk to do so while Mac continued prodding Edwin for more details.

"I actually made a call to have my alarm system upgraded. I wanted to put a motion detector in here, and maybe a camera."

"But you haven't done it yet." Mac looked around at the corners of the room's ceiling.

"No. I have the system for the house, but...well, I admit I haven't always used it lately." Edwin sighed. "I should have had the pipe in my safe-deposit box, I guess, until the security company came, but I wanted to..." He glanced ruefully at Sadie.

"He wanted to show it to me," she said. "I'm sorry, Edwin."

"It's not your fault. I should have put it right in the bank Wednesday morning, after you saw it. The auction came up so fast, and I've been so busy with all the fair-related goings-on. I thought the security system on the house was enough for a couple of days." Edwin's usually cheerful face drooped.

"What exactly have you got for a system?" Mac asked.

"Alarms on every exterior door and the cellar door," Edwin said. "All the first floor windows too."

"Obviously, none of them was triggered."

"Right."

"Motion detectors?"

"No. Not yet."

"When was the last time you saw the pipe and the case?"

"Uh…" Edwin frowned. "Yesterday, maybe? I'm not sure. Yesterday was really busy. It might even have been Thursday night."

Mac wrote it down. Sadie wished she could be more help. She'd seen the pipe Tuesday night, when Edwin had cooked dinner for her, but she couldn't vouch for anything since then.

"Now, I want you to think hard," Mac said. "Do you know anyone who might want to steal this thing?"

Edwin sighed and shook his head. "Not really. I guess any thief might break in here, especially if I left the alarm off."

"Not just any thief," Sadie said.

Mac swung around, his eyebrows arched. "You have someone in mind?"

"Well, I can think of a couple of possibilities you might want to look into. See, I don't think it was just any old thief. This person took only one thing, as far as Edwin can tell. There were several other valuable artworks in the house, though perhaps not as valuable as the pipe. But he'd also left credit cards on his dresser, and I happen to know he has a habit of leaving his checkbook in the pigeonhole here in this desk. It's there now." She pointed. "The thief didn't touch those things."

"So who are your suspects?" Mac asked.

"Number one is the mystery man at the fairgrounds."

"The man who shoved Roz last night?" Edwin asked.

Sadie nodded. "We don't know who he was, but Roz didn't recognize him. Therefore, it's likely he was from out of town. No one's been able to get a line on him since."

"I'm working on that," Mac said. "I did talk to someone who said they saw a strange car on Jefferson Avenue yesterday."

"Here on Jefferson Avenue?" Edwin stared at him. "Do you think it's possible it was the thief?"

"Maybe."

Sadie swiveled the desk chair, thinking. "Couldn't they be the same man—the one who shoved Roz and the one who stole the Arapaho pipe?"

Mac shrugged helplessly. "Anything's possible. I need to find out more about this man in the car. It could be nothing. There's no reason to think it's connected to the man at the fair yet. I only mentioned it because it came up as I was questioning people about strangers in town. But, yeah, it would be coincidental if two showed up the same day."

"Okay," Edwin said. "It makes me wonder if he came here to pull off a theft and coincidentally interrupted Roz's performance."

"There don't seem to be any signs of a forced entry here," Mac said. "And what would a thief be doing backstage at the fairgrounds, anyway? There wasn't anything valuable back there, was there?"

"Not that I know of," Edwin said.

Mac shook his head. "I don't know, Edwin. Hundreds of out-of-towners came to the fair last night. I heard the gate receipts were good. But if I find any connection between Roz's assailant and the man spotted here on Jefferson, I'll let you know. Now, Sadie, you said you'd thought of another possibility."

"That's right," she said. "I dropped by here Tuesday morning, hoping to catch Edwin before he went to the town hall, but I was too late. A young man was out back though, working on the porch. His name was...*hmm*..."

"Skip Stewart," Edwin said readily. "I did have him do some work for me. He did a nice job. Thursday was his last day here though."

"But you had gone to Arbuckle's when I arrived, and you had left the back door open for Skip. He told me I was welcome to go in and leave you a message." Sadie eyed him ruefully. She hated suggesting that Edwin, of all people, had been careless.

"That's true," Edwin said with an uneasy glance at Mac. "I did let Skip go in to use the bathroom or microwave his coffee if he wanted to. That one day, I did leave the house while he was here, and I left the door unlocked. But I asked him to lock it if he left before I came back."

"You trusted him," Mac said.

Edwin shrugged. "Yes. He seemed like a nice young man, and he did good work. He was recommended to me by Clark Langdon. He'd done some work at Clark's house and business."

"But you didn't know this Skip Stewart personally?"

"Well, no. But he started work on Monday, and he always came when he said he would. He worked four days, and he left the place looking great—no spilled paint or wood chips left around. I'm very pleased with his work."

They stood in silence for a moment.

"Right," Mac said. "I'll speak to him. It's possible he may have seen someone come around while you were out—other than Sadie, that is."

"I suppose," Edwin said. "But I'm sure the pipe was here on Friday morning."

"I thought you said Thursday night?" Mac eyed him sharply.

"Well, yes, I came in here after the rehearsal at the fairgrounds on Thursday, to get my checkbook. Skip had finished up, and I paid him, and it was definitely still here then."

"Did Skip see it?" Sadie asked.

Edwin hesitated. "Actually, I showed it to him."

Sadie clamped her lips together.

"But I'm pretty sure that it was here Friday morning, as well," Edwin said quickly. "I came in this room before I went to the office. Surely I'd have noticed if it was missing."

"But you didn't particularly notice that it was here?" Mac asked.

"Well…I think I must have." Edwin frowned.

"Did Skip show any particular interest when you showed it to him?"

Edwin shrugged. "He thought it was cool, but who wouldn't?"

"Okay." Mac pocketed his notebook. "I'll talk to him, and I'll ask the neighbors a few questions too. I'm asking people about that car that was parked on the street a couple of days ago anyway. I'll ask if they saw anyone else around your place between Thursday evening and today, just to make sure we're covering the time when it went missing."

"Thanks, Mac," Sadie said.

"Let me take a look at the back door and the porch where Stewart was working on my way out," Mac said.

"Of course." Edwin went with him, and Sadie remained in the study, gazing at the display shelves and imagining a thief entering on tiptoe and snatching up the most valuable thing in the room.

When Edwin returned, she said, "It had to be someone who knew you had the pipe."

"You mean, because that's the only thing they took?"

She nodded. "That thief knew what he wanted. He didn't mess around with anything else or leave any clues. In and out, that's all."

"I guess you're right."

"So who else knew you got it on Monday night? When you called me to tell me you won the bid, I was with Sara and Mia Garza. I told them you'd won the bid on the item you wanted. And you talked to me and Roz about the auction at the B and B Wednesday, while we were waiting for Mr. Rodin."

"I doubt either of the girls came in here and took it, and I know Roz didn't," Edwin said.

"Of course not. But it's possible they mentioned it to someone else or talked about it in a public place and were overheard. Mia could have mentioned it at her parents' restaurant, for instance. I'm not saying she did, but anyone could have overheard a conversation there."

Edwin sighed. "It gets so complicated."

"Yeah." Sadie raised her chin as another thought occurred to her. "Did you have a housekeeper come in?"

"No, nobody's been in this week for that. But I've told Kaitlyn at the office, of course, and several other people. You know…"

Sadie met his gaze. "What?"

"There was another man at the auction who really wanted the pipe."

"Who was he? Do you know?"

"David Russell. I spoke to him afterward. He's a businessman-type, said he lives in Denver."

"How badly did he want it?" Sadie asked.

"Obviously not enough to keep on bidding. And afterward, he seemed all right with my having it."

"He didn't ask where you live or anything?"

"Not specifically."

"*Hmm.* Maybe you should tell Mac about him."

Edwin winced. "I hate to cause trouble if there's none there."

"I know Mr. Waverly, the auctioneer," Sadie said. "I could make a casual inquiry about Mr. Russell. If he's a regular customer, Mr. Waverly might be able to vouch for him."

"Well…okay," Edwin said. "I trust your discretion, and I think I'd feel better about that than a police inquiry. If Mr. Waverly seems cagey about him, then I can mention him to Mac."

"All right." Sadie looked at her watch. "We'd better get going. We've already missed the Skylarks. If we want to see Roz and Rodin perform, we need to hustle."

They arrived at the grandstand just as Spike Harris and his band were taking their bows.

"I'd better go backstage," Edwin said. "I think Rodin wants me to introduce him again."

"Hurry!" Sadie gave his hand a squeeze and let go. Alice and Roscoe scooted over on their bench to make room for her.

"Hey, you're late," Alice said.

"I know. We got hung up at Edwin's house." Sadie joined the crowd in applauding the Skylarks.

The short interval between the acts dragged on a little longer than it should have, and the people in the audience began to talk and call out to each other.

"What happened?" Roscoe leaned forward to talk past Alice. "Nothing serious, I hope."

Sadie glanced around to see how many people could overhear them. "Well, kind of. Nobody's hurt, but…well, I'd better tell you later."

"Okay." Roscoe arched his eyebrows.

Alice made a face that showed her chagrin. "Mom! You can't do that. Now you *have* to tell us."

Sadie patted her arm. "After the show."

Edwin jogged out of the wings, on to the stage.

"Good evening, folks. Sorry to keep you waiting. Once again, ladies and gentlemen, for your entertainment and amazement, Silver Peak is proud to present one of America's premier magicians. He is assisted by our own Rosalind Putnam. I give you the Great Ainsley Rodin!"

As always, the words thrilled Sadie, and she clapped with great enthusiasm. It wouldn't matter how many times she saw the show, she decided, it would still be special every time.

To her surprise, Rodin changed a few of the tricks in the first part of the routine and ad-libbed several jokes she had never heard before.

"He's really funny," Alice whispered.

"Yeah, he's a real showman."

Roz, too, had learned some new intricacies, and the show went along smoothly with Rodin frequently directing applause Roz's way. The vanishing act came last, and Sadie held her breath while Roz was out of sight, but when she reappeared in the cabinet and emerged smiling and steady, she relaxed. This was how it should be.

Alice went to collect her children. Sadie and Edwin waited by unspoken agreement with Roscoe until Roz came out, a little breathless. She looked wonderful except for the telltale smudge under her left eye, a deep shadow not quite covered by her makeup. She wore white capris and a salmon-colored top with bright embroidery, and her smile was irrepressible.

"Great show," Sadie said.

"Thanks. Could you see my black eye?"

"Nope, not from the stands. I can barely see it now."

"Everything okay backstage?" Roscoe asked.

"Perfect. Steve was right there when I disappeared. He stayed back there a lot during the show, except when he had to move props and things, just to make sure nobody was hanging about."

"I'm glad," Sadie said.

Roz looked over at Edwin. "Mac Slattery came by while we were rehearsing this afternoon. He said somebody saw a strange car sitting across from your house yesterday."

"Yes, he told me," Edwin said. "He's trying to find out more about it."

"Well, if it's the same guy who pushed me last night, I'll be ready to ID him." Roz touched her cheek gently and made a face.

Alice came through the departing crowd with Sara and Theo beside her. "Okay, Mom," she said sternly. "Why were you so late?"

Sadie sighed and raised her eyebrows at Edwin. "I guess we have to tell them."

He nodded. "Seems there's no way to get out of it, though it's not a pleasant tale."

"Why don't you all come over to my house for coffee." Sadie glanced at the teenagers. "Or milk and cookies. We'll tell you the whole story."

5

On Sunday afternoon, Edwin joined Alice, Theo, and Sara for dinner at Sadie's house.

"Are you going to the fair again tonight, Grandma?" Sara asked as they enjoyed the pot roast Sadie had made in the slow cooker.

"Probably, at least for the magic show."

"Why do you go every night?" Theo asked.

"Well, Edwin has to introduce Mr. Rodin and Roz, and to be honest, I guess what happened on opening night has me a little on edge. I just want to see her come back out of that cabinet in one piece."

"That guy isn't around anymore, is he?" Sara asked.

"Oh no, I sincerely hope not," Sadie said.

"I assume he's long gone," Edwin added. He sounded a bit glum, and Sadie knew he was thinking that his Arapaho pipe had probably gone with the stranger.

Sadie stood and picked up her plate. "Ready for dessert? It's oatmeal cake."

"Yum," Sara said.

Alice patted her stomach. "You've got to stop the desserts, Mom."

Sadie laughed. "You should talk. You're the one entering the baking contest."

As Sadie had hoped, the conversation turned to more pleasant topics than the theft and the stranger at the fairgrounds. When they had finished eating, Edwin said, "That was delicious, Sadie, but I think I'd better head home now. I've got some things to catch up on before the show tonight."

"Okay, I'll see you later," Sadie said.

"Do you want me to come pick you up?" he asked.

"No, that's okay. I'm going to hang around here this afternoon and do some research for the store, and I'll drive myself over."

"All right. 'Bye, Alice. Kids."

They all called their good-byes to him, and Alice turned to Sadie expectantly. "Mom, if I load the dishwasher, would you mind getting out that pie recipe for me?"

"Thanks for reminding me." Sadie shoved back her chair. "With everything going on, I keep forgetting to look for it, but I'll do that right now."

Theo stood and began to gather the water glasses.

"Look who I found in the driveway."

Sadie paused with her hand on a cupboard door and turned toward the voice. Edwin was back, and right behind him in the kitchen doorway was Mac. He wasn't wearing his uniform, but instead had on khakis and a polo shirt.

"Well, hi, Mac," Sadie said. "What brings you out here on Sunday?"

"Nothing big, but I wanted to tell you and Edwin both that I've been working on that lead about the car on Jefferson Avenue."

"Did you find out who it was?" Sadie asked.

"Not yet, but I've talked to three different people who saw it there. They all agree it was almost directly across from your house, Edwin. Two say it was dark green, and one says black. Two said a man was sitting in it. The third one wasn't sure."

"Could they describe him?" Edwin asked.

"Not really, though one thought he was middle-aged. She wasn't really sure what made her think that, but then she said she guessed maybe his hair was white. Or gray."

Edwin sighed. "Well, I guess we know why he was so interested in my house."

"I'm still working on it," Mac said. "It's the best lead we've got on your case."

"And maybe he's the same one who hurt Mrs. Putnam," Sara said.

"Well, it's a long shot," Mac said, "but if I catch up with him, of course I will ask about that."

"Thanks for coming by and letting us know," Sadie said.

"All right, take care." Mac turned toward the door.

"This time, I'm really leaving," Edwin said.

"'Bye again," Sadie replied with a grin. She took her recipe box from the cupboard and sat down with it at the table while Alice and the kids cleaned up around her. "*Hmm*, it doesn't seem to be in here. Oh, wait, I think I know where it is." She opened another cupboard, took out a loose-leaf binder, and began paging through it. "I put a lot of loose recipes in here. Aha!" She held up a yellowed sheet of paper with her mother's spidery handwriting on it. "Got you at last!"

She handed the paper to Alice.

"Thanks, Mom!" Alice smiled as she scanned the list of ingredients. "Yellow bowl full of fresh raspberries. I don't suppose you know how big her yellow bowl was."

Sadie laughed. "I do indeed. It's this one." From another cupboard, she produced her mother's old yellow-ware mixing bowl. "I think it's about two quarts."

"I can hardly wait to see how it turns out," Alice said. "I wonder if I can make it taste as good as your grandmother did."

Sadie turned around in her chair and frowned at the worn paper. "Maybe I should type that up and put the volume in while I'm at it."

"Probably a good idea," Alice said, "though I love using Grandma's handwritten recipe."

"Bring it back when you're done with it, and I'll type it up and send you a copy by e-mail," Sadie said.

Sara hung up her dish towel. "Can we watch a video, Grandma?"

"What? On a nice day like this?" Sadie glanced toward the window. "Why don't we take Hank out for a game of Frisbee? He's getting lazy."

"We could all use a little exercise," Alice said.

Theo strode toward the living room. "I'll get the Frisbee."

A rousing game followed in the backyard, with a light breeze tempering the August sunshine. As they laughed and romped, vying with Hank to catch the red plastic disk, Sadie knew this was another moment she would cherish. She pulled out her phone and snapped a few pictures of Alice and the children frolicking with the energetic golden retriever.

When the Macombs prepared to leave a short time later, Alice wagged a finger at Sadie. "Now, don't forget, Mom. We're getting those berries tomorrow morning. Milo's at seven."

"I'll be there," Sadie said. She waved as the blue Jeep Cherokee pulled out of her driveway.

Back inside, she fixed herself another cup of coffee and settled down with her laptop. Time to get some information about those antique handcuffs. She had brought them home from the store so that she could compare them with anything similar she found online.

To Sadie, Tulley Morse's handcuffs looked a bit modern for something Harry Houdini would have used. She searched for photos of the renowned magician and carefully studied the handcuffs he used. Tulley's certainly did not look like any of those she could find associated with Houdini.

Other images of "antique handcuffs" again made Tulley's seem totally out of place. She searched cautiously for a history of shackles and handcuffs, but was appalled by some of the articles and photos that turned up on her list.

She sat back in her chair. With all the historical research she had done on Silver Peak, and in particular its opera house, wouldn't she have heard about it if Houdini had ever actually performed there?

She began reading up on the man, and was soon off on a fascinating rabbit trail about his underwater escape tricks.

This will never do, she scolded herself. As intriguing as Houdini's life and career were, she needed to know if and when he had ever been in Colorado. She couldn't find evidence of that. In fact, in 1903, the year Tulley had hazarded as the date for the Silver Peak appearance, Houdini and his wife were touring in Europe. While Houdini did appear in the western United States later in his life, and even make some movies in Hollywood, she found nothing to indicate he had come to the little town in Colorado.

She mulled that over for a while. She and Roz both remembered the magic show they had attended in junior high, so at least one professional magician had performed here prior to Rodin's appearance at the fair. It was very possible that some other conjurer had come to Silver Peak earlier. Maybe these handcuffs had been used in a performance here by someone not quite as famous as Houdini.

She decided to put the topic aside and let it simmer in the back of her mind. She needed to pick up a couple of items at the Market. While she was downtown, she popped in to see her cousin Laura, who had an apartment above the Antique Mine.

"Well, hi," Laura said when she opened the door. She gave Sadie a big hug. "Come on in. What are you up to?"

"Just running errands. Haven't had a chance to talk to you for a while, so I thought I'd stop in."

"Great! Tell me all the latest."

Sadie laughed, but sat down readily. She prompted Laura for her own news first. Her cousin was working long distance on a congressman's political campaign. When they got around to talking about the fair and Rodin, it seemed natural to introduce the subject of the old handcuffs and the dubious link to Houdini.

"What do you know so far?" Laura asked.

"They don't look like the ones in pictures of Houdini. They look more modern than that to me."

Laura's nose wrinkled. "How much have handcuffs changed over the years?"

"More than I would have thought. I may need to do some library research on this problem. Beyond that, I am reasonably certain that Houdini never performed in Silver Peak, and I really don't feel comfortable with the man who brought these cuffs in or his story."

"Maybe the best thing is simply to give them back to him and tell him no sale."

"You're probably right. It niggles at me though, that I can't find out more about them."

Laura laughed. "That sounds like you. I was thinking about having dinner at Los Pollitos. Join me?"

"Oh dear, after the big lunch I had. Well, why not? I can go to the fairgrounds from there. You said you haven't seen the show yet."

"No, and I'd love to." Laura rounded up her purse and a lightweight jacket, in case it was cool in the grandstand, and they set off on foot for the restaurant owned by the Garza family. It was across the street, beyond the bank, and they quickly reached it. Gloria Garza, who owned it with her husband, Ramon, greeted them warmly and showed them to a table.

"The girls are working this evening," she said as she handed them menus. "Mia will be right along."

"Wonderful," Sadie said. She was already planning to keep her meal light. The fair offered so many tasty treats that she couldn't trust herself not to have a rich snack later.

"*Hola*, Señora Speers," Mia sang out as she came with their water glasses on a small tray. "*Buenos noches*, Señorita Finch."

Sadie grinned. Mia was Sara's best friend, and her English was impeccable, but when she worked at the restaurant, she often gave the guests a Spanish greeting, in keeping with the cozy atmosphere of the dining room, with its terra-cotta tiled floor and bright decorations. She had managed to corral her shoulder-length dark hair into a short ponytail.

"Hi, Mia. I think I'll have a taco salad tonight."

"Very good." Mia took out her order pad and wrote it down. "You like the sour cream with it, *sí*?"

"You know me well," Sadie said.

Laura looked up from the menu. "I don't know why I'm even looking at this. I'll have a chicken quesadilla and an iced tea."

"Oh, the iced tea sounds good," Sadie said. "I'll have one too. Mia, are you ready to start school again in a few weeks?"

"Sort of." Mia laughed. "I like summer best. And it's been very exciting, with the fair and the magician…"

"How did you like the show?" Sadie asked.

Mia smiled and pushed her glasses up on the bridge of her nose. "It was very good. I'd like to see it again. Mama says maybe later in the week I can go again, but some nights they need me here."

"I haven't seen the magic show yet," Laura said. "What's the best part?"

"When he made Mrs. Putnam disappear. *Poof!*" Mia's face sobered. "But she got hurt that first night." She looked at Sadie. "Sara told me she's okay though."

"She is," Sadie said. "Nothing serious."

"You got to meet the magician, didn't you?" Mia asked.

"Yes, I did. He's charming."

Mia nodded, her eyes bright. "I met him too. It was on Friday, on the street, near where he's staying."

"Oh, really?"

Mia nodded. "My sister and I were walking past the B and B. We had seen the posters, and we saw him come out the front door. Elena said, 'Are you the magician?' He said he was, and that he was going to go and rehearse. Elena asked for his autograph, and he let me take a selfie with him."

"Wow," Laura said. "That's really special."

Mia nodded, grinning. "It came out good too. When we saw the show that night, it was fantastic, and I was really glad I met him. Now I can brag about it and show my friends when school starts. He's really good!"

"Yes, he is," Sadie said. "Do you have your phone here? Can we see the picture?"

"Sure." Mia looked over her shoulder. "Oops. Gotta go, but I'll be back. I'll show you when I bring your order." She hurried toward the kitchen.

"She's such a sweet kid," Laura said.

Sadie nodded. "And she's cute too. I know Mia thinks she's homely, compared to Elena and her mom, but I think she'll turn out just fine."

"Me too. She has an interesting face."

Mia slid their tea glasses on to the table between other chores. They continued to chat about the store, Laura's social life, and happenings in town. About ten later, Mia came back with their entrées.

"Oh, this looks so good," Sadie said.

"*Mmm*." Laura took a big whiff of her steaming quesadilla. "Thanks, Mia."

"You're welcome." Mia smiled a little shyly. "I've got the picture."

"Oh, let me see." Laura had picked up her fork, but she laid it down to take the phone from Mia.

"Oh my, he's handsome. It's good of you and Elena too." Laura handed the phone across to Sadie.

"It sure is." Sadie gazed down at the image of Rodin flanked by the laughing Garza sisters. Something else caught her eye. Just over Mia's shoulder in the selfie, the front end of a car could be seen, parked against the curb opposite. "Mia, do you know whose car that is?"

Mia took the phone back and stared at the picture, frowning. "No, sorry, I don't."

"Would you mind sending me a copy of this photo?" Sadie said. "I think that car may be of special interest to someone I know."

"Okay, I guess," Mia said uncertainly.

"Don't worry, sweetheart," Sadie assured her. "I won't pass it around, and the one person I'll show it to is very discreet."

"Sure." In seconds, Mia had sent the picture to Sadie's phone.

"Thanks," Sadie said.

Mia nodded and tucked her phone in her pocket. "Can I get you anything else?"

"I don't think so."

When she had left, Laura leaned across the table. "May I ask to whom you're sending that?"

"Mac Slattery."

Laura sat back and nodded. "Should have known."

6

"Yeah, I see it." Mac frowned at the photo on Sadie's phone.

"Can you tell anything about the car or the driver?" she asked.

"Well, it seems the people who said dark green were right. It's a Chevy, but what model or year, I'm not sure. Can't see enough of it."

Mac had come to the restaurant and now sat kitty-corner to Sadie and Laura with a cup of coffee in front of him.

"I doubt Mia and Elena can tell you any more than that," Sadie said, "but you might want to ask them."

He nodded. "Send it to my phone. Kyle may be able to enlarge it and sharpen the resolution. We may even be able to get a partial license plate number off it."

"Really? That would be great." Sadie hadn't thought the picture was sharp enough, or that the partial car visible in it was close enough for anyone to read the license plate.

Mac shrugged and handed her the phone. "Worth a try." He took a swallow of his coffee and looked around the dining room. "I'll go tell Ramon and Gloria I'd like to talk to the girls, though this seems to be their rush hour."

"Maybe you could talk to Kyle about the picture and come back in an hour or so," Laura suggested, while Sadie clicked buttons to forward the photo to Mac.

"I'll see what the Garzas think."

Mac left them, and Sadie and Laura looked at each other.

"Well, cousin, this has been an interesting meal," Laura said. "Do you want dessert?"

"No, thanks. I think I'd better get home and take Hank out for a walk before I hit the fairgrounds." Sadie also made mental plans to turn in early. She and Alice had agreed to meet in the morning to go berry picking, and she didn't want to be late.

Mia came and took their payment. As they walked toward the door of the restaurant, Mac came from the kitchen.

"Thanks again, Sadie," he said. "I'm going to take your suggestion and get this to Kyle right away. I'll come back when things are quieter here to speak to the girls."

"I hope it turns out to be useful," Sadie said.

He nodded. "Could be nothing, or it could be the best lead we've had so far on that theft."

––––––––––

The sun rose above the mountain and shone its golden rays on the green pastures behind Milo's barn. Milo leaned on the fence, grinning as Alice wheedled him for the location of the best raspberries on his land. Sadie lounged against the gate with her berry bucket hanging from her belt, content to let Alice do the bargaining.

"Come on, Milo. You said you didn't mind if we picked berries."

"I didn't say you could have all the best ones though."

"Oh, like you're going out there to pick them? You're too busy, and you know it."

"I might not be." Milo's eyes twinkled. "They sure are big and juicy this year."

"You didn't already pick them, did you?" Alice scowled at him.

"Nope, but my mother did come pick a few quarts on Saturday." He rubbed his stomach. "I can almost taste the jam she's making."

Alice turned in exasperation to Sadie. "We might as well get at it. I know there's some up the slope toward the big rock. We'll get those."

"There's an even better patch...," Milo began. He broke off and raised his chin as a pickup truck entered his driveway and rolled toward them, stirring up dust.

"That looks like Spike," Alice said.

Sadie studied the pickup. "It is Spike."

He parked next to her Tahoe and got out, wearing his customary jeans and leather jacket.

"Howdy," Milo called. He shot a sidelong glance at Alice. "You see? You're not the only one who asked if they could pick, and I gotta say, Spike was a lot more polite about it than you."

"What?" Alice stared at him in mock outrage.

Milo laughed. "Enjoy yourselves, ladies." He waved at Spike and headed for the barn.

"No, Milo, wait!" Alice took three steps after him. "Please? Pretty please? I'll bring you a piece of pie. Okay, a whole pie." She grunted in frustration as he kept walking, then she turned back to face her mother. Spike had come over to stand beside Sadie.

"'Morning, Alice," he said, gazing at her with adoring eyes, then as an afterthought, "Sadie."

"Hello, Spike. It's been a real treat to hear the band the past few nights."

"Thanks," Spike said, still looking at Alice.

"Hi," said Alice. "The kids and I went Friday night, and we enjoyed your music too."

"Thanks. I saw you in the stands."

"Are you joining us in the berry patch?" Alice asked.

"Looks like it," Spike replied. "Milo said I could get enough to make my entry for the contest."

Once again, Alice's jaw dropped. "You're entering the wild raspberry contest too?"

"Sure am. I'm making raspberry crisp. What are you making?"

Alice hesitated, then said, "Grandma Wright's raspberry pie."

"Sounds good."

"It is."

Spike nodded. "Good luck."

"You too."

Sadie cleared her throat. "So, Spike, do you know where these huge, juicy berries Milo's been teasing us about are located?"

"He told me yesterday there's a big patch of 'em around by the creek," Spike replied.

"In his north pasture?" Sadie asked.

"Yup."

"*Hmm*. Maybe we should drive over there." Sadie raised her eyebrows in Alice's direction.

"Sure," Alice said.

"Want to ride with us, Spike?" Sadie asked.

"Uh, well…"

"We might finish before he does," Alice said quickly. "I mean, there's two of us picking."

"True," Spike said with a shrug. "You go ahead, Sadie. I'll follow in my truck."

Sadie headed her Tahoe out over the dirt road that led to the north pasture.

"I found a bargain on back-to-school supplies over in Breckenridge," she told Alice. "I got some extra notebook paper and highlighters for Theo and Sara."

"That was nice of you," Alice said.

"If you want to stop by my place on your way home, I'll give them to you this morning."

They reached the gate, and Alice hopped out and opened it. She got back in the vehicle, and Sadie drove through. Behind her, Spike brought his truck through and stopped. In her rearview mirror, Sadie saw him get out to close the gate.

"I didn't expect to see him here," Alice said, looking studiously out her side window.

"Yeah, kinda funny," Sadie said. She drove across the pasture, following the grassy track Milo used only occasionally. A hundred yards away, three horses were grazing. One of them lifted its head and surveyed them calmly, then went back to eating.

Sadie drove as close to the creek as she could and parked the Tahoe. She and Alice gathered their buckets and climbed out as Spike pulled up next to them and shut off his engine. Alice didn't wait for him to get out, but headed down the creek path with quick strides. Sadie waved to Spike and hurried after her.

"Where's the fire?" she called as Alice outdistanced her down the shady path.

Alice turned. "I just want to get dibs on the best spot, that's all."

"Well, I don't want to have to run and puff and get all sweaty." Sadie caught up to her and looked up through the aspen branches overhead to the thoroughly blue sky. "It's too nice a day to get bent out of shape, honey. And there's no way Spike could have known you'd be here today. I don't think I told anyone else."

"Maybe Milo did."

"Oh, I doubt it. Why would Milo do that?" Sadie shook her head. "It's a coincidence, Alice. Come on. I do intend to be at the store by ten."

"Okay. I expect you're right about Spike. I shouldn't have been so snippy with him. Let's get at it then." Alice glanced back along the trail. Spike was just coming into view. She sighed and turned toward the creek.

The raspberry patch spread out above the bank. Sadie wondered if there had once been a homestead in here, but as far as she knew, there hadn't. The berries came every year in various patches on the mountain, of their own accord, and this looked like a good one.

The worst thing about wild raspberries was their murderous thorns. The best thing was the taste. Fat, warm ruby-colored fruit hung from the canes. She put out a hand to one, and it dropped off at her touch. Sadie smiled and put it in her mouth. Perfect.

"I'm starting right here." She set down the big stainless-steel bowl she had brought to empty her bucket into when it filled. She spotted a landmark—a clump of young aspens growing near a boulder—so that she would be able to find the bowl when she needed it, and not lose it in the tall grass.

Alice looked anxiously at the expanse of bushes before them. "Maybe there's a better spot over there."

"Fine," Sadie said. "Go find it. I'll be here picking."

Alice walked a few steps but soon gave in to the lure of the brilliant red berries and began to pick.

The bottom of Sadie's bucket was soon covered. Raspberries were soft, and you didn't want to use too big a container for them, or the ones on the bottom would be squashed by the weight of those on top.

Her father had always told her, "If a raspberry doesn't want to come off the bush easy, leave it be. The ripe ones won't object." She always followed that advice and skipped over any that clung to the stem. They'd be ripe tomorrow or the next day, but she wanted only the best, most flavorful ones.

"Hey, good patch all right," Spike said behind her.

"Yeah, these are just right," Sadie replied. "Pick a spot, Spike. But if I were you, I wouldn't get too close to you-know-who." She glanced Alice's way.

Spike sighed. "I didn't plan this."

"I know, and I told her that."

"I wish..." He let the sentence dangle and shook his head. "Well, I guess there's plenty for everybody." He edged along the patch to Sadie's right, away from Alice, and began picking.

Sadie soon lost sight of them both. She thought only of the sun on her shoulders and the warm smell of the succulent raspberry leaves and fruit, and whether she could reach that cluster without getting pricked by thorns.

She filled the bucket once, emptied it into the bowl, and went back to work. When it was two-thirds full again, she heard a stirring in the bushes to her left. "How you doing, Alice?" she called.

"Good. You?"

"Just dandy."

"I found some really big ones," came Spike's voice from farther away.

"Aren't they great?" Sadie said.

She kept picking until her bucket was full to the brim. Reluctantly, she walked back toward the path, to where she had left the stainless-steel bowl. She was surprised at how far she had worked her way from it, around the edge of the patch. Gently, she tipped the little pail and let the fruit slide into the bowl.

"Hey, yours is full too?" Alice strolled toward her, balancing her pail so that the berries heaped above the rim wouldn't tumble off.

"I should have worn long sleeves," Sadie said ruefully, looking at the scratches on her forearms.

"Yeah, I want to get into the middle of the patch," Alice said. "I saw some really big ones in there. I think I'll get my sweatshirt from the truck."

"Get mine too," Sadie said. "It's so warm, I hate to put it on, but those berries will be worth it."

"Okay." Alice emptied her bucket into the bowl and straightened.

"I put an extra bowl on the backseat," Sadie said. "How long do you want to pick?"

"I want at least one more bucketful, and I'll help you get enough for jam if you want."

Sadie looked at her watch. "Okay. It's only quarter after eight. Thanks."

Alice took the full bowl of berries and headed up the trail. Sadie began to fill her bucket again. A minute later, crackling brush jerked her to full alertness, but it was only Spike, pushing aside some stubborn canes as he made his way out of the patch.

"Guess I've got enough." His two plastic pails were nearly full.

"Good luck with the contest," Sadie said.

"Thanks." Spike looked wistfully toward the side of the patch where Alice had gone to pick earlier. "Well, I'll see ya."

Sadie almost told him Alice had gone to the car, but she thought better of it. Just this once, she would keep her mouth shut and let Alice fend for herself.

"I plan to be at the show tonight," she said.

"Great," Spike replied, but he didn't sound great. He sounded sad.

He walked away, and Sadie went back to work. She liked Spike. He was a very nice fellow, though he had had a few rough spots in his life. He had lost his wife and daughter in a car accident when he was in his twenties, but that was a long time ago. Sadie suspected the talented musician was lonely. With a sigh, she tried to put him and Alice out of her mind and think about the old handcuffs Tulley Morse had brought her, while the depth of the berries in her pail steadily mounted. It was more than half full again before she realized Alice hadn't returned. Maybe she and Spike were having a long-overdue conversation. Sadie smiled and kept picking.

A scream suddenly rent the air, and she whipped toward the path. Alice stood twenty feet away, holding Sadie's navy blue hoodie and another mixing bowl.

"Mother!" With a trembling hand, Alice pointed beyond Sadie, toward the edge of the patch where she had picked her berries.

Sadie turned her head slowly. A huge bear stood on its hind legs a dozen yards away, looking at her curiously over the tops of the berry bushes.

7

DON'T RUN.

That was the first thing that went through Sadie's mind. The second thing was, *He's big.* The third was, *Lord, help me!*

The bear let out a grunt. At least it wasn't a roar.

"Mom! Come on! Back away slowly!"

Sadie was shaking all over. She tried to remember what to do. Usually she was calm in a crisis, but she'd never been quite this close to a hungry grizzly before.

Maybe he's not hungry, she told herself. *Maybe he's already eaten a ton of berries.*

The bear lowered itself to all fours with a *thud*. Sadie's tremors increased, and her berry bucket fell from her hands. She took a step backward. She could hear the bruin shoving its way through the raspberry canes. Its thick fur would protect it from the scratches that had kept Sadie on the edge of the patch.

Make yourself look big. That was one thing she'd heard. But at five-feet-four, Sadie felt pretty small at the moment. *And make a lot of noise.* Could she even get a squeak out? The bushes in front of her swayed and then crashed apart, exposing the bear's huge head. And teeth.

From behind her, a sudden blast of sound made her jump. The bear, too, was startled. It stared and rose on its hind feet again with a roar.

Spike Harris walked past Sadie, a gleaming brass trumpet at his lips. A loud squawk bombarded her ears. In a brief moment after it ended, she heard Alice cry, "Run!" Then Spike launched into a strain of raucous jazz.

Her last impression of the bear was that it reared its head back in puzzlement. Sadie tore up the path to where Alice stood, holding her hoodie. She grabbed her daughter's hand and yanked her toward the cars. They sprinted together up the path, with Spike's jaunty music providing the soundtrack.

Panting, Sadie leaned against the hood of the Tahoe. "Get in. Maybe we can drive closer and pick Spike up."

They piled into the front seats, and she fumbled with the keys. The engine caught, and she floored it toward the narrow path. Just before she reached the tree line, she saw Spike coming and braked.

"He's not running," Alice observed.

It was true. Spike stepped briskly along, with the trumpet tucked under his arm. Every few steps, he cast a glance over his shoulder toward the berry patch. When he reached the Tahoe, he went to Alice's window.

"I think it's gone, but I'm not sure."

Sadie closed her eyes for a moment while she let out a deep sigh and a prayer of thanks. "Spike, how can I thank you?"

"It was nothing, Sadie. I mean—well, it was something, but . . ." Spike's gaze didn't meet hers, but slid off toward the berry patch.

"How did you happen to have a trumpet in your car?" Sadie asked. She knew Spike played a lot of instruments, but his usual choice was the guitar.

A smile split his weather-beaten face. "It belongs to a customer. It had a stuck valve, and she left it off for me to fix. I was going to drop it at her house after I got done here."

"I, for one, am very thankful for that." Sadie reached out the window and squeezed his arm.

"Me too," Alice said. "I don't know what we'd have done if you hadn't played cavalry for us. Thank you." She looked between the bucket seats into the back, where the bowl of berries rested. "Well, I guess we'd better cut our losses and go home."

"Yeah, I don't think you should go back down there this morning," Spike said. "How many did you lose?"

"My bucket was about two-thirds full, but that's okay." Sadie looked at Alice. "You can have the bowlful for your pie."

"But you were going to make jam," Alice protested.

"Another time." Sadie looked past her out the window. "Thanks again, Spike. Really glad you were here."

"No prob." He sauntered toward the pickup, the trumpet dangling from his hand and swinging through the tall grass.

When Sadie got home from Milo's, Alice drove in behind her. Sadie got out of the Tahoe and called, "It'll just take me a minute."

Alice got out of her Jeep and followed her into the house.

"The school supplies are upstairs," Sadie said. "Help yourself to some lemonade while I get them."

"That would sure taste good." Alice headed for the kitchen.

A minute later, Sadie came down with two bulging plastic sacks from the department store. Alice was sitting at the kitchen table sipping from a tall glass of lemonade, and she had poured one for Sadie too.

"Wow, Mom. You didn't have to buy so much."

"No big deal," Sadie said. "I know they like those view binders, and the mechanical pencils were on sale too."

"Looks like the whole stationery department was on sale. Thanks. You know what?"

"What?" Sadie asked.

"I forgot to ask Milo about the gymkhana. Sara's going to be upset."

"You can call him."

"I suppose. But he was being a turkey this morning." Alice turned toward the window. "Someone's—oh, I wonder what he wants."

"Who?" Sadie moved closer to the window and looked out. Spike was getting out of his pickup and heading for her front porch.

Sadie got to the door before he did and opened it wide.

"Well, hi, Spike. It's been ages since I've seen you."

Spike's smile flickered, but then he glanced toward Alice's Jeep. "Uh, I just—I heard Alice say you wouldn't have enough berries to make your jam, and I thought I'd give you some of mine. I have way more than I need."

"How sweet. You don't have to do that."

"It's okay. I can go back another time if I decide I want more." He held out a pail of berries.

Sadie chuckled as she took it. "Thanks. Take that trumpet if you do."

"Right. And maybe I can get back the bucket you lost."

"Don't worry about that." Sadie looked over her shoulder, but Alice hadn't left the kitchen. "Would you like some lemonade? Alice and I were just having some."

Spike hesitated, then shook his head. "Better not. I'll see you tonight."

"Right. I'll be there on time. I missed most of your act Saturday night."

He shrugged. "You've heard it enough times."

"I always enjoy your music," Sadie said. "A little bluegrass, a little country…"

That made him smile. "A little rock-and-roll?"

"You tell me."

"Yeah. Well, we're doing a different set tonight. I'd better get going. See you later." Spike walked quickly down the steps and over to his truck.

Sadie waved as he backed out, then she went back to the kitchen. "See what Spike brought me?" She held up the bucket of raspberries.

Alice's mouth twitched. "That was nice of him."

"Yes, it was. First he saves our lives, then he brings us half his berries. He's a very nice man, Alice."

"I know he is."

Sadie nodded, feeling she had said enough. She put the berries in the refrigerator and sat down opposite Alice. The first sip of lemonade slid down like nectar. "Oh, that's good."

Alice drained her glass and stood. "I'd better get out of here or I'll make you late to work."

"I'm flexible," Sadie said, but Alice was out the door with the school supplies.

"Thanks again," she called over her shoulder.

Mac Slattery's official car was parked in front of the Antique Mine when Sadie arrived, and he sat in the driver's seat with his head tipped back, enjoying a catnap.

She got out of the Tahoe and closed the door gently, but it was enough to rouse him.

"Hey, Sadie." He got out of the car and walked toward her.

"Up all night?" she asked.

"Not quite. I just wanted to let you know that I've got someone running the partial plate on the car in that photo the Garza girls took."

"Oh, good. Do you think you'll be able to track down the owner?"

"Maybe. We can see the color and the model, and we've got four characters from the license plate. That will narrow it down, at least."

"I'm glad. Is it okay to tell Roz?"

"I already did. If we find this guy, we'll want her to take a look and see if she recognizes him."

"I hope you do get him." Sadie jiggled her keys and selected the one for the store's front door.

Mac gritted his teeth and nodded. "It would be nice if we found the right man and could solve two crimes at once—the assault backstage and the theft from Edwin's house."

"That would be great police work. Hey, we saw a big bear out at Milo's place this morning."

"Oh yeah?" Mac looked suddenly more awake.

Sadie gave him a brief version of their adventure and then unlocked the store. Mac had a good laugh over her story. He got in his patrol car and headed toward his office.

When Sadie opened for business a half hour later, Laura was the first person through the door, cheerful and energetic.

"Good morning! How are you?"

"Have I got a story for you," Sadie said with a grin. She had a few gaps in her stock, due to sales she had made, and while she talked, she rearranged the merchandise and put out a half-dozen old coffee tins she had recently acquired. Laura got the longer version of the bear story and was soon laughing helplessly.

"Stop! It's not funny, but you're making me split."

"Well, I was pretty scared when it happened, but really, that animal was probably stuffed with berries when he stumbled on us."

Laura shook her head. "If you say so. That puts Spike Harris in a very heroic light."

"It sure does. He's my new superhero," Sadie said with a wink. "Trumpet Man."

Laura let out a most unladylike guffaw. "I'm sure he'll *bear* the burden of responsibility with aplomb. But speaking of berries, that's why I'm here. I wondered if you have any old pie plates."

"There's a stoneware one in the kitchen section," Sadie said.

"Oh, good. It will set off my pie. I'm entering the wild berry contest at the fair, and I . . . " Laura stopped and eyed her cautiously. "Wait a sec. Don't tell me *you're* entering the contest. Is that why you were out squabbling with a bear over a pail of berries this morning?"

"Not me," Sadie said. "Alice."

"Okay." Laura stood quietly for a moment. "I don't suppose she's making a raspberry pie?"

Sadie hesitated, then nodded. "Grandma Wright's recipe."

"I see."

They locked eyes. Laura had a tragic air about her.

"No . . . You're using it too?" Sadie asked.

"I was planning on it. Should I change to something else?"

"Why? It's all right if two people use the same recipe, and you're both family, so you're both entitled to it."

"I guess. . . I mean, everyone has a different touch with piecrust, right?"

"For sure. You and I could take the same recipe for oatmeal cookies or beef stew or—or *anything*, and it wouldn't come out quite the same."

"Right. And there will be other people entering, and they'll all be using different recipes," Laura said, seeming to gain confidence as she spoke.

"Spike's making raspberry crisp."

"A crisp?" Laura's forehead wrinkled. "I've never had that. I wonder where he got his recipe."

"He may have thought it up himself. He's very creative."

"*Hmm.* I thought it would all be cookies and squares and scones. And pies, of course."

"The rules say anything using wild Colorado raspberries."

"Yeah." Laura's mouth drooped, and her tone had gone bleak again. "I don't know. Maybe I should just drop out."

"Don't you dare," Sadie said. "You're a wonderful cook. And you know what? I'm going to give you that stoneware pie plate."

"Don't do that."

"Why not?"

"You have to root for Alice," Laura said.

Sadie made a scoffing sound and strode down the aisle to where old bakeware was displayed in a Hoosier cupboard. "That's silly. I can root for you both. I'm not one of the judges. May the best pie win."

She turned and held out the old pie plate. Laura had followed her down the aisle. She looked down at the crackled surface of the old dish and the faint flower design in its center.

Slowly, a smile curved her lips upward. "Now, that's a pie plate."

"It must weigh two pounds," Sadie said, thrusting it into her cousin's hands.

"I love it."

"So do I. And I love you." Sadie gave her a hug. "Now, go and make a wonderful pie in it."

"Thanks, Sadie."

"You're not picking your berries at Milo's, are you?"

Laura laughed. "No, I have another spot, but I'll be careful all the same. I don't have a trumpet."

———

Sara wanted to see the magic show again that night, so Sadie went to pick her up on her way to the fairgrounds.

"Are you sure you don't want to go?" she asked Alice, as Sara came tearing down the stairs.

"I'll sit this one out, thanks," Alice said.

Sadie wondered if she just wanted to avoid Spike again.

"Maybe tomorrow," Alice said. "I'm working on lesson plans tonight. Only a couple more weeks until school starts."

"Okay."

"I'm ready, Grandma," Sara said, zipping her sweatshirt.

"Let's go, then." Sadie started toward the door with her, but turned back. "I guess I should tell you, so you don't find out from somebody else…"

"What?" Alice asked, frowning.

"Laura is entering the wild berry contest."

Alice shrugged. "So? More power to her."

"Yeah, well…" Sadie took a deep breath. "It seems she had Grandma Wright's recipe too. She's using the same one you are."

Alice's eyebrows shot up almost to her hairline. "You're kidding."

"No, I'm not. And I encouraged her to do it. She offered to withdraw when I told her you were using it too."

"Well, I guess it's her right." Despite her words, Alice looked the way she used to when she was a girl and felt utterly frustrated.

"Yes, it is. Laura had already decided to enter and what she would make before she told me. I wasn't about to tell her otherwise."

"Of course not." Even so, Alice's face scrunched up as though she had just taken a swallow of pickle brine.

"You'll both make delicious pies. The judges will have a tough decision."

Alice gave her a halfhearted smile. "It's good that she's taking part in the fair and feeling at home here."

"I think so too." Sadie walked over and gave her a warm hug. When she pulled away, she turned to Sara, who waited by the door, watching her mother anxiously. "Well, what are we waiting for? The bright lights await us!" She grasped Sara's hand and pulled her out the door.

8

At the fairgrounds, Sadie and Sara slid into their front-row seats in the grandstand with Edwin and Roscoe.

"I sure hope nothing goes wrong tonight," Roscoe said. "The magician had Roz over here almost all afternoon, practicing new tricks."

"Then we're in for a treat," Sadie said. She was glad Rodin was taking the trouble to vary his performances.

Edwin looked tired, but he smiled and squeezed her hand. "How was your day?"

Sadie chuckled, realizing he didn't know about her adventure. "I had a close encounter with a bear this morning. Otherwise, it was great."

Edwin's jaw dropped. "Please tell me you're joking."

"Would I joke about something like that? I can *barely* keep a straight face."

"Where did this happen?"

"Out at Milo's," Sadie said with a teasing smile. "It was a *berry* interesting excursion."

"Grandma." Sara tugged on her sleeve and nodded toward the walkway before the grandstand. "There's Sheriff Mac."

Sure enough, Mac Slattery strolled along toward them as though he hadn't a care in the world. Rays of the setting sun glinted off his badge.

"Hi, Mac," she called.

He homed in on her face and strode toward her. "Evening, folks. I suppose Roz is backstage."

"Yes, they do her makeup and all that while the Skylarks perform," Roscoe said.

"Well, I'll tell you then, Roscoe. Maybe I'll get a chance to speak to Roz later. Edwin, I know you'll be interested in this too. We've got a possible hit on that partial license plate number."

"Who is it?" Sadie asked.

"There were several possibilities, but the most likely one is a man who lives in Denver. Our suspect seems to be a con man named…"

"A *con man*?" Roscoe almost roared.

Mac winced, and Sadie put her hand on Roscoe's shoulder to help calm him. "Mac, you were saying?"

"His name is Murray Lithgow. He was recently released from prison."

"Okay," Edwin said. "Have you arrested him?"

Mac shook his head. "The Denver police went to his address, but he wasn't home. In fact, they haven't turned up any trace of him since last Thursday."

"Last Thursday?" Roscoe echoed. "Roz was assaulted on Friday night."

"And my Arapaho pipe was stolen between Thursday night and Saturday," Edwin added.

Mac nodded. "I know. They're still following leads. They're sending photos, and my deputies and I will start canvassing here, to see if anyone in Silver Peak has seen him. Edwin, we might get a positive ID for him being the one sitting outside your house last week."

"If there's anything I can do to help, let me know," Edwin said.

"Sure. And I'll bring pictures around tomorrow to show you folks."

The Skylarks began to play their first tune, and Sadie smiled at Sara. "I love this one."

"Me too," Sara said. "It's one of my favorites."

After the musical show, Edwin's introduction of Rodin and Roz brought a gust of excitement. The crowd tensed, expecting to be amazed. Even though she had now seen the show three times already, Sadie still had some adrenaline-filled moments. Rodin had added several new places where items disappeared, but reappeared in unexpected places.

The trick that astonished her most was when Rodin sent Roz to the grandstand to collect a dollar bill from a viewer. Roz chose Chad Pearson, who sat one row behind Sadie and Edwin. Julie and her husband had brought their twin boys, Brody and Logan, to see the show. Chad cheerfully signed his name across the dollar he handed to Roz.

"Now, be sure you bring that back," he told her in a teasing voice. "It's my last buck."

"You can count on it," Roz said with a smile. She turned in a flutter of netting and silk scarf and strode confidently back to the stage and up the steps in her four-inch heels.

"I don't know how she does it," Sadie whispered to Edwin. "I'll take my sneakers and hiking boots, thank you."

"Oh, I've seen you swanked up," Edwin said. "Even wearing heels. Don't be so modest."

Sadie smiled and squeezed his hand.

While Roz was collecting the money from Chad, Steve had helped Rodin arrange his props onstage, the largest of which was a plump watermelon.

"That thing must weigh thirty pounds," Roscoe said.

Sadie leaned past Sara. "Where did they get it? Do you know?"

"From the Market."

"I'm going to get one for this weekend," Sadie said.

Sara licked her lips and grinned. "Can't wait, Grandma."

Rodin accepted the dollar from Roz and walked to the edge of the stage. He held it up and met Chad's gaze.

"Now, Mr. Pearson, can you see your signature on this dollar bill?"

"Yes, I can," Chad called.

"So this is the same dollar bill that Rosalind borrowed from you a moment ago?"

"It sure is."

"And you have not discussed this trick in advance with me or Roz or anyone else involved in the show?"

"No, I haven't."

"Very good. Now, I need a volunteer to hold on to this for me."

Sara jumped up and waved her arm wildly.

"Yes, the young lady in the first row."

"Oh, wow! He picked me, Grandma!"

Sadie only had time to give her a quick pat on the back. Sara dashed to the steps and scrambled up onto the stage.

"Hello," Rodin said. "What is your name?"

"Sara."

"Sara, would you please hold the dollar for me?"

Rodin rolled the bill up from one end and passed it to her. Sara held it out where the audience could see it, while Roz stood near the table that held the watermelon, smiling. Rodin took a bright blue scarf from a pocket inside his jacket. He flicked it open and let it flutter in the air, then brought it down over Sara's hand. Almost immediately, he whisked the scarf away.

"Open your hands," he said.

Sara's jaw dropped, and she turned to face the audience, with both hands held up, spread wide—and empty.

"Where is the money?" Rodin asked.

Sara shook her head, with a baffled expression. "I don't know."

"Not skimming, are you?" Rodin asked.

The audience laughed, but Sara only looked puzzled.

"Did you put it in your pocket?" the magician asked.

"Most certainly not!" Sara sounded offended. "I had it right here in my hand, but it's gone."

"Aha. That, my dear, is the beginning of magic." He looked over at Roz. "Now, Rosalind, take the knife from the table and show the audience."

Roz picked up a wooden-handled butcher knife with a huge blade and brought it to the edge of the stage. She held it up with both hands and displayed it to the left, right, and center parts of the audience.

"Well, folks," Rodin said. "We have a problem. I wouldn't like to accuse Sara of taking Mr. Pearson's money, so I guess we'd better find out where that dollar went, eh?"

The audience clapped, and Rodin walked over to where the watermelon sat.

"Sara, would you like to join me?"

Sara walked to the table, and Rodin positioned her so that she could watch his actions but not block the audience's view.

"And now, the knife." He reached toward Roz, and she placed the butcher knife's handle in his hand.

"Watch carefully, now, Sara." Rodin glanced up. "Mr. Pearson, would you like to observe too? You may come up on the stage if you would."

Chad left his seat. Julie stayed with the boys, who writhed with excitement. He bounded up the steps on to the platform, and Roz positioned him next to Sara.

"All right," Rodin said. "Mr. Pearson and Sara, do you agree that this watermelon has not been cut open yet?"

Chad chuckled, but he and Sara leaned close and looked at the melon. Chad curled his fingers and thumped on the melon.

"Sounds ripe."

"Yes, it does." Rodin raised the butcher knife. "Mr. Pearson, would you like to do that cutting?"

"If you want me to," Chad said. "I've cut a few watermelons in my day."

"Oh, good. I'll let you do the honors. Just cut it in half, please, right down the center. Stand back, Sara." He handed the knife to Chad.

Chad leaned over the melon for a moment, studying it, then placed the knife on top and pushed the blade down, slicing quickly through the middle. Rodin leaned over the table and set the two halves of the big melon apart.

Chad and Sara stood for a moment, gazing at the pink flesh of the fruit.

"See anything?" Rodin asked.

"Yeah," Chad said.

Sara pointed to the half on the left. "There's something stuck in it."

Rodin took the knife from Chad. With the tip, he carved out a small piece of the pulp. Then he reached over and extracted something dark from the melon and handed it to Chad.

"I believe this is yours, sir."

Chad took the item and carefully worked at it with his fingers, unrolling a dollar bill.

"Is it your dollar?" Rodin asked.

Chad nodded, staring at it.

"Do you see your signature?"

"Yeah."

Rodin stepped back with a triumphant sweep of his arms. "Would you please show the audience?"

Chad walked to the front of the stage and held up the bill so the crowd could see the side with his name scrawled on it. Roz followed him with a microphone.

"Would you like to say anything to the audience?" she asked him.

Chad bent his head toward the mic. "I have absolutely no idea how he did it."

"Sara?" Roz turned to the girl.

"Me either," Sara said, shaking her head. "That was awesome!"

Everyone laughed and cheered.

"And would you prefer a dry dollar bill that isn't sticky, Mr. Pearson?" Rodin asked. "I don't want to make you put that one back in your wallet."

"No, this is fine," Chad said. "I'll keep it for a souvenir."

"Thank you. Now, both of you, take a bow."

Chad and Sara complied, and the crowd applauded vigorously as they left the stage.

Sara plopped down beside Sadie. "I just can't believe it, Grandma. How do you think he did that?"

"I couldn't begin to guess," Sadie replied.

As their final trick, Rodin and Roz vanished in a flash of light and smoke. The people in the grandstand began to rise, gather their belongings, and pick up sleepy children.

"I saw him cut that melon open, and the dollar bill was there," Sara said uncertainly. "But magic isn't real. Is it?"

"Not in the supernatural sense," Sadie said.

"What do you mean?"

Sadie looked helplessly at Edwin.

He smiled. "Well, Sara, I think your grandmother's right. So-called magic—the entertaining form that we love to watch—involves making people believe that what they see is all that happens."

Sara frowned. "So there's more to it than what Chad and I saw?"

"I think that's probably a fair assessment."

"But what?" Sara persisted. "I mean, how did he get the dollar into the watermelon?"

"That I don't know, but I don't think it was actual magic," Edwin said.

"So…" Sara was still puzzling over the trick as she zipped up her hoodie.

"He fooled us," Roscoe said with a grin. "He fooled us all."

Sara eyed him keenly. "Maybe Roz will tell you."

"Oh, I'm sure the magician has sworn her to secrecy. Even if she knows, she probably took an oath not to tell anyone."

Roz came briskly from the stage wings, wearing a dark raincoat over her costume.

"Hey! How did you all like the show tonight?"

"Fantastic," Sadie said.

Edwin nodded. "It was great."

"You did great, sweetheart," Roscoe added.

Sara was still frowning. "I sure don't know how he got that dollar into the melon."

They all laughed.

"You keep thinking on it," Roz said. "I wondered about stuff like that for almost fifty years, after that magic show Sadie and I saw in junior high."

"Oh yeah, me too," Sadie said. "I never figured out those tricks either, and that guy wasn't as good as Rodin."

"Do you all want to wait ten minutes for me, and we'll go to the Depot for ice cream?" Roz asked.

After a quick consultation, they decided that would be nice.

"You'd better call your mom and tell her," Sadie told Sara.

Roz was about to hurry back to the dressing room when Mac Slattery approached them.

"Got a minute, Roz?"

"Sure," she said.

Mac took out his phone. "I told Roscoe earlier, we've got a possible ID on the owner of the car that was seen on Jefferson Avenue last week. He's a convicted felon named Murray Lithgow."

"That's kind of scary," Roz said.

Roscoe moved closer to her and slipped his arm around her.

Mac pushed a few buttons on his phone. "I got some pictures of him this evening, and I had the dispatcher send them to my e-mail. Does this guy look anything like the man who pushed you down Friday night?"

Roz took the phone and looked at the screen. She caught her breath. "That's him!"

"Are you sure?" Mac asked. "Take your time. There's another picture, but it's a mugshot, so not too flattering." He swiped the screen for her.

"Yeah, I'm sure," Roz said. "What did he do?"

"He's served time for fraud and theft. He was released not long ago, and he returned to his home in Denver. Unfortunately, the police haven't been able to find him since I alerted them to what's been going on here."

"What was he doing here?" Roz asked.

"I wish I knew." Mac took the phone back and passed it to Edwin. "You and Sadie take a good look and see if you recognize him. Roscoe too."

They all studied the pictures, but none of them could say for sure that they had seen the man. He was thin, with light brown hair and a lined face. Sadie didn't think his features were especially memorable.

"You said he had a beard." Sadie looked questioningly at Roz. "He doesn't have one in the first photo."

"He did. A short one, like in the mugshot. I'm sure that's him.

"I don't recognize him," Edwin said.

Roscoe shook his head. "Me either."

"Well, thanks for trying," Mac said. "I'll keep you posted. And stay aware of who's around you. If you see anything that doesn't look right—anything at all—call me."

9

ON TUESDAY MORNING, SADIE WENT TO THE STORE AN HOUR
before opening time. She had told Edwin on Saturday that she
would try to find out more about David Russell, the man who had
bid against him at the auction, but she had put it off. She had been
to several auctions run by the company that presented Edwin's
artifact for sale. It was time to make good on her promise, so she
looked up auctioneer Ron Waverly's phone number and called him.

"I wondered what you could tell me about David Russell," she
said after they had exchanged greetings.

"David? He's a good customer," Mr. Waverly said. "He was at
my last big auction."

"So he buys from you often?" Sadie asked.

"Oh yes, all the time."

"And you've never had any problems with him?"

"None. Why, are you doing some business with him?"
Mr. Waverly asked.

"No," Sadie admitted. "I was just curious. A close friend of
mine bought a piece from you, and he was very happy with it, but
it was stolen a few days later. He remembered that Mr. Russell was
one of those who had bid against him."

"Oh. Well, I'm sorry to hear his item was stolen, but I wouldn't look David Russell's way. As far as I'm concerned, he's as honest as the day is long."

"I was actually hoping you would say that," Sadie said. "This whole thing has been trying for my friend, but the police are working on it. In fact, they have a lead that may pan out soon."

"Let me know if I can be of any assistance," Mr. Waverly said. "What was the item?"

"A ceremonial Arapaho pipe in a beaded case."

"Ouch. That was a beautiful piece."

"Yes," Sadie said. "My friend was shocked when it went missing."

"Well, David never has any trouble paying for the things he buys from me. If he loses out at an auction, it doesn't upset him. He has more of a you-win-some-you-lose-some personality."

Sadie hung up feeling better about her inquiry. David Russell seemed to be above suspicion. Edwin would be glad to hear that the man from the auction was probably not involved in the theft of the pipe. She hoped Mac could find out more soon about the con man who had been seen in Silver Peak.

Julie arrived, and after they opened for business, Sadie divided her time at the store between customers and a restoration project she was doing for a client. The small child's chair needed to be stripped and refinished before it was sent to another craftsman to have the seat caned.

Before starting the job of removing the old paint, she put in a call to Roz.

"Hi. Just wondering if there's any word from Mac on that con man."

"No," Roz said. "I spoke to him about a half hour ago, and they still haven't found him."

"He's got to turn up sooner or later," Sadie said.

"I suppose so. Are you coming to the show tonight?" Roz sounded as eager as a teenager.

"Of course! Every night, you get better and better. I can't stay away."

She hung up a moment later, smiling at her friend's enthusiasm for the show, and took out some rubber gloves, rags, and a jug of stripping gel. She set the little chair on newspapers on her worktable and hummed as she began to brush the compound on the slats of the chair's back. Sadie loved working on old furniture in her back room. She could picture the delight on the faces of the chair's owner and his grandchildren when they saw it restored.

After a while, her mind drifted to Tulley Morse. She hadn't yet been able to uncover any solid information about the handcuffs he had brought her. Maybe she ought to contact him and tell him she didn't want them. He was right that now was the time to find a buyer, but Sadie didn't suppose they would be a popular item, even with Ainsley Rodin in town. A tourist might buy them as a souvenir of the Old West, she supposed, but she had serious doubts about their age.

Julie came to the doorway of her workroom and smiled.

"Hey! That looks good."

Sadie stood back and eyed the chair. It did look a lot better, now that the green paint slopped on it in the 1980s had been removed.

"The kids are out front," Julie said.

"Theo and Sara?"

Julie nodded.

"Oh, great. I'll be right there."

Sadie put away her supplies, washed her hands, and took off her smock. When she walked out into the store, Sara was rummaging happily through a box of dollhouse furniture, and Theo stood on a step stool, lifting down a framed watercolor that hung from the picture rail above the display shelves. He handed it to a customer who stood waiting beside the stool.

"I hope you enjoy it, ma'am," Theo said.

"Thank you, young man. I'm sure I will." The gray-haired woman's smile told Sadie that she had spotted the watercolor of an old homestead and fallen in love with the scene. And she was getting a bargain. If Sadie had marketed the watercolor online, she probably could have doubled the price.

Julie walked toward the woman. "Thanks, Theo. Just set the stool out back, would you please?"

"Sure." Theo collapsed the steps and picked up the stool.

"All set, Mrs. Cunningham?" Julie asked.

"I believe I am."

Sadie waited until they had passed her on the way to the checkout and joined Theo.

"Good morning! What are you two up to?"

Sara heard her and hurried to her side. "Hi, Grandma."

"Hi, honey."

"Mom's busy planning her strategy for the pie contest," Theo said. "We were hoping Julie could stay here and you could…"

"And you could go riding with us," Sara broke in.

"Horseback riding?" Sadie looked down at her outfit. Knowing she would be working on a messy project this morning, she had worn jeans and a presentable but functional shirt. She kept a pair of riding boots and a cowboy hat in Milo's tack room. "You know, that sounds like fun."

"Yay!" Sara bounced up and down. "It's been ages since you've ridden Scout."

"Well, not ages, but a while." Sadie smiled. "How about you, Theo? Are you ready to give Bronco a workout?"

"Oh yeah. I'm past ready." The tall boy cracked his knuckles and put on a nonchalant air.

Sadie laughed. "Well, then, put the step stool away and let's get going. I'll let Julie know and meet you out back. My Tahoe's parked out there today." She handed Theo her car keys.

Sara's energy didn't abate, and she kept Sadie entertained all the way to Milo's ranch by telling her stories about her pets' latest antics and Theo's attempts to help one of his friends resurrect an old jalopy that had belonged to the other boy's uncle.

"It's going to be awesome once he gets it running," Theo insisted.

Sara made a face. "If you say so. Right now it looks like a piece of junk."

"Vintage cars are like that," Sadie said. "Think of it as an antique that's been neglected. A little love and restoration can bring it back to its glory."

"I s'pose. Anyway, Mia is going camping next weekend with Nicole and her family."

"That's nice," Sadie said.

"They're going over to the national forest for three whole days. I wish Dad would take us camping." Sara bounced a little in the backseat as she continued to complain about how few vacations her family took together, and then launched into an animated tale of how her friend Nicole had gotten sick while on one of the carnival rides at the fair.

"And her dad told her she couldn't go on any more rides this week. Period. At all."

"That is so lame," Theo said.

Sara punched his shoulder lightly. "You wouldn't think so if you were thirteen. When we're your age, Nicole and Mia and I will be able to go on all the rides we want."

"Right," Theo said with evident disinterest.

"Anyway, if Mom lets me go to the fair tonight, I'm going to do the shooting gallery. I know I can win one of those teddy bears."

Sadie hoped Sara would calm down a little before mounting her horse, Daisy, but she didn't say anything. Seeing Sara carefree and happy was priceless.

"By the way, honey, I sold that Centennial thimble that you found in the Monopoly game."

Sara's eyes flared, and she grinned. "Wow! That was fast. How much do I get?"

"Half of twenty dollars. I'll pay you when we get back to the store."

"Awesome! Thanks."

"You sold that thimble for twenty bucks?" Theo asked.

"Colorado Centennial," Sadie said, with a quirk of her eyebrows.

She parked in Milo's yard, and Sara hopped out and ran toward the barn. Theo walked more sedately beside Sadie across the barnyard, his green eyes thoughtful. "Do you think they'll catch that guy who stole Mr. Marshall's Indian pipe?"

"I think they will, given time," Sadie said, glancing up at her tall grandson. "I guess you've heard that Mac Slattery has some clues, and the state police are looking for the man whose car was parked near Edwin's house on Friday."

"Yeah."

They stepped into the dim barn. The air was cooler inside, and the smells of horse, leather, hay, and manure greeted them.

"Best smell in the world," Theo said.

Sadie chuckled. "Amen to that—although baking bread would be a close second for me."

"Pizza," came Sara's voice from the tack room. Sadie laughed and shook her head.

They saddled up and headed out along a trail they seldom took. It curled around the base of the mountain and approached a shimmering stream.

"I love it out here," Sara said, leaning forward to pat Daisy's neck as they ambled along.

Bronco was more fidgety, and Theo had to fight to keep him at the leisurely pace.

"Did your mom talk to Milo about the gymkhana?" Sadie asked Sara.

"Yup. He's taking me and Daisy over. It's going to be great!"

"Race you to the stream," Theo called. He slipped the reins so that his black gelding could gallop.

"Hiya!" Sara squeezed Daisy with her legs and set off after them.

Scout didn't need any encouragement to pick up the pace, and Sadie and Sara barreled along in Bronco's wake.

They could ford the water, or cross it on a bridge that was part of a rural road, and then get back on to Milo's property just beyond the bridge. Theo reined in his horse when he came to the place where they sometimes walked the horses across the stream. He waited for them to catch up.

"The water's higher than I expected. Want to cross here or go over the bridge?"

Sadie brought her five-year-old chestnut gelding up beside Bronco. The bridge was visible about a hundred yards downstream.

"Let's do the bridge today," she said. "I haven't had Scout out for a while, and I'd hate for him to get fussy in the middle of the stream." She didn't really think Scout would dump her, but she was actually concerned about Bronco. The young horse was still prancing and eager to run. A misstep in the rocky creek bed could send Theo flying.

"Okay," Theo said. He was off almost at once, loping Bronco toward the near end of the bridge.

Sadie smiled ruefully at Sara. "Looks like we're playing catchup today."

"I don't mind. I don't think Daisy does either." Sara's bay filly snorted and tossed her head. "Oh, you want to go some more, huh? Well, let's go then." Sara loosened her reins and took off after Theo.

To Sadie's surprise, Theo had pulled up near the stream bank, still twenty yards short of the bridge. She thought he was just waiting for them, but as she approached, she saw that he was easing Bronco closer to the stream. Daisy and Scout's arrival drew his attention, and he turned Bronco to face them.

"Grandma, there's a car down there, half in the water."

"Really?" Sadie rose in her stirrups, peering toward the shadows under the bridge. As she got closer to Theo, she saw a darker green spot beyond the bushes that lined the bank. She urged Scout forward, and he took a few more steps. The glint of sun on chrome and glass startled her, even though Theo had warned her. "Whoa, boy." She could only see the back end of the car, which appeared to be tilted up at an angle, with its nose in the water.

"What do you think, Grandma?" Sara rode Daisy up beside her and shielded her eyes as she looked under the bridge.

"We should tell Milo," Sadie said. She glanced at Theo. "When was the last time any of us came out here?"

"We rode this trail a couple of weeks ago. It wasn't here then," Sara said.

"No, we would have seen it," Theo confirmed. "Mom was with us, and we all rode over the bridge."

"We let the horses drink on the other side," Sara added. "There wasn't any car there that day."

"Was it here when you and Mom picked raspberries?" Theo asked.

Sadie shrugged. "We didn't come this way. We drove into Milo's north pasture. There's a berry patch near the creek that flows into this. That's where Milo told us the best bushes were."

Sara smiled faintly. "And the bears apparently agree with him."

"Yeah, they gave it a five-star review," Theo said with a chuckle.

"Well, we should definitely tell Milo," Sadie said, unable to shake her uneasiness. "It must be a recent accident, but I didn't hear anything about it in the news."

Sara's face sobered. "It's a little scary, thinking someone could have a wreck out here and nobody knew about it." She shuddered.

Sadie gazed at the car, knowing what she should do, but Theo voiced her thought.

"I think we should check and see if anyone's inside."

"Yes, we should." Sadie lifted her reins. "There could be someone down there."

"I'll go," Theo said. Bronco pranced in place, as though eager to carry out his master's plan.

"Are you sure?"

"Yeah. You stay here with Sara."

Sadie hesitated only a moment. Theo, at seventeen, was nearly a grown man. He wanted to be a police officer, and he had faced some difficult moments in his young life. Now he wanted to protect her and Sara. She decided to give him that chance.

"Okay, go ahead."

Bronco moved out eagerly at a trot, and Theo kept him on a tight rein. Sadie urged Scout a little closer to the stream bank, so that she could watch Theo when he dismounted. He hopped down and looped his reins over a small alder.

Sara moved Daisy up beside Scout. "What will we do if there's somebody in there?"

"The same thing we would have done if there wasn't," Sadie said calmly. "Tell Milo. He'll take care of it." She watched Theo make his way carefully down the steep bank below the bridge piling. Another glance at the car made her catch her breath.

"What?" Sara asked anxiously.

"The license plate," Sadie said, squinting at it and trying to make sure of the characters, but even from this distance, she knew she was right. "I think that's the car Sheriff Mac has been looking for."

Sadie and Sara waited on their horses while Theo lumbered down the steep bank to where the green car rested. He stooped and peered in through the back window, then carefully stepped along the side of the car until he was even with the front window on the driver's side. Sadie's heart thundered.

Theo straightened and put his hands to his mouth, making a megaphone. "There's a guy in here. I think he's alive."

Sadie pulled out her cell phone, but the mountain was between her and the nearest tower. She turned to her granddaughter. "Sara, I don't have a strong enough signal to call nine-one-one. Go get Milo. Fast. Have him call for the sheriff and an ambulance."

10

SARA'S FACE HAD PALED, BUT WITHOUT ANOTHER WORD, SHE pivoted Daisy and pushed the horse into a canter. As they tore for the ranch house, Sadie turned her attention back to Theo. She rode Scout closer and dismounted, leaving her gelding to browse near Bronco.

The grass and weeds grew high up to the stream bank, which dropped off about four feet. The descent was steep, and the water below swirled over rocks, but it was less than a foot deep in most spots near shore. She could see the rocks beneath the surface. Theo was tugging on the driver's door handle when Sadie reached the edge.

"I sent Sara to Milo's for help," she called.

Theo looked up at her. "I can't open this door. Should we wait?"

"I don't know. He's probably been in there a while." Sadie's mind whirled. If this was the car belonging to the man who had stolen Edwin's Arapaho pipe, he may have been trapped here for several days. Would another half hour matter? On the other hand, she knew a little bit about emergency medicine, and every fiber of her being cried out to act as quickly as possible.

She walked cautiously along the bank for several yards, until she was beneath the bridge and could see the passenger side of the car.

"This side is mostly clear of the water. Maybe we can open this door."

"Okay, I'm coming around."

While Theo carefully edged around the front of the damaged car, Sadie scrambled down the bank, holding on to a flimsy bush for a little support. She landed with one foot on a rounded rock and the other boot in six inches of water.

She hopped across three rocks until there was no helping it—if she wanted to get to the car, she had to step down into the water. It came nearly to her boot tops with the first hesitant step. Theo was rounding the front of the car, hanging on to the hood ornament.

"How deep is it out there?" Sadie called.

"Maybe a foot and a half." His jeans were soaked past his knees.

That settled it. Theo already had wet feet, and a man's life was at stake. Sadie gritted her teeth and waded out. The current wasn't very strong, and by feeling her way among the rocks in the stream bed, she made it to the car's rear passenger door. It was completely above the water, while a small part of the front door panel was submerged. She took hold of the nearer door handle and pulled, but it didn't give. She leaned against the glass and peered inside. She couldn't see the driver. The high headrests blocked her view, and she supposed he had slumped low in the seat.

"I think this door's locked," she said to Theo, who had nearly reached her.

He came even with the front door and tugged at the handle. "I guess they all are. We'll have to break a window." He stooped and felt about in the water for a small rock.

"Don't break the front one," Sadie said. "You might cut him."

He fished about a little longer and came up with a stone the size of a baseball.

"Stand back." He smashed it against the rear passenger window, and the glass cracked but didn't give way.

"Safety glass," Sadie said.

"Okay, get out the way."

She stepped on to a rock near the bank. "I wish we had one of those glass-breaker tools." She had one in the glove compartment of her Tahoe, but that was back at Milo's.

Theo waded a few feet away from the car and fished for another rock. He flung it at the window he had cracked. The window shattered, and hundreds of small pieces collapsed into the car.

"I should be able to unlock it now."

"Wait," Sadie said. "I have a pair of gloves in my saddlebag. Let me get them for you, just to be on the safe side."

She struggled up the bank to where they had left the horses. She always left a few items in the pouch on her saddle, just in case—leather gloves, a hoof pick, a small bottle of sunscreen, and a couple of granola bars. Today she had added a plastic bottle of water, and she grabbed that along with the gloves. She almost tumbled down the bank in her hurry to get back to Theo.

"Careful, now."

"I will be." He pulled on one of the gloves. "It's a little tight, but I can make it work." He tugged the second one on with his teeth. He approached the window and brushed the small pieces of glass on the edge away. Sadie held her breath as he unlocked the rear door and levered it open. From there he could lean in and reach the release for the front door.

He backed out and leaned into the passenger compartment in the front. Sadie stepped carefully through the water and climbed into the tilted backseat, carrying the water bottle.

"Sir," Theo said. "Sir, can you hear me?"

The driver moaned.

Sadie hitched up over the back of the seat before her. The man had light brown hair sprinkled with gray. His thin face was bruised and smeared with dried blood across his cheeks and into his short beard. He reached feebly toward Theo.

"Who...who?"

"I'm Theo Macomb. We're getting help for you, sir."

The man's lips moved, but no sound came out. Sadie unscrewed the cap on the water bottle and held it out.

"Give him some of this."

"Sir, would you like some water?" Theo asked.

The man jerked his head in an abbreviated nod.

Theo carefully tipped the bottle up until the rim touched his swollen lips and a small amount of water flowed into his mouth. A few drops spilled down on to his olive jacket and blue shirt. The man swallowed, licked his lips, and leaned forward for more.

After his second sip, Sadie said, "Sir, I'm Sadie Speers. If we help you, do you think you can get out?"

"No." His breath came fast and shallow, and his eyes clouded. "My legs. Can't move."

Theo hunched down for a moment, looking under the dashboard and steering column.

"He's bled a lot, Grandma. I think one of his legs is smashed. Maybe both. There's a lot of water down around his feet, and I can't really see very well in here."

"All right." Sadie touched the man's shoulder. "Don't you worry. We've sent for some paramedics. They'll have the equipment to get you out of there without hurting you worse than you are."

He gave a little groan, but didn't answer.

Sadie looked at Theo. "You stay with him. "I'd better ride Scout up to the road and guide them in. You okay with that?"

"Yeah, that's good," Theo said.

Sadie gave him a pat and eased to the edge of the seat, then lowered herself gingerly into the stream bed.

By the time she got up to the horses, she could hear a faint siren in the distance. She tied Bronco so that he wouldn't follow her and led Scout in a circle until the ground sloped down and she could mount easily. She trotted quickly toward the ranch and stopped the horse when she could see vehicles coming.

Scout stood majestically in the middle of the road, with Sadie in the saddle. Milo's pickup came first, and as it approached, Sadie made out Milo driving and Sara in the passenger seat. Behind them came Sheriff Mac's car with the light bar flashing, and then the ambulance with its red lights and wailing siren.

Sadie waved and moved Scout to the side of the road as Milo slowed and stopped the pickup. He lowered his window.

"You probably want to drive on over the bridge," Sadie said. "Right at the near end of the bridge is the closest the EMTs will be able to get."

"Okay. I'll park on the other side and leave my flashers on, just in case a car comes along from that direction while they're loading, but this road doesn't get much traffic."

"Sounds good," Sadie said.

He drove on, and she trotted Scout along behind him until she got to the bridge.

Milo paused, and Sara hopped out of the truck and came around to stand by Scout while Milo drove on across the span. "What should we do, Grandma?"

"Probably just stay out of the way. Here, you take Scout over on the other side of the road, where there's some grass, and then take Bronco over there too. No sense in the EMTs having to worry about horses between them and the creek."

Sadie dismounted and gave Sara Scout's reins. Sara led him off as Mac left his car a few yards away, parked at the edge of the road to give the ambulance room to pass him.

"Whatcha got, Sadie?"

"There's a man trapped in his car down there." Sadie pointed. "Theo and I broke a back window, because everything was locked. We got in and gave him some water. He says he can't move his legs. I think he's dehydrated and disoriented."

"Sara said it could be Murray Lithgow, the con man we've been looking for," Mac eyed her closely.

"I think it's the license plate number you gave me. Didn't you say Lithgow's number started with four-C-two?"

"That's right. Do you know how long he's been out here?"

"He didn't say, but if it's Lithgow..."

"Yeah," Mac said. "Nobody's seen or heard from him in Denver since last Thursday. Why don't you take me down there? Is there a path?"

"Not really. Theo and I walked down over here."

The ambulance driver had cut off the siren, and the vehicle nosed up close to where they stood talking.

Sadie told the EMTs where the patient was and led the way, with Mac close behind. The two medical specialists grabbed their portable equipment packs and followed.

"There," Sadie said, when the back end of the car was clearly in view. "We only saw it because we were riding that trail, down there near the stream. I'll stay up here with Sara and the horses. Theo is probably still in the car with him. Let me know if there's anything we can do."

"You got it," Mac said. He and the EMTs made their way down to the edge of the stream.

Sadie turned back and met Sara where she was collecting Bronco.

"I found a place for Scout," Sara said. "There's enough good grass to keep them happy for quite a while."

"Thanks. Let's get Bronco over there. We'll only be in the way if we go closer."

————

While Sadie and Sara waited with the horses, Sara described her adventure.

"When I got to Milo's, his truck wasn't there, so I called nine-one-one like you said, and they put me through to Sheriff Mac. He said he'd get right out to the ranch, and almost as soon as I hung up, Milo drove in."

"That was fortunate," Sadie said.

"Yeah. I wanted to ride right back here, but he told me to put Daisy away and I could ride in his truck. He thought Mac might not know which way to go to get out here, and we ought to wait for him. But he was there in a few minutes." Sara's eyes were huge, and Sadie patted her shoulder.

"You did just right, honey."

"What did you and Theo do?"

Sadie smiled. "Broke one of the car windows with rocks, so we could unlock the doors."

"Cool. Grandma, can we pray for him?" Sara asked.

"Of course, honey." Sadie took her hand and offered a short prayer for the man in the car. Sara added her plea, and she gave thanks for the quick responders.

Milo strolled toward them over the bridge. "No traffic on this road today, as usual, but I'll keep the truck there until the ambulance crew is done."

One of the EMTs labored up the stream bank, took something from the back of the ambulance, and hurried back down toward the wrecked car. A few minutes later, Theo came up and looked around.

"Over here," Sara called, waving to him.

Theo ambled across the road. "Here are your gloves, Grandma. Thanks."

"No problem." Sadie took them and opened her saddlebag. "How is he?"

"Fading in and out, but he was talking to the sheriff when I left them. The EMTs put an IV line in his arm first thing. They think they can get him out without doing more damage. If not, they'll have to send for special equipment."

"I can help, if they need extra hands," Milo said.

"I told them I could too," Theo replied. "I guess they'll ask us if they need us."

Shortly afterward, Mac toiled up the bank and went to his car, where he talked on the radio for a few minutes. When he got out and walked over to where they stood, Sadie greeted him.

"Is he going to be okay?"

"Well, he's pretty torn up," Mac said. "One knee is shattered, and they said there could be internal injuries. I expect he'll be in the hospital for a while. They might even decide to transfer him to Denver, but they'll take him to Silver Peak first thing."

One of the EMTs came up to the road again. "One of you fellows want to help get the stretcher down there?"

"I'll go." Milo seemed relieved to actually be able to do something physical.

Sadie turned back to Mac. "So…is it him?"

"Yeah," Sara said. "Is it the con man?"

11

MAC PUFFED OUT A DEEP BREATH AND GAZED TOWARD THE bridge."Yeah. It's Murray Lithgow. Looks like he's been out here since Friday night."

"That's awful," Sara said.

"After the magic show?" Sadie asked.

Mac nodded. "After his little run-in with Roz backstage, he ran out to his car, thinking someone would catch him and he'd be in trouble again. He didn't want to go back to the slammer, so as soon as he got off the fairgrounds, he tore out of town. Took a wrong turn, and... well, this is the result."

"That's almost four days," Theo said.

"Yeah. Lucky you folks found him. The EMT said another day or two would have done him in. There was water inches away, but he couldn't get to it."

"That is so sad." Sara had tears in her eyes.

"It is," Theo told her, "but keep in mind that he's a crook. He hurt Roz, and he may have stolen Mr. Marshall's Indian artifact."

"You can be sure I'll search the car thoroughly once they get him out of there," Mac said. "We'll have it towed to the sheriff's office today. I've already requested a tow truck." He looked at

Sadie. "You can tell Edwin and Roz, if you don't mind. I'll contact them if I find out anything else that relates to them. I still don't know what he was doing at the fairgrounds that night."

"I'll tell them," Sadie said. "I know they'll be glad to hear he's been found."

"So what made you ride out this way?" Mac asked.

Theo shrugged, and Sara said, "We hadn't been out here for a while, and we like variety."

Mac laughed.

"I was only along because the kids coaxed me out of the store on this beautiful day." Sadie glanced at her watch. "I'd better call Julie. We've been gone quite a while, and I probably won't get back there for at least another hour."

"Your cell phone won't work out here, remember?" Sara said.

"Oh, right." Sadie gritted her teeth. "Maybe we should take the horses and go back to the ranch."

Sara's face drooped. "I left Daisy back there. Should I wait for Milo?"

"You can ride double with me," Theo said. "Bronco's had some exercise, so he's calm now. It'll be good practice for the gymkhana."

"I don't know," Sara said. "I think I'd feel safer with Grandma on Scout. Can he carry both of us?"

Sadie smiled. "Sure, he can."

Mac said, "Well, you be careful. I'll say one thing: That man is lucky to be alive. You can all be proud of yourselves for what you did today."

Sadie started to protest, but Mac shook his head.

"None of that. I don't care if it was coincidence that you rode today, or that you chose that trail, or that you spotted the car, or that you even bothered to go down and look inside. It's what happened, and you all acted commendably."

"Thank you," Sadie said. She decided not to downplay the incident, though her natural modesty called for that. The kids deserved to be praised. Today would help mold them into responsible and caring adults who would take the time to stop and see whether someone needed help.

———————

Sadie couldn't sleep that night. She was physically tired, but the image of Murray Lithgow, injured and imprisoned in his car, kaleidoscoped 'round and 'round in her mind. Sleep eluded her so long that at quarter past midnight she rose, threw on her housecoat, and opened her laptop. If she couldn't rest, maybe she could find out something about the old handcuffs.

For fun, she began reading sites about Harry Houdini. She found several dedicated to him, his art, museums holding collections related to him, and even sites telling about his wife and his brother. She found that Houdini's early handcuff escapes had made him famous. Later he went on to other things, but handcuffs were often one component of more complicated escapes. He might be handcuffed and shackled, then placed in a large wooden box that was locked and encircled with chains, or handcuffed and shackled and hung upside down in a container of water. But he always got out of them. Even police departments that ordered special handcuffs made just to test him were outsmarted by the great Houdini.

Houdini, it seemed, was extremely secretive and jealous of keeping the workings of his tricks to himself, true to the magicians' code. He was also very choosy about who was allowed to handle his equipment. That made Sadie think of Rodin, insisting that only Steve Parrish could carry his luggage. After reading this in several different accounts, she was convinced that Houdini would not likely have given away a set of handcuffs during his lifetime.

She delved deeper into his travels and decided that Houdini couldn't possibly have performed in Silver Peak. His brother Dash, however, might have done so. Dash, as Theodore was known, had performed with his brother before Harry got married. After the wedding, Harry made his wife, Bess, his onstage partner. But later, Dash took the name Theodore Hardeen and became famous in his own right. Sadie couldn't pin him down precisely, but she decided it was quite possible that Hardeen had performed in Silver Peak between Houdini's death in 1926 and Hardeen's final show in 1945.

That narrowed things down somewhat. She ought to be able to check in the records held by the Historical Society. If Hardeen had never performed here, then she would assume the handcuffs Tulley Morse had brought her had no connection whatever to Houdini and were practically worthless.

She went back to bed, and this time she slept through until morning. After a cup of strong coffee, a walk with Hank, and a good breakfast, she was ready to go to work.

When she turned the sign on the door to "open," Pete Osborn was one of the first people to come into the Antique Mine.

"Hi, Pete!" Sadie smiled at him and eyed the cardboard carton he carried. "Do you have something for me today?"

"Maybe so." He set the box carefully on the counter. "See what you think of these." He took out several small square books, each an inch or two thick, and lined them up before her.

"Big Little Books! One, two three…eight! Where did you get them?"

"Not telling," Pete said. "I assure you it's all nice and legal, but I don't want to give away my source. She's got some other things she might sell me if I make a good deal on these."

"Okay, that's fair." Sadie scanned the titles and noted that most of the books were in very good condition. "*Popeye, Donald Duck*—those are fun, but not really valuable. The detective stories and *Jungle Jim* would be worth more." She clicked on her computer and skimmed through a few listings. "How does thirty dollars for the lot sound?"

Pete frowned. "I'd like to give her that much, but I need to make something too."

"Well…hold on." Sadie did a little more checking. She could give Pete a little more margin, she decided. "Okay, I'll give you ten each for *Buzz Sawyer* and *Dick Tracy*, and twenty-five for the other six books as a group."

Pete pursed his lips and nodded. "We'll take it. Thanks, Sadie."

"No problem." She wouldn't make as much as she would have liked on the purchase, but Pete was a loyal supplier, and she wanted to keep the goodwill she had earned in the community. She took the money from the cash register and handed it to him. "Let me get this in the computer, and I'll print you a release to sign."

A moment later, she handed Pete the slip of paper describing the items she had bought.

"Say, Pete, a fellow was in here last week who says he knows you."

"A lot of people know me," Pete said.

Sadie smiled. "That's true. This guy's name was Tulley Morse."

"Oh, him." Pete's slight frown raised a warning flag in Sadie's mind.

"So he's not a friend of yours?" she asked.

"I wouldn't call him a friend exactly. Did he say that?"

"No. He only said you'd told him that I sometimes buy old things from people, and that's true. I do."

"I might have mentioned you to him. I hope that's okay."

"It's fine, Pete. But the thing he brought me was a pair of handcuffs. He claimed they'd belonged to Harry Houdini, and…well, I just can't find anything to make me think his story is true."

"Huh. Wouldn't surprise me a bit."

Sadie arched her eyebrows at him, waiting for more of an explanation.

"I don't like to trash-talk anyone," Pete said. "Just beware of his—what you call provenance for stuff."

She nodded. "Thanks. I'll do that very thing."

Pete nodded and gave her a little salute with the receipt in his hand.

Julie came to the front with a customer who was buying an old hayfork. Sadie vacated the space behind the counter and left Julie to take care of the sale. No one else seemed to be in the store at the moment, so Sadie turned toward her workroom. Behind her, the bell over the door jingled. She turned back and was pleased to see Roz enter.

"Hi," Sadie said. "Come on out back with me."

As soon as they were in the back room, Roz said, "That was some adventure you had yesterday, lady!"

"Yes, it was."

"Well, I'm glad you found that car. Mac says the driver's definitely Lithgow, and he's admitted that he was the one at the fairgrounds Friday night, so I don't have to ID him or anything."

"That's a relief."

"Yeah."

"I wonder if he found anything in Lithgow's car?"

"He didn't say anything to me about it, if he did," Roz replied.

Sadie nodded. "Maybe I'll touch base with Edwin after lunch, to see if Mac's said anything about his pipe."

She heard the bell on the door jingle again and looked out the workroom door to see if new customers had come in, or if the woman Julie had been attending had gone out. Jane Remington had entered. Julie was still with her customer, and Jane stood looking around the store.

"I'd better get going," Roz said, giving Sadie's shoulder a gentle squeeze. "Roscoe asked me to help him at the hardware store for a couple of hours. He has a dental appointment."

"Okay, I'll see you later."

They walked into the store, and Roz greeted Jane and then slipped out the door.

"Hi, Jane," Sadie said. "Nice to see you."

"I sneaked off for a break," Jane confessed. "We've been full up all week with fair people, and the laundry and cooking have kept me pretty busy, but Jerry insisted I take this morning off. He even loaded the dishwasher after the guests finished breakfast."

"Isn't that sweet of him?" Sadie said. "So you have other guests, besides Mr. Rodin and Steve Parrish?"

"Oh yes! If I had half a dozen more rooms, I could fill them too. I've sent two couples to Wade Marley to see if he had any cottages free for them. We've got the man in charge of the midway rides, and a couple with a concession stand. Then there's a couple who came here to hike. Summer is winding down, you know. Everyone wants to get their mountain weekend in before school and cold weather come back. I'm not complaining, you understand," Jane added quickly.

"I feel the same way when a bus full of seniors parks out front. I know it'll be chaotic for a few hours, but we love to see them coming. Do you want to look at anything particular?"

"One of our guests mentioned that she collects cranberry glass. I thought I'd ask if you had any, so I could tell her if you did."

"I have a few pieces, as a matter of fact. Over here." Sadie led Jane toward the section where she displayed china and glassware.

When they reached the area, Jane lowered her voice. "I also heard about you and the kids finding that man in his car. Sadie, how awful."

"Well, it could have been worse. I'm glad we were able to get help for him."

"Yes, of course." Jane shook her head. "Mr. Rodin was glad to hear they'd caught that fellow. Found him, I mean. At least now, he knows that man won't be trying to interrupt the show."

"I think he and Roz are safe. Mr. Lithgow won't be going anywhere for a while."

"That pitcher's really pretty," Jane said, studying the pieces of cranberry glass Sadie had shown her. "I like the serving bowl too. I'll definitely tell my guest that she ought to stop in here."

"Thanks," Sadie said. She and Jane chatted for a few more minutes, mostly about the Remingtons' illustrious guest, Ainsley Rodin.

"He's not difficult at all," Jane said. "He always seems to like what we serve for breakfast. He's a little fussy about his things though. He won't let anyone touch his luggage, and we can't go in to clean unless he or Steve is there."

"I guess magicians have to be really protective of their secrets," Sadie said. "I read an article last night about Houdini, and he was the same way."

Jane smiled. "You're probably right. If everyone knew how they did their tricks, they wouldn't pay to see them perform."

"How about Steve?" Sadie asked. "Do you clean his room when he's out?"

"Yes, he's no problem," Jane said. "Of course, we don't touch his personal things. He doesn't talk to us much, but when he does, he's very polite. He's a good guest." She looked around for a moment. "Well, I think I'll go over to Material Girl now and look at fabric. I want to make some new cushions for the love seat."

"Okay. Have a good day, Jane."

When she had gone, Sadie and Julie were alone in the store.

"It's kind of slow today, isn't it?" Julie said. "Not like it was last weekend."

"Do you want the afternoon off?" Sadie asked. "I was thinking of asking Edwin if he could have lunch with me, but if you'd like to go home..."

"I'd love to put in a few more hours, actually," Julie said. "Why don't you go to lunch, and if it's still slow in here afterward, I'll take off."

Edwin readily agreed to meet Sadie at the Depot at noon. She walked to the restaurant, and he arrived soon after she took a booth. While they waited for their spaghetti, they nibbled garlic breadsticks and thoroughly hashed over the latest developments concerning Murray Lithgow.

"Mac said he's talked to him a little, but Lithgow's really not up to an in-depth interview yet," Edwin said. "No visitors either. I got the impression he's sedated."

"Did Mac say anything about the car?" Sadie asked.

"Only that he'd searched it, and there was nothing inside that appeared to be stolen. No sign of my pipe."

"That's odd," Sadie said. "Did they find out if he was staying around here? Maybe he had a hotel room and left stuff in it."

"Mac didn't say." Edwin broke his breadstick in half. "I talked to the insurance company yesterday. They said to file for the loss, but I hate to. I keep thinking Mac is going to find it any minute. I guess I have to face reality."

Sadie reached for his hand. "It's probably for the best if you go ahead and file. I did talk to Mr. Waverly about David Russell, and he seemed to think Russell is about the last person on earth who would steal an antique. He's known him awhile and done a lot of business with him."

"Thanks." Edwin sighed. "You're right. I'll call my insurance company when I get back to the office. So are you coming to the show tonight, or are you bored with it?"

"I'll be there." Sadie smiled. "Roz and Rodin seem to be taking pains to make it a little different every night. And she's still excited about it."

"I thought she'd be tired of it by now," Edwin said.

"She doesn't seem to be. Maybe she missed her true calling and should have gone into show business."

"She does seem to enjoy the spotlight."

"I think it's a nice diversion for her, but I know Roz," Sadie said. "Nine nights in a row is probably enough. When it's over, she'll rest for a few days and then be ready for the next adventure. Now, Roscoe, on the other hand, may be counting the days until the fair closes." She looked up as the waitress came toward them with their plates on a tray. "Oh boy, here's our spaghetti."

"I'm glad you're going tonight," Edwin said after the waitress had left them. "I don't mind going and doing the intro, but Roscoe let on to me that he's a little nervous about it. He doesn't want Roz to be there alone, but he gets up pretty early to open the hardware store every morning. I think he's tuckered out."

"Why don't you stop at the store and tell him we'll keep an eye on Roz tonight?" Sadie suggested. "We could give him a night off, and he could go to bed early."

"I don't know if he'd do that," Edwin said. "The whole thing is irrational, now that Lithgow is incapacitated, but he's still feeling a little overprotective of Roz."

"Maybe he'll feel better once Lithgow is out of the hospital and in police custody. Mac is going to arrest him, isn't he?"

"I'm not sure if they can prove he did anything illegal, other than pushing Roz," Edwin said.

"That's assault."

"Well, yes. I guess we'll have to wait and see what happens."

Sadie enjoyed the evening's show. Roz exuded charm and enthusiasm, and she played a major role in a new trick Rodin had taught her. She did a short but beautiful routine where she tied colored scarves together and then magically untied them without seeming to touch the knots. She laid the scarves one by one on a chair, and a moment later picked them up to reveal that they were again tied together. The crowd applauded loudly, and Roz took two bows before they quieted down for Rodin's next trick. Even Roscoe, who had dark circles beneath his eyes, clapped and gave a piercing whistle.

Roz carried herself like a professional and seemed to have lost her self-doubts about performing. Sadie knew the black eye was still colorful under the makeup, but either it had faded considerably, or Roz was getting better at doing her stage makeup. The bruises were hardly noticeable from the front row of the grandstand.

Sadie had just let Hank out for a run the next morning when her phone rang.

"Well, hi, Mac," she said into it after a glance at the screen.

"Good. You're awake."

She laughed. "Barely, but yeah. I'm up."

"The hospital says Lithgow can talk to me this morning, but he also would like to see you."

12

"Me?" Sadie squeaked. "What does he want with me?"

"Well, you and Theo," Mac said. "Mr. Lithgow would like to thank you for saving his life."

"I see. Theo's going to Denver today with some friends."

"Okay. What about you?"

Sadie's impulse was to say no. She didn't want the con man's thanks. But her natural curiosity got the better of her.

"Sure. What time?"

"Nine okay?"

"I'll be there."

She called Julie to tell her she might be slightly late arriving at the store.

"I can be there to open," Julie said. "No problem."

Sadie toasted a bagel and poured herself coffee. She looked down at her jeans and print blouse and decided she didn't need to dress up for the hospital visit.

Mac's official car was already in the parking lot, and Sadie found a space not far away. She stopped at the front desk for the room number and learned that Lithgow was in the intensive care unit. She took the elevator to the fourth floor and walked to the nurses' station there.

"Sheriff Slattery asked me to come in and see Mr. Lithgow," she told the nurse, who was one of her former high school students.

"Oh yes, Mrs. Speers. He told me you were coming." She pointed to one of the units, which had a glass wall on the front so that the nurses could see into the patient's room. However, a curtain was now pulled across the glass, blocking the view. "He's in there. You can go right in. The sheriff is with him."

Sadie walked to the open doorway and looked in. Mac sat beside the bed, with his back to her. Murray Lithgow lay on the white sheets. He had a thermal blanket over him, and sensors were hitched to his hand and chest. An IV pole stood close by, and the tubing from that went to his collarbone, where Sadie assumed he had a subclavian portal for the intravenous fluids. A monitor registered his pulse, blood oxygen level, and respiration rate. His face was still pale, and his skin looked taut across his cheekbones, but he was alert and speaking to Mac. His eyes flickered to Sadie, and he paused.

Mac turned around and nodded at her. "Hi, Sadie. Thanks for coming in. You've met Mr. Lithgow."

"Very briefly." Sadie stepped forward. "How are you feeling?"

"A lot better than the last time I saw you."

She smiled. "Good. I'd be worried if you weren't. My grandson, Theo, was the one who spotted your car, and the one who broke the window so we could get to you. He's out of town right now, but I'll tell him you expressed your thanks."

"Good, good." Lithgow shook his head. "I still don't know how I got into that fix. Guess I was just in too much of a hurry. My night vision's not that good either."

"I didn't see any skid marks," Mac said. "There's a curve in the road, but it's not too serious. It looked to me as though you didn't realize the road narrowed there, and you shot past the bridge rail on the right side."

"Probably so. It's all kind of hazy now."

"What about the mayor's house? Is that hazy?" Mac asked.

Lithgow frowned. "I'm not sure what you mean."

"Yes, you are. We talked about this before. You were parked in your car across the street from Mayor Marshall's house on Friday."

"I don't know who that is, but I told you, I wasn't watching him or his house."

"You did say that." Mac's voice held infinite patience, but Sadie had the feeling his frustration was just beneath the surface. "What you didn't tell me is why you were there. If you weren't planning to break into the Marshall house, what were you doing on Jefferson Avenue?"

Lithgow let out a deep breath and lay back on the pillow, closing his eyes. Sadie looked at Mac in alarm. Mac put a finger to his lips, signaling for her to stay quiet. Sadie studied the older man's features. He looked completely played out. Maybe it wasn't such a good idea to try to pump information out of a man in the intensive care unit.

His eyes fluttered open. "All right, Sheriff. You might as well know. But I'm telling you right now, I didn't do anything wrong. Well, I slammed into that woman backstage at the fairgrounds.

Didn't mean to do that, at least not that hard. But I didn't go to Jefferson Avenue to case your precious mayor's house. I went there looking for Ainsley Rodin."

———————

Sadie and Mac paused in the wings of the stage. Rodin was out front, demonstrating a trick involving large metal rings to Roz.

"I don't know, I just can't seem to get the hang of it." Roz sounded discouraged. She took the three hoops from him and stood center stage as she attempted the maneuver that would somehow hook them together into a chain. Of course, they were both standing behind the main curtain, which was closed, to prevent anyone outside from watching them rehearse.

Steve Parrish watched them from the other side of the stage. He stood patiently, holding Rodin's wand and the silk scarves Roz had used in her routine last night. He noticed Sadie and Mac before the performers did, and raised his chin.

"Hey, boss, looks like you have company."

Rodin looked at Steve, and Steve pointed toward the visitors. Rodin turned toward them, his magnificent, bushy white eyebrows raised.

"Ah, Sheriff! And Sadie! Welcome. How may we assist you this morning?"

Mac ambled out on to the curtained stage, and Sadie followed.

"Hi," Roz said with a grin. "Did you come to see me fumble through my new trick?"

"Now, now," Rodin said. "It is always a challenge to learn something new. But you catch on very quickly. You've done a new trick every night this week, and you have never made a mistake during the show."

"That's right," Sadie said. "I don't know how you do it, but you've been great, Roz."

"Well, thanks. I feel like a butterfingers, but with everyone cheering me on, I keep at it until somehow it goes right."

"You're too modest," Rodin said. "Pretty soon, you will go on the road with your own show."

"Oh, I don't think so." Roz blushed a little, which made her look even prettier than usual. "I'll never forget this week though. It's been an honor to work with you."

"It's been fun," Rodin said. "But now, I'm sure the sheriff would like to do business. Otherwise, he wouldn't be here."

Mac pushed back his cap and scratched his temple. "Now that you mention it, I do have a little news and some questions."

"Please proceed," Rodin said with a hint of a bow. Steve moved a few steps closer.

"The man who was in the wrecked car out beyond Milo Henderson's house has admitted that he was the one who came here last Friday night. The one who shoved Roz while she was backstage during her disappearing act."

"Yes, you told us this," Rodin said.

"He was also the man several people saw sitting in a car across the street from the mayor's house earlier that day."

Roz and Rodin nodded as if synchronized.

"Well, this morning at the hospital, he told me that he wasn't there to watch the mayor, or even the mayor's house."

"Why was he there?" Roz asked, her eyes wide behind her glasses.

Mac's gaze settled squarely on Ainsley Rodin. "He was looking for you."

"Me?" The magician touched his chest, his lips parted and his blue eyes guileless. "I don't understand."

"Oh, come on," Mac said. "You have a history with this man."

"I'm sorry," Rodin said. "I'm not following you."

"I showed you his picture a few days ago. I told you his name. You said you didn't know him."

"I don't."

Mac shook his head, his lips pressed tight together. "I'm not buying that. Murray Lithgow said you testified against him in court five years ago. Because of that, he spent the last five years in prison. And you don't remember?"

"Lithgow." Rodin gazed up toward the lights overhead as though searching for a memory. "You're right. I exposed him. But he was using a different name."

"You must have heard his real name in court," Mac said.

"I suppose I did, but I assure you that when you asked me about the man who came here, I didn't make the connection."

"I showed you his photo."

Rodin shook his head. "It must have been a poor likeness. I'm sorry, Sheriff. I didn't recognize him, and I let you down."

"So tell me about it. What happened five years ago?"

"He was bilking people. I saw him going around pretending he could help people, and he got them to invest in things, telling them they would get a huge return. He would say that he could influence things in their favor, but he couldn't. He would just take their money. When things didn't go their way, he made excuses. Old people would trust him and place their entire savings in his hands."

"And you exposed him."

"Yes. He was a fraud. I talked to a few of his victims and got details about the claims he had made. I'm not an expert in finances and investment, but I am pretty experienced with making people think something's true when it's not. I told the police in Los Angeles. They looked into it and found he was using aliases. He'd cheated dozens of people. By then, he had moved on to Denver. But eventually they caught up with him and arrested him."

Mac nodded. "He served five years. But he got out of prison a few weeks ago, and he wanted to get back at you."

Rodin spread his hands helplessly. "I didn't know. When Roz had her encounter with the stranger, I didn't think of him. I supposed he was safely behind bars. I thought his sentence was a lot longer than that."

"Well, he probably got it reduced for good behavior or something like that," Mac said. "Somehow he found out you were appearing at the fair in Silver Peak this week, and he followed you here. Took a hotel room in Breckenridge. He drove up here Friday and made some discreet inquiries. He found out where you were staying and parked his car across from Mr. Marshall's house, which is just down the street from the Remingtons' B and B. He sat there, watching for you."

"I'm so sorry to have brought trouble to Silver Peak."

"You had no idea," Roz said, patting Rodin's shoulder.

"What did he plan to do?" Steve asked, his voice tight. "Was he going to hurt Ainsley?"

"He hasn't admitted to that," Mac said. "He did tell me that he'd decided to publicly humiliate Mr. Rodin by ruining his show. I think he had some vague plan of cutting some cables backstage, or maybe damaging the apparatus somehow, so that something would break during the show and embarrass him."

"He had a knife when I saw him," Roz said.

"Yeah. I found a hunting knife in his car." Mac looked at the magician. "He says he didn't intend to hurt anyone with the knife, but he did take it backstage, and he had it in his hand when he pushed Roz. You could have been seriously hurt, Roz. Or even Mr. Parrish, if he'd seen Lithgow back there and tried to stop him."

"I wish I *had* been there," Steve said. "I never dreamed anyone would do something like that. And if I'd been able to stop him then, you wouldn't have had to look for him all this time, Sheriff, and he wouldn't be in the hospital today."

"What happens now?" Rodin asked.

"I'm detaining him when he's released from the hospital, and he'll have a bail hearing as soon as he's able. I told the district attorney I think he should be charged with aggravated assault. I may ask him to add a stalking charge, based on what he's said about watching for you, Mr. Rodin. He was lying in wait, but he won't say specifically what he wanted to do to you."

"I should have spotted him," Steve said bitterly. "A lot of other people saw him sitting in his car, apparently. I should have been more alert."

"I didn't hire you as a bodyguard," Rodin said. "Besides, we were both preoccupied with the opening."

"And I don't think he was actually there all that long," Mac added. "He might have sat there two or three hours, but you were probably at the fairgrounds during most of that time, setting up for the show and rehearsing."

"Wait a minute," Roz said. "Are you saying Lithgow wasn't the one who broke into Edwin's house?"

"He says not. I'm not sure I believe him, but so far I haven't found any evidence that says he did, other than his being in the area on Friday. It could be he had nothing to do with the theft, and somebody else pulled that one off."

"I'm so sorry," Roz said, looking at Sadie. "I'd hoped that if they caught the guy who pushed me, they'd find he was also the thief."

"It made sense," Sadie replied. "At least it seemed to."

"What will you do now, Mac? About Edwin's stolen pipe? That seems more serious than the little 'ruin the show' game Lithgow was playing." Roz leveled her gaze at Mac.

He inhaled deeply. "I'll keep working on it. I have a few other leads, but I admit they look pretty slim."

"Wasn't Lithgow trapped in his car through most of the window for the theft?" Sadie asked.

"Edwin couldn't be sure he'd seen the pipe after Thursday night," Mac said.

"But if Lithgow stole it before Friday afternoon, why would he sit in his car near Edwin's house afterward?"

"I know," Mac said. "I'm inclined to think he's telling the truth about that. I found absolutely nothing in his car, and his hotel room in Breckinridge has been searched too. Nothing there, except a few clippings about Mr. Rodin and notes about his appearances." Mac met the magician's eyes. "He's been watching to see where you'd be. Silver Peak was perfect, from his perspective. It's a small town, and you weren't taking your usual entourage with you. That would make it easier for him to get at you. He only had to get past Mr. Parrish."

Steve shook his head. "I didn't think we needed security here, and I knew your department was patrolling the fairgrounds, Sheriff. But I should have been more careful."

"It's not your fault," Rodin said. "I told you we didn't need private security for this gig."

"And ordinarily, you wouldn't. But Lithgow had it in for you." Mac looked around at the others. "Well, I'd better get back to my office and catch up on some things. Sadie, you want a ride back to Main Street?"

"Thanks." Sadie smiled at Roz. "I'll see you tonight. And don't worry—you'll catch on to that new trick."

She rode back into town with the sheriff, and he stopped in front of the Antique Mine.

"Thanks for being so diligent on this, Mac," she said, reaching for the seat belt release.

"Hey, I want to see this case solved as much as you do. And, Sadie?"

She paused with her hand on the buckle. "Yeah?"

"If you see or hear anything that might help—even something small..."

"I know. I'll call you."

Inside the store, Julie was holding her own among a small influx of shoppers. Sadie waved to her and walked slowly around the display areas, stopping to greet acquaintances and ask if she could help anyone. An hour later, they had sold several items, and only three parties were left browsing the aisles. Sadie was about to suggest that Julie take her lunch hour when her phone rang.

"Hey, it's me." Roz sounded a little out of breath. "We're going to take a break and meet back here at two. Can you get lunch with me?"

"Uh, sure, I guess so," Sadie said, glancing about at Julie and the remaining customers. "Where and when?"

"Twenty minutes from now, at my house? That is, if you can stand leftover lasagna from last night."

"Sounds delicious. I'll be there." She hung up, puzzling over this exchange. Roz's suggestion that they eat leftovers together had surprised her. She had expected her friend to suggest Los Pollitos, the Depot, Sophia's, or even the Market, where they could get a sandwich on Maggie Price's homemade artisan bread.

As soon as Julie was free, Sadie filled her in on the situation.

"I promise not to be gone long, and when I get back, you take a long lunch, or even the rest of the day if you want."

"That would be great," Julie said. "I've got a decorating project I'm doing, and I'd love to have a few hours to work on that."

"Consider it done," Sadie said. "I'll try to have you out of here by one thirty. Two at the latest."

Julie smiled. "Thanks. Oh, and I want that framed sampler for my client. I put it under the counter, and I'll settle up for it before I leave."

"Okay by me." Sadie grabbed her purse and keys and headed out the door again with a wave.

Roz's car wasn't in the Putnams' driveway when she arrived, so Sadie waited in her Tahoe. Peonies and chrysanthemums flourished in the flower beds lining the walkway to the cottage. Once again, the weather held perfect for the fair.

Sadie took out the small notebook she always carried in her bag. It seemed the mystery of the man who had assaulted Roz was solved, but the theft at Edwin's house was further from a solution than ever. The pipe had been stolen nearly a week ago, and as Mac had said, the leads were slim. Especially now that their number-one suspect seemed to be out of it. Time to write down what she knew about the theft.

Edwin last saw the pipe on Thursday evening, nearly a week ago now. He thought he might have seen it early Friday, or at least would have noticed if it was missing, but he wasn't a hundred percent sure. Skip Stewart had been at Edwin's Monday through Thursday, and he had been left alone for several hours, with the back door unlocked. The pipe had not been stolen during that time, but Skip could have entered the house and observed Edwin's possessions. Murray Lithgow had been seen near Edwin's house at the right time, but he denied even knowing about the pipe, and Mac could find no evidence that he'd had anything to do with the theft. It wasn't much.

She was still thinking about it a few minutes later, when Roz pulled in. They both got out of their cars. Roz wasn't wearing her heavy stage makeup, and in the bright sunlight, Sadie could see the dark blotch of the bruise around her eye through her foundation, but it looked much better than it had even yesterday.

"Sorry I'm late," Roz said.

"It's okay. But what's up? You sounded—I don't know—worried?"

"Come inside," Roz said.

More curious than ever, Sadie followed her to the door. It wasn't like Roz to be secretive. Had she chosen to eat at home because she knew it was private, and their conversation wouldn't be overheard?

13

"Okay, spill it," Sadie said over the warmed-up lasagna and garlic bread. "What's going on?"

Roz sighed and laid down her fork. "It's this." From her pants pocket, she drew out a folded and crumpled piece of paper. Sadie unfolded it. The sheet of plain white notepaper was from a five-by-eight-inch tablet. A message was written on it in black ink in a distinctive script that incorporated some printed letters and some cursive, but was easy to decipher. Sadie read it out loud.

"*I know you're angry, but this is for the best. Believe me, if I had known your feelings, I would have done things differently.*" She frowned. "It's not signed."

"Where did it come from?"

Roz drew in a deep breath. "I found it on the floor outside the dressing room under the stage. I've got a new overskirt and headpiece that I'm debuting tonight, and Ainsley wanted me to wear it for part of the rehearsal, to make sure the feathers wouldn't get in the way during one of the tricks."

"Feathers?" Sadie asked with a laugh.

"Ha-ha, yes. They're on the headpiece. Ainsley suggested it. It makes me look very vaudeville-esque. Anyway, I came out in my costume, and that note was lying on the concrete by the steps that go up to the wings."

"So...who dropped it?"

"I'm thinking Steve. While I was changing, I had heard someone out there moving things around. I assumed it was Steve, getting the table and the riser for one of the tricks."

"I thought Rodin didn't bring much equipment," Sadie said.

"He didn't, but Steve has rounded up a few props since we got here, and he picked up some scrap lumber for a couple of items."

Sadie thought about that. "Would you recognize Rodin's handwriting?"

"I doubt it," Roz said. "Steve's either. I haven't seen many things they've written."

"So three possibilities." Sadie ran a hand through her short hair. "Either Ainsley wrote it, Steve wrote it, or someone from outside wrote this note to one of them."

"Well..."

"You're right," Sadie said, even though Roz hadn't expressed her thought. "It could be totally unrelated to the magic show. Somebody working at the fair might have dropped it."

"And it seems to me it wouldn't be all folded up and creased if it hadn't been sent yet. So probably it was delivered to the person for whom it was intended, and he dropped it." Roz quickly added, "Or she."

"Yeah, that makes sense to me. But..." Sadie shook her head. "It could be nothing. Nothing serious, I mean. It could be any one of the fairgoers, really. Hundreds of people—maybe thousands—have been through the fairgrounds this week. And the band has been all over that stage every night—probably down below too."

"True." Roz pushed back her chair. "Dessert? I haven't baked all week, but I've got ice cream in the freezer."

"Sure. And coffee, but I'll get it."

"Pour me some too," Roz said.

They sat for another fifteen minutes, enjoying their ice cream and coffee and talking about the note. Finally they had to admit they had no idea where it had come from.

"I need to get back to the store and let Julie go," Sadie said, "But what if I came to the show early tonight?" Sadie asked. "Maybe I'd have a chance to talk to Steve."

"Do you think we should show him that note?"

"Maybe. In itself, it seems pretty innocuous. What do you think?"

Roz frowned. "I guess it couldn't hurt. Or maybe I should give it to Mac."

A shadow of guilt crossed Sadie's mind. She hadn't even considered that course of action.

"But it can't have anything to do with Edwin's pipe. I mean, no one would write a note saying that stealing it was for the best."

Roz wrinkled her nose. "I guess you're right. Maybe we're just a couple of busybodies."

"I've been called that before." Sadie grinned. She picked up her dishes and carried them to the dishwasher. "Let me talk to Steve. I'll be discreet. What time will you get to the stage tonight?"

"Around five, so we can go over that new trick again."

"I'll be there as soon as I can, and I promise to stay out of the way."

"Okay." Roz pointed to the note. "Take that with you, if you think it will help. It's probably nothing, and I panicked for no good reason."

"I don't blame you for being on edge after what happened to you last week. Now, I'm going back to the store." Sadie kissed Roz's cheek. "Thanks for lunch. The lasagna was terrific."

———

Sadie closed the store an hour early and went home for a short walk with Hank. "There, boy, I've been neglecting you, haven't I?" she said as she snapped on his leash. "I promise that when the fair's over, we'll have a long ramble together. Maybe I'll even take you over to Alice's Sunday afternoon. Would you like that?"

She opted for a quick snack rather than a meal and arrived at the fairgrounds a little before five. The stage curtain was closed, but she could hear Roz and Rodin's banter as they rehearsed the trick, then the clash of metal on metal and wood. Roz must have dropped the rings again. Sadie winced. Maybe this wasn't the best time to make herself known.

Clark Langdon, a member of the city council who was also on the fair committee, was ambling about, making a few adjustments here and there. He stooped to pick up something off the ground, and when he rose, he saw Sadie in front of the lowest row of the grandstand.

"Hi, Sadie."

"Hello, Clark." She walked over to talk to him. "This place will be filled up in a little while."

"Yup. Only three nights left for the show. Saturday night, it's all over, and the midway will be struck, all the animals will go home, and the workers will clean up all the trash."

She smiled. "It's been a good fair."

"Hasn't it? I think everyone's especially enjoyed the magic shows. Although the gymkhana on Saturday and the wild berry baking contest both have a record number of entries."

Talking to him made Sadie realize just how many people had walked through the area recently.

"They don't give out the ribbons from the livestock shows here, do they?"

"No, that's done over at the show ring. But the baby contest will be held here tomorrow, and then we have extra musical acts on Saturday, before the headline show, and sometimes the community awards and best in show from the fruits, vegetables, flowers, and arts and crafts are presented here. It depends on how big a turnout we have."

"So attendance has been good?"

"It's been great," Clark said. "Roz has been so busy with the magic show, I've been keeping track of attendance and gate receipts for her. Anne's been helping a lot too. Things have gone smoothly so far."

"Isn't Roz great in the show?" Sadie couldn't hold back her grin.

"She sure is. She's just blossomed this week. And funny! I knew she had a great wit. I've seen her do some theater over at the opera house, but this is something really different for her."

"She's having a grand time," Sadie said. She chatted with Clark for a few more minutes and turned the topic to local handymen. "Edwin told me you've hired Skip Stewart to do odd jobs for you."

"More than odd jobs," Clark said. "He's good at repairing and building stuff."

"And you like his work?"

Clark nodded. "He's terrific. If you need something done, he'd be a good one to call. I've never heard any complaints about him."

"Thanks."

The music from the rides on the midway reached them, and they could hear young people screaming as they whirled around on the octopus ride. Farther along, past the steam engines and tractors on display, the petting zoo and livestock barns were alive with participants and spectators who had come for the evening's events.

Sadie left Clark and walked around to the back of the stage and in beneath the structure. She easily found the steps that led up to the wings, but she turned away from them and looked around. In her previous involvement in fairs and shows on the grounds, she had gone backstage and beneath the structure several times, but now she took a new interest. Odd things were going on here this year, even if only small things, like a dropped note.

Murray Lithgow couldn't have dropped that piece of paper during his meddling, she reasoned as she scanned the floor. Roz or Steve would have found it before now. But she was probably wasting her time, thinking she could find out who had lost it.

She walked quietly up the steps to the wings on the performers' left side of the stage. Steve Parrish sat on a stool behind one of the flats that made up the wings, his head bent over something in his lap. On the floor at his feet was a rectangular wooden box about two feet long, with leather handles.

As she stepped closer, he looked up, saw her, and quickly dropped the thing he was working on into the box and closed the lid.

"Hi, Sadie."

"Hello, Steve. You look busy."

"Just working on a new trick." He smiled, but he glanced nervously toward the box.

"How's the rehearsal going?" Sadie asked.

"Good. Roz is turning into a real pro."

Sadie decided to be open with him. The note Roz had found wasn't threatening. If Steve had written it, would it matter if he knew they had seen it? And if he hadn't, he might be able to shed some light on it. She took the note from the pocket of her jeans.

"This was lying on the floor downstairs."

Steve looked at it, frowning. "What is it?"

"A note. I wondered if it was yours."

He unfolded it slowly and gazed down at the words, his forehead furrowed. "It's not mine."

"Okay. I've been trying to figure out what it means, and who could have lost it."

Steve hesitated and glanced down at the paper again. "Could be anyone, I guess."

Sadie frowned. "Yeah. But I don't suppose it has anything to do with Murray Lithgow. I mean, he hasn't been back here since Friday night, and one of you would have seen this earlier if he'd dropped it then."

"Yeah, the cops went over this place pretty thoroughly after that incident." Steve rubbed the back of his neck and looked down at the paper. "*If I had known your feelings, I would have done things differently.*"

"Do you think Ainsley might have written that?" Sadie asked.

"No, it's not his handwriting," Steve said immediately.

"He could have received it though."

"I...suppose so." He looked into Sadie's eyes. "Does it matter?"

"I'm not sure." She had the funny feeling Steve was holding back something.

"There were a couple of maintenance men around here this afternoon while I was setting up," he said.

Sadie nodded. "Could be one of them dropped it. Thanks, Steve."

"No problem. Oh, wait a sec," he said as Sadie turned away.

"What?"

"Ainsley did get a letter from that Lithgow guy once. It wasn't like that. It was a real letter, a couple of pages, and very bitter. He wrote it while he was in prison. Ainsley showed it to me once."

"Do you think the handwriting is the same?"

"I don't know. That was a long time ago. Three or four years, at least. But it didn't sound like this at all. This writer seems to be apologizing, sort of. Lithgow wanted blood."

"So he really has been planning some sort of revenge on Ainsley for exposing him as a fraud?"

"I think so. If he hadn't driven off that bridge last week, who knows what he would have done. That man is dangerous. I told Sheriff Slattery as much."

Sadie thought about that. "So do you think Ainsley really did recognize the name and picture when the sheriff showed it to him?"

Steve lowered his eyes. "I couldn't say. He did tell us Lithgow used a different name when he knew him." Steve shrugged. "I wasn't with Ainsley when all that started. I can't really speak for him."

"Sure, I understand."

"Oh, Steve," Ainsley Rodin called from onstage.

"Be right there." Steve looked down at the note, but said, "Hey, can I hang on to this?"

"Why?" Sadie asked.

"I could show it to Ainsley later."

"Well…all right."

He tucked the note in his pocket, stooped, and flipped a latch on the wooden box. He moved the box over to where he would be able to see it from center stage and walked out to see what the magician wanted.

Sadie felt a little slighted. Steve didn't trust her. Just to put his mind at ease, she went down the steps and out to the front. She headed toward the livestock barns. She hadn't gone in to see the 4-H livestock entries yet. Patting a few goats and horses should calm her down.

The cryptic note had nearly lost her interest—until Steve asked to keep it. Did he really want it so he could ask Rodin if he'd dropped it? Or was he hiding something more?

It probably *was* nothing. The letter Steve had told her about was more thought-provoking. Lithgow had written a threatening letter to Rodin from prison. Why hadn't Rodin told Mac about that as soon as they learned someone had been lurking backstage? And had he truly forgotten the man's real name?

Or had Steve told her about the letter to draw her attention away from himself?

14

SADIE STROLLED ABOUT THE FAIRGROUNDS THINKING ABOUT Steve Parrish's words and his actions. After viewing the animals, she wandered among the booths of the vendors, games, and refreshment providers. Families and groups of young people roamed the grounds together, talking loudly against the background of carnival music. The smell of the fried dough lured her, and she hovered on the verge of having some, even though she knew it was packed with fat, when her phone rang.

"Hi," Edwin said. "I saw your Tahoe in the fairgrounds parking lot. Are you here already?"

"Yeah," she said. "Where are you?"

"Just came through the main gate. Thought I'd browse a little before I go to the stage."

Sadie glanced around her. "Well, I'm about halfway down the midway, opposite the bumper cars."

"I'll find you if you don't stray far," Edwin said.

"Good. You just saved me from succumbing to the wiles of fried dough and cotton candy."

He laughed. "You must be hungry. No supper?"

"No, and that was foolish of me."

"I'll take you out after the show."

"Oh, thank you! That's very sweet of you."

"Have to do my bit."

Sadie could see him now, walking toward her through the crowd, and she waved. Edwin looked especially debonair tonight in khakis, with a Fair Isle sweater vest over a blue Oxford shirt. She felt a little casual in her jeans, but after all, this was the fair, and Edwin had to go onstage before a crowd to make introductions.

She slid her phone into her pocket and hurried to meet him.

"You're here early." He planted a kiss on her cheek.

"I've been talking to Steve while Roz and Ainsley rehearsed."

"Oh, it's Ainsley now." Edwin's thick, silver eyebrows arched playfully.

Sadie smiled. She supposed she had become more comfortable with him as the days had passed.

"Would you like to ride the Ferris wheel and tell me about it while we take in the view?"

"I'd love to."

The Ferris wheel had always been one of Sadie's favorite carnival rides. Not only did she get a fantastic bird's-eye view of the fair and the massive mountains surrounding the little town, but she got an enjoyable ride in the swaying seat, as well. Sitting close to Edwin was a bonus. They got their tickets and stood in line for only a couple of minutes before sliding into the seat.

"Remember when we did this last?" Edwin asked, bending so close to her ear that his breath tickled her.

She smiled. "Unless I'm mistaken, it was about a month before you went away to college."

"That's the time, all right." He sat back with a sigh and put his arm around her. "We never know what God will do with our lives, do we?"

"That's for sure," Sadie said. She had gone to the fair several times with T.R., and later with Alice and her family. But somehow, being here with Edwin, she felt she had come full circle.

"I'm glad He brought me home," Edwin said, echoing her thoughts.

She smiled and leaned back against his arm, enjoying the swoops and rises of the wheel. As they headed downward the third time, Edwin said, "Looks like people are starting to go to the grandstand."

"We'll get right over there as soon as this is over," Sadie assured him.

"So tell me about Steve Parrish."

Sadie told him about the note Roz had found and her conversation with Steve. "He said it wasn't his, and that it wasn't Ainsley's handwriting. Roz and I are probably making too much of it. But I am starting to wonder about Steve."

"Why is that?" Edwin asked.

"He wanted to keep the note. If he truly thinks it's nothing, why would he do that? And he's got this wooden box, and he's very careful not to let anyone see inside it."

"What kind of a box?"

Sadie described it to him, ending with, "I think your Arapaho pipe would fit nicely in there."

Edwin's eyebrows shot up. "Surely you don't think he stole my pipe?"

"Not really. But then again, why not? He came to town Wednesday, and we have no idea what he did after he and Ainsley settled in at the B and B. He had plenty of time to scout the town before the first rehearsal on Thursday night, I'm sure. Not to mention all day Friday."

"The more I think about it, the more certain I am that the pipe was there Friday morning before I left the house."

"But there's still the box," Sadie said.

"It's probably some of Rodin's equipment. You know he takes care of all the props, and he's fussy about who touches Rodin's things."

"*Rodin* is fussy about who touches his things." Sadie shrugged. "But you're right. Steve said whatever was in the box was a new trick he was working on, or something like that." She frowned, not really upset to have such a simple explanation. She thought Steve was probably telling the truth about the box, but she could speculate. "I suppose it makes sense that he'd want to ask Mr. Rodin about the note."

"It does to me," Edwin said.

Their seat on the giant wheel slowed as they came down toward the platform, and the young man operating the machine stopped it so they could climb out.

"Thanks," Sadie said as he unlatched the safety bar on their seat.

"Good job," Edwin added.

"Thanks, Mr. Mayor." The young man grinned and lifted the bar. They walked carefully down the steps as more riders climbed up on the other side to take their seats.

Edwin took Sadie's hand. "It's almost time for the Skylarks to start. Let's book it for the grandstand."

Sadie hurried along beside him. When they got to the area between the stage and the bleachers, she spotted Alice on the lowest row.

"Looks like someone's saving seats for us," Edwin said.

They reached Alice just as Theo and Sara walked toward them from the opposite direction. Theo carried a cardboard tray of drinks.

"Hi, Mom." Alice jumped up for a hug. "Iced coffee?"

"Sounds wonderful," Sadie said.

"Edwin?"

"Sure. Thanks."

Alice and Sara handed the drinks around while Theo patiently held the tray. Onstage, the band was warming up.

"I didn't know you were coming tonight," Sadie said to Alice.

She shrugged. "Sara wanted to see the show again."

"Aw, Mom," Sara said, "you wanted to hear the Skylarks again, and you know it."

Alice smiled at her indulgently. "Oh, cut it out. They're pretty good, but that's not why I'm here."

Sadie smiled at Sara. "I think they're good, too, but I really came for Roz and the magic show."

"You don't think they'd call on me again, for the watermelon trick, do you?" Sara asked. "I really want to figure out how they do that."

"I'm not sure they're even doing that one tonight," Sadie replied. "I don't think I saw any watermelons when I was backstage earlier."

Spike Harris looked toward them and nodded at Edwin, who handed Sadie his cup.

"Oops, I'm on. Would you hold this for a minute please?"

"Sure thing." Sadie watched with pride as Edwin mounted the stage, had a word with Spike, and turned to the microphone.

"Good evening, folks. Looks like we've got a good crowd tonight. Thank you for coming to the Silver Peak Fair. We hope you'll enjoy the show and spread a little love to the vendors afterward. I hope you like bluegrass, because our opening act is the hometown band we love, the Skylarks, and Spike has just told me they'll be doing a six-city tour next month!"

Everyone applauded as Edwin scurried down the steps to rejoin Sadie and the others. He took his cup from her and settled down on the bench.

"You did great," Sadie said, swiveling her head. "And it does look like a good crowd. The grandstand is nearly full, and we're an hour from the headline show."

"Spike and the boys have gained a lot of fans," Edwin said. "One of the T-shirt vendors has shirts with their logo."

"That's cool," Sadie said, but she decided she wouldn't mention it to Alice. Her daughter had made it clear in many ways that, while she liked and appreciated Spike, she wasn't interested romantically, and any hints to the contrary might get her dander up.

The magic show went flawlessly. Roz performed her new trick with the interlocking rings as though she had been doing it for years.

"She didn't look the least bit nervous," Sadie said to Edwin as they clapped. "This morning she was sure she'd never get it right."

"She's a quick study," Edwin agreed.

To Sadie's delight, the disappearing cabinet was once more part of the show.

"I'll bet Steve's backstage keeping a sharp eye out," Roscoe said when Roz stepped into the cabinet. He watched anxiously until she stepped out of the box once more, smiling from ear to ear. The entire crowd cheered and clapped.

"She did great, Mr. Putnam," Sara said.

"I think I was more nervous than she was," Roscoe admitted with a laugh.

"Well, she looks wonderful too," Alice said. "In my opinion, she's been a big asset to the show. Her costumes have been fabulous, and she really adds class to the act."

Steve, dressed in black, drifted on to the stage to remove the cabinet and set up for Rodin's next trick.

"Let's see if we can take Mr. Rodin out to dinner after the show," Edwin said to Sadie. "We won't have many more chances."

"Great idea," she said. "I'd like to talk to him again. Every time I come around here, he's busy rehearsing or performing."

When the show ended, the crowd applauded so long that Roz and Rodin took two curtain calls. At last, people began to filter out of the grandstand.

Sadie called good night to Alice and the kids and went backstage with Edwin. Roscoe went to the dressing room to find Roz, but Sadie and Edwin found the magician backstage, discussing the setup for Friday night's show with Steve.

"Terrific show," Edwin said, nodding to both men. "Mr. Rodin, Sadie and I wondered if you'd join us for a late supper at Sophia's restaurant?"

"You know, I am a bit hungry," Rodin said. "Thank you, I accept."

"Great," Edwin said. "Steve, would you like to come?"

Sadie held her breath. She really wanted a chance to talk things over with Rodin while Steve wasn't present. To her relief, Steve had other plans.

"Oh, no thanks, Mr. Marshall," he said. "I ate during the music show. I'm going to put things away here and then turn in early."

"I just need to change out of this," Rodin said, waving a hand to indicate his formal tailcoat and cape.

"Take your time," Sadie said, though by now her stomach was clamoring for food.

She and Edwin found no shortage of friends to talk to while Rodin was in the dressing room. Everyone seemed delighted with the evening's entertainment.

A short time later, they were seated at a table in the beautifully decorated Italian restaurant. The waitress came to take their orders and brought them an appetizer plate of cheese, olives, and vegetables, and a basket of crusty Italian bread. Sadie dove in, glad to at last have some solid food before her, and Edwin watched her with twinkling eyes.

"Good, eh?"

"I'll say." Sadie smiled "Rodin, won't you have some too?"

"Oh yes. I am so hungry." He took a slice of bread on his plate and added a few cubes of cheese. "And I've eaten here several times now, so I know I won't leave hungry."

"That's certain," Edwin said. "Ainsley, I read Troy Haggarty's article about you in the *Sentinel* yesterday. That was a fascinating piece."

"Thank you."

"I had no idea your parents were immigrants to this country."

"On my father's side," the magician said. "My mother's people have been here since colonial days."

Sadie reached for her water glass. "That's interesting. Whereabouts did they live?"

"I believe they first came to New England. They were in Connecticut for about a hundred and fifty years. Then, around the mid-eighteen-hundreds, my branch moved to Ohio. Later generations spread out, and I have some extraordinary ancestors."

"I've done some work on my family history, and the more I dig, the more quirky stories I find," Sadie said.

Edwin smiled. "I guess we all find some nuts in the tree, if we shake it hard enough."

"That's true." Sadie rolled her eyes. "But I found some very admirable ancestors too. And Edwin, your people were no slouches. Some of your forebears had significant roles in the period of westward expansion."

"Yes, and I love reading about them," he admitted.

Sadie turned eagerly to Ainsley. "Who was the most outstanding of your ancestors that you know of?"

"I did have some folks who fought in the Revolution," he replied. "My mother was very proud of them. She was a DAR member. But I think the one who intrigues me the most was Uriah Dawson, the famous mountain man."

Edwin's eyebrows shot up. "You mean old Grizzly Dawson?"

"He's the one." Rodin chuckled. "Guess I'm lucky to be here at all, since he was nearly killed at least twice before he was married—once by Indians, and then by the bear that gave him his nickname."

"I think there's a chapter about him in one of my books about Colorado lore." Sadie skewered a cheese cube from her plate with a toothpick. "He was an amazing man."

They talked about the mountain man and other oddities in their family trees until their entrées arrived.

Later, the conversation turned back to the show at the fairgrounds.

"I hope you and Roz feel safe now while you're performing," Edwin said. "I know the sheriff's deputies have tightened their patrols during the shows this week."

Rodin nodded. "We've been fine since Roz's scare last Friday. Steve is very good, and he's been keeping an eye on her when she's backstage."

"How well do you know Steve?" Sadie asked. Edwin glanced at her, but said nothing.

"Pretty well, I'd say. He knows my biggest professional secrets."

"So you trust him completely," Sadie said.

Rodin nodded. "That's a fair statement."

"How long has he been with you?"

"Over four years now. He was working as a stagehand at a theater in San Francisco. He helped me out with some shows that involved about three times the equipment we've got here and some tricky changes onstage. I asked him afterward if he wanted to go on the road with me. He did, and eventually I made him my main technical assistant."

"He goes everywhere with you, then?" Edwin asked.

"Oh yes. All over the country, the Bahamas, Japan, and Europe most recently. I've never had another prop man as good as Steve."

The waitress came to the table and asked cheerfully, "Anything I can get you folks?"

"I'd like some coffee," Edwin said. "Sadie?"

"Yes, please."

"Decaf for me," Rodin added.

The waitress nodded and turned away.

"I guess magicians have to be pretty careful with their equipment for their tricks," Edwin said, and Sadie gave him a grateful smile. She didn't want to end the conversation about Steve Parrish, but she didn't want to seem too snoopy either.

"Oh yes." Rodin blotted his lips with his napkin and leaned back in his chair. "You have no idea how cutthroat this business is. People are always trying to steal my secrets. Everybody does certain tricks, or variations of them, but there are a lot of so-called magicians out there who want to take shortcuts. The best professionals practice constantly. We always want to make it look better, look easier. And we're always on the lookout for a fresh trick, or a new twist on an old favorite."

"I don't think I've seen you slip up all week," Sadie said. "Every trick is flawless."

"Thank you. I've been doing most of them for years." Rodin smiled.

The waitress brought their coffee, and after she had left them, Rodin continued, "When I was a young man, starting out, it wasn't always that way. I would make a mistake, or I'd think something was hidden from the audience's view when it really wasn't. Even nowadays, things go wrong once in a while."

"But you know how to cover it when that happens," Edwin said, smiling.

"Oh yes. You keep on with the show, and you also learn how to make a mistake seem part of the plan."

Sadie frowned. "Like when Roz dropped the flowers the other night?"

Rodin laughed. "That really was a mistake. But you're right. I used it to say, 'Oops, that's not right,' and pull out a second bouquet."

"But you had to have that second one ready," Sadie said.

"Sure. I always have several backup devices ready to bring out—coins in place to feed into my hand, cards in various pockets, a fan or a scarf that's bright and flashy to distract the viewers for a moment."

"I guess that's all you need to put things right—a moment," Edwin said.

"Usually."

"What would you have done if Roz hadn't reappeared in the cabinet Friday night?" Sadie asked.

Rodin sighed. "As soon as Steve gave me the tablet that Mrs. Remington wrote on, I knew he would go backstage. I could count on him to handle whatever was wrong. If she hadn't returned within that first minute or so, I'd have launched into another routine that takes about three minutes, and I would have apologized so profusely to the audience so that they would think we had planned all along for her to fail to appear. And Steve would have given her some props to carry when she finally came out again. Maybe a nail file, and she could say something like, 'Sorry I'm late, Mr. Rodin. I went to get my nails done.' Or she'd be wearing a policeman's hat and say, 'So sorry. I got stopped by a very handsome officer, and I had to talk him out of giving me a ticket.' Something silly, but the audience would just accept it."

"Have you ever had a real emergency before?" Edwin asked. "I mean, what if your assistant had a heart attack or something?"

Rodin frowned. "We have a contingency plan, for Steve to come out instead of the girl. But I'm not sure I'd use that in the case of a real tragedy. I'd probably stick my head through the curtain after a while, get the scoop on what was going on, and then tell the audience we'd had a mishap and would have to close the show. It depends, really. If it was near the beginning, we'd refund their money. But I'm thankful to say that's never happened to me. I like to think we would handle it gracefully."

His words sobered Sadie. She couldn't help thinking how badly things might have ended on Friday night if Murray Lithgow had succeeded in his purpose. What if Roz had been badly hurt, and Steve had come through the cabinet instead? Was there some more to this that she wasn't aware of? Somehow, she was sure Edwin's Arapaho pipe figured into this, but she couldn't think how.

15

Sadie went early to the store on Thursday to put a final coat of finish on the antique child's chair she was restoring. She hoped to return the item to the owner soon. She and Julie had set up the day's schedule so that both could have some free time. Sadie would man the store until one o'clock, when Julie would take over until closing time.

She worked until ten, and then went to the door to unlock it and change the sign to open. She stepped outside and went to the edge of the sidewalk to gaze at the current display inside her plate-glass window. She loved the items they had showcased that month, including a washboard, tub, and several old flat irons, crocks, and canning jars. Old-fashioned clothes pegs held several vintage pieces of children's clothing on a short piece of cotton clothesline. But it was time for a change, and several things that were originally part of the display had been sold.

Cars rolled down the street behind her, and she glanced around the block. Across the street and down a bit, Steve Parrish was just coming out of the Music Emporium. He was carrying one of Spike's retro brown paper bags stamped with a guitar motif. Sadie hoped Steve had found something he would enjoy.

He crossed the street and ambled her way. Surprised, Sadie waved.

"Morning, Steve."

He noticed her and smiled, walking toward her. "Hi. I've been meaning to stop by your place. Are you open now?"

"Yeah. Come on in." Sadie held the door open for him.

Steve crossed the threshold and paused to look around. "You don't have any small wooden boxes, do you?"

Sadie smiled. "Lots of them. Could you be more specific?"

"Yeah, I'm working on something, and I need a box about this long." He measured with his hands awkwardly, with the bag from Spike's dangling from his grasp. "I could build one, but I thought maybe I could find something already made, and it would save me time."

"Come on back to the tool area." Sadie led him down the aisle. "I get a lot of miscellaneous containers. If you see anything on the way that looks like a possibility, just tell me." She stopped by kitchenware. "Like this cheese box, for instance?" She held up a small, rectangular box with an open top and "Kraft cheddar" stamped on the side.

"A little bigger," Steve said, "and it needs a lid."

"What's it for?"

He hesitated. "I can't tell you exactly, but it's for a magic trick I'm working on."

"Okay. Over here, there's one with a microscope inside it, but that might be too small." She took him to another set of shelves and took down a heavy wooden box about ten inches long and four inches square on the ends.

"A microscope." Steve sounded amused. He opened the sliding lid. "Reminds me of high school biology lab. But you're right, it's too small."

"Well, in the tools, there's a set of chisels in a wooden box, but I hate to sell it without the chisels."

"But you wouldn't care what I did with them if I bought them." He was smiling broadly now.

"Just don't tell me."

"Okay, let's see it."

She took him to the tools but suddenly whirled. "Hey, what about that box you had backstage yesterday?"

"Yeah. Something about that size would be perfect. Only that one's already in use."

She nodded, hoping he'd tell her what was in it, but he didn't.

"Here's the chisel set." She reached for the box and put it in Steve's hands.

"*Hmm.* Maybe." He hefted it and turned it around. "A little flatter than I wanted, but I think it's deep enough." He opened the lid. "I could put a latch on it."

"I have some vintage hardware out back," Sadie said. "I'd throw in a latch if you want to buy it. In fact, I'll give you twenty percent off, because I know you really only want the box, not the chisels."

Steve squinted at the sticker. "You don't have one just a little bigger, do you?"

They kept on rummaging in the tool corner. More customers entered the store, and Sadie walked a few steps toward them. "'Morning, folks! I'm back here, if you need me."

Finally, Steve pulled a small tool chest out from under a pile of old harness.

"What's in this?"

"To be honest, I can't remember."

He raised the lid. "How about that?"

Sadie leaned in and looked over his shoulder. "Empty."

"Yeah." Steve pulled it out into the aisle and looked at every side, then tipped it up for a moment. "I don't see a price."

"Steve, for you, I'll give it to you, on one condition," Sadie said.

"What's that?"

"Tell me what you're going to use it for. What are you working on?"

He smiled. "Can't tell you."

"Why not?"

"You know magicians..."

"Oh yes, I know," Sadie said. "Magicians can never reveal their secrets. But you're not a magician."

"I sort of am," Steve said. "In all the time I've worked with Ainsley, I've learned a lot about the business. I can do magic tricks. But I'll never be as quick and skillful as he is."

"Even if you practice?"

He shook his head. "Some people are naturals at it. I'm not. Besides, I don't want to practice sleight of hand for hours every day. I'd much rather make things. And that's what I've started doing. I'm making new tricks for Ainsley, and I've even sold a few to other magicians. I think when Ainsley retires and doesn't need me anymore, I'd like to open a magic store and sell my original tricks. But that's all I can tell you."

She sighed. "All right. You take the box."

"You sure?" he asked.

"Yeah, I'm sure. Did you show that note to Mr. Rodin?"

"I didn't have a chance last night," Steve said. "I'll try to remember later."

It must not seem very important to him, Sadie thought. "Oh, there's one more question you *might* be able to answer."

"If it's not a *trick* question." He winked at her.

Sadie laughed. "You're too much. No, I was just wondering about last Friday night."

He sobered. "What about it?"

"After the show ended, and after we all talked to Sheriff Slattery about what happened to Roz, Edwin and I invited you and Mr. Rodin to go get some ice cream with us and my daughter and her children. Mr. Rodin said he wanted to get right to bed. You said you'd take him back to the B and B."

Steve frowned as if thinking about it. "That sounds right."

"So my question is what did you do after you took him there? Did you stay in for the night?"

Steve closed his eyes for a moment. "Nope. I went out again." He opened them and returned her direct gaze.

"Do you mind telling me where?" she asked.

"I went out with Spike."

Sadie blinked. She hadn't expected that answer. "Spike Harris?"

"Yeah. He and the band were going to get some pizza, and they'd asked if I wanted to tag along. We went to that Italian place."

"Sophia's?"

He nodded. "It was good pizza too."

"How late were you out?"

"I don't know. We talked quite a while. Maybe midnight?"

Sadie sighed. Edwin was home long before midnight that night, and if Steve was out with the Skylarks, he couldn't have stolen Edwin's pipe, at least not that night. She could confirm his story easily with Spike, but it had the ring of truth.

————

Julie arrived at one for the afternoon shift, and Sadie was ready. She had eaten a sandwich in between customers and formulated her plans for the rest of the day.

In her mind, Steve Parrish was not a prime suspect in the theft any longer, but she had put off investigating another person who seemed more likely. She caught Julie up on the sales of the morning and went out the back door to her Tahoe.

The drive to Skip Stewart's house took only ten minutes. As Sadie had hoped, his pickup was in the driveway. Edwin wouldn't be happy if he knew she had come here. She sat for a moment, questioning her own motives and reviewing the evidence—or lack of it—concerning the theft. Skip was the one person they knew had access to Edwin's house, and nobody had ruled him out as the thief.

Lord, I don't want to snoop into other people's business when I'm not wanted, she prayed silently. *But Edwin spent a lot of money on that pipe, and I was the one who told him about Ron Waverly's auction. I hate to see him take such a loss, especially when I feel like it was my fault.*

She sat for another moment, but no flashes of inspiration came to her. She pulled in a deep breath and got out of the vehicle. On her way to the small brick house, she walked past Skip's truck, and a book on the front passenger seat caught her eye. *Plains Indian*

Art. Had Skip been reading up on Indian—Arapaho, perhaps?—arts and crafts?

She went to the door and knocked. Skip opened it and eyed her in surprise.

"Mrs. Speers?"

"Hello, Skip. I wondered if I could talk to you about the time you worked at Edwin Marshall's house."

His chin rose a fraction of an inch. "What do you want to know?"

"Well, I wondered if you ever saw the Arapaho pipe he bought at an auction earlier that week."

Skip's eyes narrowed. "Yeah, he showed it to me. I talked to the sheriff about that. Why are you asking?"

"I—I'm just a friend of Edwin's, and I'm trying to help him figure this out."

"Well, I didn't go inside the house when Mr. Marshall wasn't home. He said I could, but I didn't."

"Never?" Sadie asked.

"No. It's a policy of mine. It saves me a lot of headaches to just keep out of the employer's space unless they invite me in."

"But Edwin said you could go in."

"Yeah, he did. But I never took him up on it."

"Okay."

Skip frowned. "Even if I did go inside, I would never touch anything I wasn't supposed to."

She considered asking him about the book in his truck, but decided she had already raised his hackles and it might be best to let the matter rest. "All right, thank you. I appreciate your talking to me."

He shut the door without saying any more, and Sadie turned toward her vehicle. *Next time I get these impulses, Lord, please stop me.* Skip seemed like a nice person. She had upset him, and probably he didn't deserve her suspicion.

She sighed and headed back toward Main Street. Edwin was right. She should leave this alone. Mac was good at his job, and she should step back and let him do it, without annoying the people he interviewed. Even if she wondered about their truthfulness.

She rolled slowly past her store and Putnam & Sons Hardware. Would a Silver Peak resident walk into the hardware on Main Street to make a duplicate of someone else's house key?

There was another hardware store in Breckenridge, and a large building supply store. She circled the block and pulled in behind the Antique Mine and went inside to look them up. She decided to call and make a simple inquiry.

The woman who answered at the big box store transferred her call to the clerk on duty in the department where keys were made.

"We get quite a few people in here for keys," the man told her. "Of course, we have a self-service machine now too. Some people use that, but a lot of folks still prefer to have us do it for them."

"Could you tell me if you had someone make a house key there within the last week?"

"Probably about a dozen or so. Could you be more specific?"

"This man is about thirty. He's blond, about five-nine, and maybe a hundred and sixty pounds."

"Doesn't ring a bell," the man said.

"Okay, thanks." Sadie hung up. It probably wouldn't be ethical for him to tell her, even if Skip had made a duplicate key there.

Discouraged, she called the other number anyway. She would wonder if she didn't check.

The hardware store manager answered on the second ring.

"I was wondering if anyone had come in this week to have a duplicate house key made—a young man about thirty, blond hair…"

"I've only made one house key lately," the man said. "Most people go to the building supply. They've got a machine there, so you can do it yourself. I might stop doing it."

"Well, the one that you made," Sadie persisted.

"It was an older man."

"Oh." Sadie processed that. "Did he have a beard?"

"Nope, no beard."

"Did you know him?"

"Never seen him before. Nice-looking chap though. He paid in cash."

"Okay, thank you." She hung up. That person was probably someone local. If Skip wanted to make a key, he would probably use the self-service option. The machinery wouldn't intimidate him. She couldn't see any way to tell for sure if he'd made a duplicate or not. She could ask Roscoe, but she seriously doubted he would do it right there in Silver Peak.

With a sigh, she headed homeward. She had time for a nice, long walk with Hank before she fixed her supper and went to the fairgrounds.

———————

The next morning, Sadie went to the Antique Mine early to catch up on her consignment records. Julie was coming in after lunch again, to give her free time in the afternoon. A stream of customers, both local folks and tourists, flowed through the store. Sadie almost wished she had scheduled Julie for the whole day.

She was talking to Marge Ruxton about the merits of a vintage pine blanket chest when her phone rang. Sadie took it out and glanced at the screen. "Sorry, it's my daughter and I need to take it."

"Okay. I think I'll take the chest if you can fix the lock like you said."

"You got it. Thanks, Marge." Sadie turned away and pushed the button on her phone. "Hi. Alice." She glanced toward new two customers who came in, but both began exploring the merchandise and talking to each other. "What's up?"

"I'm having the worst time with my piecrust," Alice said. "It won't hold together. Should I put more shortening in it?"

"Are you using Grandma's recipe?"

"Of course."

"Well, that's usually no-fail. I guess you could try more shortening, but if you measured carefully, it should be right."

"I double-checked everything."

"Maybe try a trickle of cold water and see if that helps. If not, I think I'd start over."

Alice groaned.

"I know, I know," Sadie said. "I can't make it for you, or I would."

"Thanks. The judging is tomorrow. I have to get this done! Oh no."

"What?" Sadie asked.

"Milo's out front with his horse trailer. Sara's riding Daisy in the gymkhana tomorrow, and Milo's taking them over to the fairgrounds this morning. They're allowed to practice today. Sara!"

Sadie winced and held the phone out away from her ear. She could still hear Alice yelling up the stairway. "Sara! Milo's here! Get the lead out."

"Are you going with her?" Sadie asked.

"What? No. I should be." Alice moaned. "Mom, it's this pie. Why am I doing this? I should be out there watching Sara practice, or watching Theo...whatever he's doing right now. Is a pie really more important?"

"Now, hold on," Sadie said. "Overall, I'd say that's true. The kids are definitely more important. But the pie means a lot to you, for several reasons. Am I right?"

Alice sniffed. "Yeah, I guess so. I was all excited about using Grandma's recipe. It's a family heritage sort of activity. It's also something I can do just for me."

"You don't get enough me-time," Sadie said.

"I don't know about that," Alice said. "Picking berries with you was fun. Until the bear came."

Sadie couldn't help chortling. "That's right, and since you contended with a bear for your berries, you can hardly drop out of the contest now. It wouldn't be honorable."

She thought she heard a small chuckle. "Okay, Mom. I'll finish my pie, even if I have to start over with the crust. But after that, I'm going to spend the rest of the day with my kids."

"Good. Are you going to the show tonight?" Sadie asked.

"I don't think so. We went last night, and tomorrow's going to be a long day."

"It's going to be a big day for Sara," Sadie said. "I will definitely be there for the gymkhana, to cheer her on. And at the judging of the baking contest."

"Thanks, Mom. If the kids want to go to the final show tomorrow night, I'll take them. But tonight, I think we should stay home and just be together, without all the crowds and the noise and the brouhaha."

"I think that's wise," Sadie said. "I'll see you at the gymkhana, if not before."

"Okay. I'm going to finish my pie. Thanks, Mom. Wish me luck."

Sadie went to see if her customers needed assistance. Traffic through the store was light for the rest of the morning. Around noon, a truck pulled up outside. The driver had a large delivery of merchandise for her. She asked him to stack the eight cartons out of the way, near the door to the back room.

She had no customers at the moment, and she called Roz.

"Hi! Not out at the fairgrounds yet?"

"No, we're meeting for a rehearsal at three, but Ainsley said we don't need to work all day. He thinks I'm pretty good."

"You're fantastic," Sadie said. "Listen, Julie doesn't want to work tomorrow. Her boys want to spend most of Saturday at the fairgrounds. I wondered if you'd possibly be willing to tend the store for a few hours while I catch Sara in the gymkhana."

"Of course," Roz said. "You've been supporting me all week. I'd be happy to do that. You need to be there to watch Sara, and to see Alice take home the blue ribbon in the baking contest."

"Don't say that too loudly," Sadie told her. "You know Laura and Spike are in the contest too?"

"Them and about three dozen other people," Roz said. "Clark Langdon told me yesterday that the response to the contest has been almost overwhelming."

"Is he in charge of it?" Sadie asked.

"That and a lot of other things. I've been so busy with the show that I've had to delegate a million things to the other committee members and enlist more helpers."

"That's what you're supposed to do," Sadie said. "It's part of the chairman's responsibility to delegate. And the fair has been great."

"And no accidents," Roz added. "I think my bump on the head is the worst injury we've had, praise the Lord."

"That is wonderful. If you can come in at ten tomorrow, I'll try to have you out of here by two, so you have plenty of time to unwind before the show."

"Three o'clock would be fine," Roz said. "Stay for all of Sara's classes if you can."

The door opened, and three couples came in, including Lillian Devine, who worked at the Market. Sadie quickly ended her call.

"Hi, Lillian," she sang out.

"Hi! Nathan and I are going to the fair with some friends," Lillian told her. "We thought we'd stop in here first. My friend Diane here is an avid antiquer."

Sadie greeted them all as if they were guests in her home. "Is there anything special you're looking for?"

"I just love to browse shops like this," Diane said.

"Well, feel free. I'll be right up front if you need anything." Soon the newcomers were scattered throughout the store, exclaiming over various finds.

Sadie took her post behind the counter and occupied herself with slitting open the newly delivered boxes and making a quick inspection of the contents. This was going to be a lot of fun.

As she worked, her mind went back to the theft at Edwin's house. Steve Parrish had seemed like a possible culprit, and she still wasn't satisfied with his actions when she showed him the note Roz had found. That might be insignificant, but she wasn't sure. But even with him and Murray Lithgow low on her list, that didn't mean she was left without suspects. She still had Skip Stewart. If only she could be sure he was telling the truth when he said he didn't enter the house when Edwin wasn't home.

Lillian and Diane came to the counter carrying several items. "I can't believe you had a Kennedy's Coffee tin," Diane said.

"We get quite a few tins through here," Sadie said with a smile.

"And I found this." Lillian laid a milk glass cream pitcher on the counter. "Nathan said he'll buy it for my birthday. I think he he's found some tool or other he wants too."

The two couples left with half a dozen purchases among them, and Sadie was pleased with the sale.

Julie arrived to take over for her, and Sadie showed her the boxes of new merchandise. "Feel free to start getting it out. I just want to finish the restoration on that child's rocking chair before I go. Then I'm out of here!"

She only needed twenty minutes to complete the job, and when she was done, she stood back to assess her work. She might be prejudiced, but it looked great. She cleaned her brush and put away her supplies. When she went out front, she found Julie gleefully inspecting the contents of the first box, which held mostly vintage jewelry.

"This stuff is great! How did you get it?" Julie asked.

Sadie grinned. "An old acquaintance of mine decided to close her online store. She wanted to get out quickly because she's going to move to Alabama to live with her daughter."

"So she had to unload her inventory fast," Julie said, holding up a jeweled turtle scatter pin encased in an acrylic box.

"That's about the size of it. I made her an offer on all the jewelry, books, and tinware. I didn't want to take a chance on shipping a lot of dishes and china, but I did also get one box lot of kitchen utensils."

"It's going to be so much fun unpacking it all." Julie glanced at the mountain of boxes.

"You can work on it this afternoon, if you have time," Sadie said. She opened a computer file and showed her how to list each item with its source and description. "Here are the prices Anne had on each piece when she had them listed retail. Of course, she gave me a big discount. You can tag them with the same prices she used, and I'll go over them this weekend and see if I want to change any. I want to get them out for sale as soon as possible. You can call me if you have any questions."

"Got it," Julie said in perfect contentment.

Sadie looked toward the front display window. "And do the tinware next, if you finish the jewelry. Tins are hot sellers right now, and I think I'll put some in the front window. It's nice and colorful."

"We could do a kitchen display," Julie said.

Sadie nodded. "There should be some nice biscuit tins and coffee cans in those boxes. We could set up a cute 'coffee time' display, with mugs, coffeepot, tins, a small table, and chair."

"Sure," Julie said. "That little drop-leaf table would fit in there. And maybe even a whatnot shelf holding some cookie jars and cookie cutters."

"Maybe Arbuckle's will want to coordinate with us. You think about it," Sadie said. "I've got to run."

She went home, changed her clothes, and took her lunch out to the backyard. The weather had been clear and sunny all week, perfect for the fair, but now gray clouds gathered over the mountain. A cool breeze fluttered the grass and the aspen leaves. Sadie hoped it wouldn't rain out any events at the fair.

Hank also liked being out in the fresh air, and after a few minutes, he brought Sadie a much-chewed rubber ball and coaxed her into a game of fetch.

"You know I haven't been getting enough exercise lately, don't you?" she said. She pushed up from her patio chair and flexed her throwing arm. Other than the horseback ride with the kids on Tuesday, her playtime with Hank and moving boxes at the store were about the only physical activity she'd had this week.

When Edwin came by for her at two o'clock, she was relaxed and ready to go to the fairgrounds. The sky was grayer than before, and as a precaution, she tucked her umbrella between the seats in Edwin's car.

"They're awarding Best of Show ribbons for the arts and crafts, canning, and vegetables at three," Edwin said. "I need to be there for that."

"I can't wait to see if Harry Polmiller's corn wins this year," Sadie said with a smile. Harry, at ninety-four years of age, far outdid her in the gardening department. Presenting his best vegetables at the fair was a highlight of the summer for him.

Sadie loved this part of the fair, but her mind was still buzzing with the odd goings-on in town too. She told Edwin about Steve Parrish's visit to the Antique Mine. "I was a little suspicious of him before that, I'll admit," she said. "Now I mostly think he's okay."

"Mostly? Steve seems like a solid guy," Edwin said.

"Seems like. But that's the thing with career criminals. They *seem* normal. Nice. Charming, even. That's how Murray Lithgow got away with conning people."

"Well, Ainsley Rodin saw through him," Edwin pointed out. "Don't you think he'd know if Steve was doing something underhanded?"

"I suppose so. They've worked closely together for a long time." Sadie eyed Edwin cautiously. She told him about the mysterious note Roz had found, and Steve's reaction.

"So?" Edwin said.

"It seemed odd to me that he wanted to keep the note."

"He didn't want to keep it. He wanted to show it to Ainsley."

"Maybe. Or maybe he just wanted to get it away from me so I wouldn't show it to Mac."

Edwin's face wrinkled up. "Aw, it didn't sound like something incriminating. Do you really think the thief might have written it?"

Sadie sighed. "Unlikely, I guess. Have you thought any more about Skip?"

"What about him?"

"As possibly having stolen your pipe?"

"I've thought about it," Edwin said, "and I don't think he did it. I trust him."

"But you don't know him very well. He could have gone all through your house while you were at the office, and you wouldn't know it."

"I was there most of the times he came to work, and Mac said he didn't turn up any evidence pointing to Skip. He had the opportunity, I'll admit. But I don't think he's lying."

"He could have made a duplicate key and come back some other time," Sadie persisted. "Like while you were at the fairgrounds, or the town hall. You're not exactly unpredictable."

"I do keep an extra key on a rack in the kitchen. But I just don't believe Skip would do that. He's worked for a lot of people in this town. He does good work, and I haven't heard any complaints about him." Edwin pulled into the field used as a parking lot for the fair, parked, and turned to face her. "Look, Sadie, sweetheart, would you do something for me?"

"What?" she asked.

"Just forget about the theft for a while. Relax. Enjoy the rest of the day with me."

His words struck Sadie to the core. He sounded like Alice, lamenting that she no longer got to spend much time with her children and was missing out on some important moments in their lives.

She pulled in a deep breath. "Okay."

"Thank you." Edwin leaned across the seat and kissed her. "Ready to go spread some cheer?"

"I sure am."

16

As Sadie and Edwin walked toward the grandstand, where the presentation of the Best of Show awards would take place, they passed Milo, driving slowly off the grounds in his truck. Sara was seated beside him, and she rolled down the window.

"Hi, Grandma! Hi, Mr. Marshall."

"Hi," Sadie said. "Did you get to practice?"

"Yeah. I had to wait in line, but it was worth it."

"All set for tomorrow?" Edwin asked.

She nodded eagerly. "Daisy loved it. I think she's got a good chance at some of the games. And we're leaving her here overnight in one of the stalls."

Cars were accumulating behind them, so Milo moved his truck forward with a final wave.

"This will be a good experience for Sara, even if she doesn't win," Sadie said.

At the grandstand, the bleachers were sparsely populated. The presentations didn't seem to be as popular as the evening shows, Sadie noted, but that was all right.

The regular ribbons for each class had been attached to the winning exhibits earlier in the week, but the Best of Show prizes were for outstanding items in each overall exhibit group, and each one came with a check for the winner.

Jenna Henderson took the ribbon and prize money for Best of Show in arts and crafts, for the magnificent pictorial quilt she had made. Sadie clapped loudly, proud of the young woman. Jenna had worked on the scene depicting their mountain all winter, and it had come out beautifully. She certainly deserved the prize.

Harry claimed the vegetable prize. Clark Langdon presented the award. "This is not just for your corn, Harry," he said into the microphone, "though that's truly superior. It's for your entire exhibit. You not only entered twenty-two categories, but you presented your vegetables in an attractive manner, and you've supported this fair for many, many years. We all love you, Harry Polmiller!"

Everyone cheered as Harry went forward to accept the blue ribbon rosette with flowing blue-and-white streamers, as well as a certificate and his check.

Clark also announced the Best of Show winners for canned goods, which went to a local rancher's wife. Sadie was happy to see her pleasure in accepting.

"That's it for now, folks," Clark said, "but I don't want you to forget that tomorrow our Colorado Wild Raspberry Baking Contest will be judged at eleven o'clock in the tent near the exhibit hall. That's going to be very exciting, and the winner and his or her recipe will be featured in *Colorado Mountain Life* magazine."

The spectators drifted out of the grandstand, and Sadie and Edwin strolled around the grounds together. They paused at each vendor's booth, and Edwin spoke to the merchants, thanking them for their part in the fair's success.

At five o'clock, Sadie asked, "Are you going to do the introductions again tonight?"

"Yes, Mr. Rodin seems to like the way I do it. Do you want to stay through? We could get something to eat now."

"Sure," Sadie said. "Roz is covering for me tomorrow at the store, so I want to be sure to see her act tonight and show my support."

"You're a good friend, Sadie." He leaned over and kissed her temple.

Sadie smiled up at him. "Thanks. So what do you want to eat? Maybe we can get some chicken at the firemen's barbecue."

"That sounds really good," Edwin said. "I hear they've got corn on the cob too."

They got in line near the huge grill where several of the volunteer firefighters were cooking the chicken. Some of the firemen's wives were serving corn, chips, and soft drinks to go with the chicken.

"Such a nutritious meal," Sadie said with a laugh.

"It's only once in a while," Edwin reminded her. "We don't eat like this every day."

"Good thing. I'm going to make myself eat a salad-only lunch tomorrow. Unless I forget."

He laughed. They carried their plates and drinks to a picnic table and sat down with the fire chief and his wife, one of the school board members, and Sadie's old schoolmate Rita Dodd, who was now the receptionist at Doc Conroy's office. They enjoyed their meal together and chatted about the fair, town happenings, and their memories of bygone times.

When they had all finished eating, the group ambled toward the grandstand together. Sadie took up her usual place in the front row. The Skylarks were tuning up, and Roz and Rodin were not anywhere in sight.

A few minutes later, Edwin went onstage to introduce the band, then returned to the bleachers. Sadie enjoyed the music, clapping along with some of the songs and humming the familiar tunes. Edwin smiled. He caught her hand for a moment and squeezed it.

The Skylarks were finishing their last set when Roscoe slid into the seat beside her. He leaned close to her. "Hi, Sadie. I'm running late tonight."

"It's okay, but I hope Roz isn't just getting here."

"No, she left hours ago. I was making out orders for new stock at the store and lost track of the time."

When the band finished playing, they joined the applause, and Edwin made his way on to the stage to remind folks of the extra musical acts performing Saturday and to introduce the magic show.

Sadie said to Roscoe, "Hey, I was wondering if you'd made any house keys for anyone lately."

"At the store?" Roscoe shook his head. "It's been at least a couple of weeks. Why?"

"Just wondering. I suppose you know about those self-service key-making machines?"

"Yeah, they're pretty good on standard keys," he replied.

"Are they going to put you out of business?"

Roscoe laughed. "Making keys is a very small part of my trade. Getting smaller all the time, what with machines like you mentioned and electronic locks."

"And now, ladies and gentlemen," Edwin intoned, "together again, I present to you the resplendent Rosalind Putnam and the Great Ainsley Rodin." The crowd erupted in boisterous approval.

"You changed your intro," Sadie noted when he rejoined her.

"Rodin's request," Edwin said, clapping along with the rest of the crowd as Roz and the magician walked on stage and bowed. "He's really impressed with Roz's work this week, and he wanted to give her a little more acclaim."

"Well, she's eating it up." Sadie grinned and clapped louder, watching Roz's radiant face as she bowed once more and waved to the audience, then walked gracefully to her mark for the first trick.

The performance was seamless, and yet it was different from any other night's. The best tricks the pair had presented were brought out again, and they even added a new mind-reading stunt that seemed to Sadie a variation of the watermelon trick. This time, Rodin showed a sealed envelope he claimed contained his predictions. He had Roz set it in plain view on an easel to one side. Later, he drew a sheet of paper from the envelope. It contained the information given to him by a woman in the audience.

Everyone was properly astounded, but Sadie was beginning to think she understood at least the rudiments of how that trick was done. She still wasn't sure how the magician put the dollar bill into the watermelon, but she was beginning to look beyond the obvious. She never saw Steve Parrish during the show, but she had a feeling he was lurking backstage, dressed all in black. But she might be wrong.

After the show, Edwin and Sadie stayed long enough to congratulate Roz and Rodin.

"Only one more night," Roz said. "It's kind of sad."

"Are you tired?" Sadie asked.

"Exhausted. But I'll still miss it after the fair closes."

"How about you, Mr. Rodin?" Edwin asked.

Ainsley sighed and smiled at him. "I admit I'm tired too, but it's been a very good week. I've made a lot of new friends here."

"Well, we hope you'll come back again," Sadie said.

"Oh, I've got something for you," Roz said. She opened the large tote she had carried her extra clothes and cosmetics in and fished to the bottom. She pulled out a book and passed it to Sadie.

"What's this?" Sadie asked.

"After we got talking about the old magic show we went to, and the funny handcuffs, I asked Kimama if she could order anything for me on Interlibrary Loan."

"Theodore Hardeen," Sadie said, reading the dust jacket of the hardcover book. "Houdini's brother."

"Yeah. I thought it might go into more detail than you've been finding online. She got me another one on old vaudeville shows, too, but it doesn't have much on magicians. Only one small section. I'm reading it for the stuff about the old variety performers. I'll swap with you when I'm done, if you want."

"Thanks," Sadie said. "This should be interesting."

She and Edwin went to Arbuckle's for coffee, but she was careful not to bring up the subject of the Arapaho pipe. When she'd arrived home, she decided to continue following Edwin's advice. He wasn't agonizing over the theft of the pipe, or at least, he wasn't talking about it much. She suspected he was deeply disappointed. But Edwin wasn't one to moan about his own troubles.

She wondered if his homeowner's insurance would cover the loss. Maybe not, since he'd only had the pipe for a few days.

The book on Hardeen had a table of contents in the front, and Sadie skimmed the chapter titles. This would be a fun read. She only wished she was more in the mood for it. At the bottom of the page, she noticed that an index and several appendices were listed. Curious, she flipped to the back of the book. One of the appendices was a schedule of Hardeen's performances, as far as could be documented. Her excitement rose as she went through it.

"Denver area," she said aloud, when she spotted an entry for 1937. Was Silver Peak close enough to the capital to be included? She turned quickly to the page referenced and read for several minutes. At last, she sat back, smiling and holding the book close to her chest.

It was too late to call Roz, or even Edwin.

"Hooray," she said in muted victory.

Hank, who had been napping on the rug at her feet, opened one eye.

Sadie grinned at him. "He was here, Hank. Hardeen was really here."

17

Knowing Roz would arrive at the store by opening time at ten, Sadie went in early on Saturday morning. She had a couple of things she wanted to do before leaving for the fairgrounds, and one of them was settling once and for all whether the handcuffs Tulley Morse had brought her had any connection with Houdini's brother, Theodore Hardeen.

The knowledge that "Dash" had performed in Silver Peak in 1937 gave her more hope that they might have some historical significance. However, all the references she had found so far indicated that the handcuffs were newer than that. Installed in the Antique Mine with the door still locked, she put in a call to Tulley Morse. Remembering what he had said about buying more minutes for his phone, she held her breath, but to her relief, he answered after five rings.

"Took you long enough," he said when she had told him who was calling.

"I'm sorry, but I've been trying to learn as much as I could about your handcuffs."

"You mean Houdini's handcuffs," Tulley said.

"No, I don't think so. Harry Houdini was never in Silver Peak, as far as I can tell."

"Oh yeah?"

"That's right. But I learned last night that his brother was here in 1937."

"His brother?" Tulley sounded doubtful.

"He was called Theodore Hardeen, and he was a famous magician in his own right," Sadie said. "But I'm still skeptical about the handcuffs. I think they're too new, even for Mr. Hardeen's show."

"Well, I was told they belonged to Houdini."

"I know," Sadie said, "but sometimes when people want an item to seem more valuable than it really is, they bend the truth a little. Could you tell me who you got these from?"

Tulley sighed. "Okay, but he swore Houdini used them."

"Just give me the name."

"George True."

"Thanks. I know who he is. I'll call him."

"Oh, uh…"

"Yes?" Sadie waited.

"I was just thinking," Tulley said. "Maybe he said Houdini's brother, like you were telling."

"Think so?"

"I'm not sure now."

"Okay. I'll let you know what I find out, Tulley."

Sadie picked up the old handcuffs and examined them once more. After her reading on the subject, she really thought they belonged more to the 1960s, the era when she and Roz had attended the magic show at the opera house.

She looked up the telephone number for George True, a mechanic who lived on the edge of town, and punched it in on the store's phone.

"Those old handcuffs?" George said when Sadie had explained why she was calling. "Tulley came around asking if I had any scrap metal or old junk, and I let him take those."

"Did you tell him they belonged to Houdini?"

George laughed. "That's a good one. No, my dad got those after he saw a magician perform here in Silver Peak."

"What year was that?" Sadie asked.

"I don't know. Maybe fifty years or so ago. He said he was all gung-ho on being a magician for a while. He practiced card tricks too. Got pretty good at that, and he would do them at parties. But I don't think he had much success with the handcuffs and escape tricks."

Sadie smiled. "I don't suppose you remember who the magician was?"

"Oh, let's see. Marvin the Marvel or something like that."

She laughed out loud. "I saw that show. Roz Putnam and I went to it when we were in junior high."

"Yeah?" George said. "Say, Roz is doing great in the show at the fair this week. Have you seen it?"

"Oh yes, I've seen it," Sadie said. "She and Rodin are terrific."

"Tonight's the last night," George said. "My wife and kids want to go see it again. We went last Saturday."

"I was there too," Sadie told him. "They've been adding new tricks. I'm sure you won't be disappointed if you go again. So is there anything else you can tell me about the handcuffs, George?"

"Naw, Dad had them just for kicks. My brother and I used to play with them when we pretended to be cowboys. They didn't belong to anybody famous."

"That's about what I figured," Sadie said. "Especially not Houdini. They're too new for him to have used them."

A little digging online rewarded Sadie. She found a few brief mentions of Marvin the Marvel, and on an auction site she located a handbill from one of his shows. From what she could tell, he hadn't performed beyond the 1980s. Still, it was fun to see a picture of him again and recall her and Roz's astonishment when they saw him perform. In one photo, Marvin was wearing a set of handcuffs that looked a lot like the ones lying on her counter.

She made herself a note to offer Tulley Morse ten dollars for the handcuffs. She wasn't sure she could resell them for that, but she had kept them a lot longer than she had expected to, and she didn't want to cause hard feelings.

She still had about an hour, and her thoughts drifted back to Edwin's loss. She checked online and found that the catalog for the auction from which he had bought the pipe was still available for viewing. She scrolled through it until she found the Arapaho pipe in its intricately beaded case. The colorful beads formed distinctive geometric patterns and small figures of people and animals. It was a beautiful piece of artwork. Where was it now? Had the thief sold it to another private collector, or would it surface in the black market for Native American artifacts?

As she had noted earlier, the pipe was part of an estate collection. The name of the deceased wasn't given, but she read the short blurb introducing the two dozen articles offered for sale by the estate's administrator. The original owner, it seemed, was descended from a mountain man who received the pipe as a gift from an Arapaho chief.

Sadie frowned and read the description again. Edwin had mentioned that. Sadie continued her reading and followed a link to a modern association of the Arapaho people. She decided it couldn't hurt to inquire there about the story concerning the pipe. They might be able to tell her if it was true or not.

She crafted a note carefully and typed it into her e-mail program. As she finished her message, a brisk rap on the front door interrupted her. Roz was outside, waving at her through the glass. Sadie clicked "send" and went to unlock the door for her.

"Hi! Thanks for coming."

"No problem. Anything I should know?"

"Nothing special. If Tulley Morse comes in for his handcuffs, they're down here, below the counter. I decided to offer him ten bucks for them. He'll probably be insulted, but if says he'll take it, give him a ten from the till and make me a note." Sadie stepped behind the counter to shut down her computer.

"Okay." Roz came around and peered at the Web page she was about to close. "Chief Niwot?"

"Yeah," Sadie said with a rueful smile. "I'm looking for stories about an Arapaho chief's son being saved by a white man."

Roz frowned. "I get it. Edwin's pipe."

"Yeah. So far, I haven't been able to pin down that story. But I *have* learned a lot about the Arapaho."

Roz chuckled. "No one could ever say you're not tenacious." She waggled her eyebrows at Sadie. "That's a big word for stubborn."

"I can't just sit by and do nothing. I'm the one who sent Edwin to that auction."

"You feel responsible."

Sadie nodded reluctantly.

"Don't. From what I've heard, it's Edwin's fault for leaving his burglar alarm off."

"I don't know about that." Sadie let out a big sigh. She didn't like to think of Edwin as careless. In fact, he was usually much more careful than that.

"People do get lax about security measures after a while, if they seem unnecessary," Roz said gently. She slapped Sadie playfully on the shoulder. "Hey! You've got a fair to go to."

"Right." Sadie clicked a couple more buttons and closed the laptop.

"Not expecting any tour buses today, are you?"

"No, but anything can happen. It *is* the last day of the fair, and it's Saturday. If you get swamped, call my cell. I can be here in ten minutes. Fifteen if I get hung up in fair traffic."

"Okay, I'll keep it in mind. Now get out of here."

Sadie gave Roz a hug. "I'll see you later." She took her purse and went out to her Tahoe. The last day of the fair. She would be glad in a way when the bustle and stress had ended, but she would miss it too. The excitement. The new friends she had made. The chance to be amazed every day.

As soon as she had parked and was walking on to the midway, she phoned Edwin. The music from the rides muffled his voice, but she made out the fact that he was already at the tent where the wild berry contest was to be judged. Sadie hurried her steps. Alice would never forgive her if she missed the dramatic moment.

She spotted Edwin at the entrance to the tent, waiting for her. He waved, and she strode toward him.

"Hi! Is Alice here?"

"Yes, and the kids." He took her hand and drew her inside the large tent. They managed to get a spot from which they could watch the three judges at work. They had already begun examining the pies and other goodies, making notes on their clipboards. When they had circled the long table where all the entries were laid out, a helper cut small pieces from each entry and put them on paper plates. A photographer popped in to snap photos of them tasting the bite-size servings. Troy Haggarty was also on hand with his notebook at the ready, but was less obtrusive than the photographer.

"I'm so glad I'm not judging this," Edwin said. "Can you imagine having to taste more than thirty desserts?"

"Looks like they're taking tiny bites," Sadie observed. Across the group, Theo caught her eye. Sadie waved, and then Alice and Sara joined Theo in waving.

Laura squeezed between onlookers until she was next to Sadie.

"Hi," Sadie said. "What's your number?"

"Pie #7," Laura said. "They seemed to like it, but it's hard to tell."

"Impossible," Sadie agreed. "Your filling seems to have set up well."

"Yeah, I'm glad it's not too runny," Laura said. "What's Alice's number?"

Sadie glanced across the tent toward her daughter and grandchildren. Alice's face was tense as she watched the judges moving along toward her entry. Sadie didn't suppose it would matter if she shared that information with Laura.

"She's pie number fifteen. She brought it in at the last minute yesterday."

Laura sighed. "I don't begrudge Alice the ribbon if she wins. I just hope one of the pies from Grandma's recipe wins."

The judges seemed to take their job very seriously. The sixteen pies, four cobblers, three danish pastries, three varieties of cookie squares, two plates of tarts, two crisps, two types of muffins, and lone trifle each had their moment. Each entry got as much attention as the others.

"I wonder if that photographer is from *Colorado Mountain Life*," Sadie said as the cameraman moved in for a close-up of one of the judges.

"Wouldn't it be great if Grandma's recipe was in the magazine?" Laura said dreamily.

"It sure would."

After they had completed the round, the judges huddled for several minutes and then passed a sheet of paper to Anne Hastings, who was representing the fair committee as hostess of the event.

"We have progress," she said into her portable microphone with a smile. "Our judges have narrowed down the entries to four finalists. They are muffin number two and pies numbers seven and fifteen, and tart number one."

A collective sigh went up from the audience. Laura grabbed Sadie's arm. "Alice and I are both in the finals!"

"Yes." Sadie smiled at her. Were the two pies so similar the judges could barely tell the difference? She doubted that. One would edge out the other.

Edwin leaned toward Laura. "Congratulations."

Laura nodded. "It's an honor to make it this far."

On the other side of the crowd, Sadie spotted Spike. He spoke to the fellow beside him and shrugged, then made his way toward Alice. He said something to Alice, and she responded with a smile and then turned her attention back to the judging.

"Spike is out," Sadie said softly.

"Too bad," Edwin said.

"I guess raspberry crisp doesn't measure up to the pies," Laura said.

Edwin smiled. "I'm a pie man myself."

"So I've gathered from observation," Sadie replied drily. She glanced back toward Alice. Her daughter was waving and trying to point discreetly. Sadie frowned and then caught on as she noticed movement in the crowd. Sara was winding her way through the closely packed spectators. A moment later, she emerged, smiling and panting.

"Excuse me. Excuse me." Sara looked at Sadie and grinned, exposing her braces. "Hi, Grandma! I've got to go get Daisy ready for the gymkhana now. Are you coming over there to watch?"

"We'll be there as soon as the judges announce the winner here," Sadie promised, giving her a quick one-armed hug.

"Good luck, Sara," Edwin said.

"What's your first class?" Laura asked.

"Pole bending. We've been practicing, and Daisy's pretty good at it. It's fourth on the schedule."

"We'll be there," Sadie said, hoping she wasn't being rash with her promise. If the food judging dragged on too long, she might have to leave Laura to report for her.

"Do you need any help?" Edwin asked, and Sadie wished she had thought of that.

"Milo said he'd be there to help me tack up. He's been great about this whole thing. I think he wishes he was entering." Sara smiled broadly. "See ya."

Before Sadie could say anything more, the girl was gone, sidestepping onlookers and wriggling between those who wouldn't move.

Laura's fingers dug into her wrist. "They're going to announce it!"

Sadie patted her cousin's hand. "Ease up a little."

"Oh, sorry."

The head judge handed a piece of paper to Anne and said something to her. Anne turned on the microphone and smiled at the crowd.

"Folks, I know you've all been waiting for this. Ribbons will be awarded to places one through four. I'll announce them, beginning with fourth place. But first..."

A moan rippled over the audience.

"Sorry," Anne said. "I just want to tell you that portions of the entries will be sold at the Historical Society's booth, just across the path." She adjusted her glasses and looked down at the paper. "In fourth place, muffin number two, Andi Taylor."

Everyone clapped as Andi made her way to the podium. Watchers parted to make a path for her.

"I thought she was the barbecue queen," Laura whispered to Sadie.

"She's legendary at barbecue," Sadie replied. "Apparently her muffins are up to par too. I don't know as I've never tasted them."

The head judge passed a white rosette with long, flowing streamers to Andi and shook her hand.

"I'll bet the tarts win," Laura said. "They're unusual."

"I wondered about the trifle," Sadie replied.

Laura shook her head. "The pound cake is the only baked part. The raspberries weren't in that, just in the sauce. I guess it fit the rules, but maybe not the expectations."

Sadie considered that and glanced at Edwin.

He shrugged. "I'm sure they're all tasty."

"In third place," Anne said into her microphone. She paused, and Sadie looked across the tent, where Alice and Theo were standing. Alice looked interested, but not totally invested. Was she wishing she was over at the stable, helping Sara prepare for the gymkhana? Laura, on the other hand, seemed about to pass out from the tension.

"Pie number fifteen, Alice Macomb."

Alice smiled and walked forward to accept her yellow ribbon. She shook the head judge's hand and thanked her, then walked over to stand by Sadie, Laura, and Edwin.

"Congrats," Sadie said.

"Thanks. Looks like it's you and whoever made the tarts, Laura," Alice said with a smile. "Good luck." She gave Laura a hug.

"Thank you, honey."

Theo worked his way around the outside of the crowd and joined them just as Anne announced, "The final two entries are pie number seven, by Laura Finch, and tart number one, by Marisol Vidal."

"Marisol!" Sadie looked joyously at Alice and Laura. Whoever won would be a friend.

"Hector and Luz are over there." Edwin nodded to one side, and Sadie followed his gaze to see the couple standing with Marisol. "I wonder who's minding the store at Arbuckle's today."

"Maybe they closed for a while," Alice said.

Sadie shook her head. "I doubt it. They have a couple of part-timers, and probably one of them is holding the fort." She turned her attention back to Anne Hastings.

"The judges tell me the decision was very difficult, but they have chosen a winner. The blue ribbon goes to Marisol Vidal for her tarts, and Laura Finch is runner-up, for her pie. Would you both please come forward for your prizes?"

Laura huffed out a breath.

"Second is good," Alice said, patting her shoulder.

"I know. Thanks. And I'm happy for Marisol. She can use the money for her college bill, I'm sure." Laura walked to the podium and received her red ribbon, then headed back to where they stood. Meanwhile, Marisol slowly made her way to the front, trying to respond to the many congratulations she received along the way. Her lovely face was flushed, and her eyes sparkled as she reached the judges.

"Thank you! Thank you so much."

Anne said, "Marisol, congratulations. The reporters from *Colorado Mountain Life* and the *Silver Peak Sentinel* are eager to speak to you, right over here."

"Guess we'd better get over to the riding ring for the gymkhana," Alice said.

"Go ahead, honey," Sadie told her. "I want to make sure Laura's not feeling too let down."

Alice pouted her lips. "What about me?"

Sadie chuckled. "I know you. You'll land on your feet, and you're dying to get over there and cheer Sara on."

"Come on, Mom," Theo said.

"Save us seats," Sadie called after them, as Theo took his mother's elbow and herded her toward the opening in the tent.

She and Edwin soon joined them in the bleachers facing the show ring. Dozens of local teenagers, children, and adults were in various stages of preparing their horses. Gymkhana games were a fun outlet for riders of all skill levels.

"Hey, look," Edwin said. "Skip is helping set up for the pole bending."

Out in the ring, Skip and another young man were positioning the upright poles that the horses would weave their way around for the timed race.

The announcer called the riders to line up. One by one, they entered the ring. At the signal to start, each horse tore to the far end of the arena. The rider turned the animal, and the horse wove its way down the line of evenly spaced poles toward the start. At the end of the line of obstacles, they circled the final pole and wove their way back, darting in and out between the poles, all the way to the far end. There they turned homeward and raced back to the starting line. The announcer called out the time for each horse.

Sara was the sixth rider of fourteen in the class. Sadie found herself yelling and cheering not only for Sara, but for several other riders she knew. To her delight, Sara and Daisy picked up a red ribbon in pole bending. In a later class, they earned a white ribbon for fourth place in the egg and spoon race. They placed out of the ribbons in barrel racing and several other games. As the final class approached, Theo handed Alice his bag of popcorn.

"I've got to go get ready."

Sadie arched her eyebrows at Alice, seeing Theo hurry away toward the starting area. "I thought he wasn't riding today."

"He's not, except for this one class. Sara begged him to help her with the Rescue Race."

Edwin leaned toward her. "Is that where one rider gallops down the field and picks up the other one, and they ride double back to the start?"

Alice nodded. "It's fun, and it's hectic. But I'm sure they'll be fine."

Sadie agreed. The kids had done this stunt many times, and Daisy was calm.

Even so, the tension mounted as twelve young people walked the length of the ring to stand behind a line at the far end and a dozen horses lined up at the start. This many mounts galloping at once could be chaotic, Sadie realized. It wasn't like a choreographed ride where each horse and rider was expected to be in a certain position every moment. These kids and horses were all scrambling to be first at the finish, and that could lead to some upsets.

"Come on, Theo," Alice yelled. "You've got this." He heard her and gave her a salute from his place on Daisy's back at the starting line.

"He should have brought his own saddle," Sadie said. "Those stirrups are too short for him, even on the lowest notches."

"He'll be okay," Alice said.

"Get ready," came the announcer's voice. Everyone tensed, and the riders tried to quiet their horses, lining them up to face their goals. The partners they were to rescue, generally the smaller and lighter of each pair, took up their preferred positions beyond a line of powdered chalk on the ground at the far end of the arena. Sara stood leaning forward, her hands braced on her knees, focusing on Theo and Daisy.

"Get set." A cap gun fired, and the twelve horses bounded forward, one with a buck that upset his closest neighbor. That horse squealed and leaped away, colliding with the Appaloosa on his left.

Theo and Daisy managed to avoid the fray and head straight down the field. They were among the first three to reach the goal, almost at the same second. Sara stood and reached toward her brother with one arm. When Daisy charged up beside her, Theo grasped Sara's wrist and swung her up behind him. She landed on Daisy's haunches, just behind the saddle, and wrapped her arms around Theo's waist.

"Go, go, go!" she yelled.

Meanwhile, two other horses had jostled each other as they turned, and one began to buck and kick with a vengeance, tossing its rider off over its head.

18

THEO PIVOTED DAISY AND PUT HIS HEELS TO HER SIDES, AT THE same time slackening the reins so she could lower her head and streak for the finish line. Sara clung to him, her hair flying out behind them like a pennant in the wind of their speed.

Skip ran out from the sidelines to grab the loose horse's reins, and another official hurried to help the fallen boy off the field and out of harm's way. Sadie's heart was in her throat, but the boy who had been thrown didn't seem to be seriously hurt.

Daisy and the Appaloosa were halfway down the field now, running neck and neck. Sara stuck to Theo like a leech, and Theo leaned low over the saddle horn, squeezing the mare's ribs with his boots. They edged ahead of the Appaloosa as they crossed the chalk line.

"And the winner is number six, Daisy, by a nose," the announcer intoned. "In second place, number seven, Speckles, and a distant third is the number two horse, Joe Friday."

The other horses thundered across the line, and the riders pulled them in, forcing them to slow down.

"They won!" Alice jumped up, waving her arms and yelling. "Yay, Sara! Yay, Theo!"

Edwin took Sadie's hand. "Well, that was sure exciting. Haven't watched a race like that in years."

"I'm so proud of them," Sadie said. "And Daisy! She's probably not the fastest horse here, but she stayed out of trouble and followed the signals Theo gave her."

"She's a great horse," Edwin agreed.

Alice threw her arms around Sadie. "Sara's going to be so happy with that ribbon!"

"Don't they both get one?" Edwin asked.

"No, the prize is for the horse in this one. The team only gets one blue ribbon. Theo won't mind. He's got bragging rights. That's more important to boys."

They watched the kids receive their prize. Theo stood on the ground now, and he led Daisy forward. Sara, in the saddle, grinned as she leaned down and took the blue ribbon from the judge. Sadie, Edwin, and Alice walked around to the gate to meet them as the participants left the ring. Sadie hugged Theo and reached up to squeeze Sara's hand.

"Good job, you two! I was yelling so hard, I'll probably be hoarse for a week."

Sara laughed. "I could hear you, Grandma."

Sadie patted Daisy's nose. "You did a good job too, Daisy."

"Best race since American Pharoah won the Triple Crown, huh?" Theo said, his smile almost as wide as Sara's.

"It sure was," Alice said.

Edwin slapped Daisy's withers. "Good horse. How about some lunch, gang? It's after one o'clock. Shall we grab a hot dog at the Historical Society's booth? My treat."

"Sure," Sadie said. "Then I'd better head back to the store. But I'll be back this evening for the show."

"Mom said we could spend the day here," Sara said.

"You've got to get Daisy home and comfy," Alice reminded her.

"I'll go with Milo," Theo said. "Sara can stay here with you, and I can drive my car back."

"Thanks." Sara gave him a mock punch on the arm. "More time for me with Mia. We're supposed to meet by the shooting gallery at three."

"Well, let's go get those hot dogs, then," Sadie said.

On their way to the booth on the midway, they ran into Clark. "Hey, Clark. Good job on the baking contest," Edwin told him.

Clark paused and grinned. "Thanks, Edwin. I heard the Vidal girl won."

"That's right," Edwin said.

"I had Anne host that while I was over to the livestock ring for the calf show. This week has been fun, but frankly, I'll be glad when we close tonight."

Sadie realized Clark was the perfect one to ask about a question that had been niggling at her. "I saw Skip Stewart working at the gymkhana. Is he volunteering?"

"No, he's paid help," Clark said. "He's actually put in several days this week. He's a good worker."

"He's done some work at my house," Edwin said. "I was happy with what he did."

"Yeah, he's dependable." Clark glanced toward the show ring. "He's done a lot of the muscle work for the livestock shows. I'd better move along. Good to see you."

They left Clark and walked along in the teens' wake. Sadie frowned.

"What are you thinking?" Edwin asked.

"Just that if Skip was into stealing valuable items from people's houses, he probably wouldn't be out here doing hard physical labor. He'd be scouting around for marks in town while half the homeowners are out here having fun at the fair."

"That makes sense to me," Edwin said. "But I never suspected Skip in the first place."

"I know." The disappearance of the pipe still bothered her, but she knew better than to launch a discussion of possible suspects.

Sara and Theo had reached the hot dog stand. Alice, Edwin, and Sadie joined them.

"Get whatever you want, kids," Edwin said, taking out his wallet.

"Fried dough too?"

"Oh, Sara," Alice said. "Really?"

"It's yummy!"

"The fair is only once a year," Edwin said, smiling.

Alice sighed. "I guess so."

After they all got their hot dogs and drinks, they strolled along, stopping at various booths for Sara's fried dough, onion rings for Theo, slices of pie for Edwin and Alice, and a caramel apple for Sadie.

"Cotton candy, anyone?" Edwin asked.

Alice moaned.

"No thanks, but I could eat an ice cream sandwich," Theo said. "That is, if we haven't broken your wallet yet."

"No problem," Edwin said. "Anyone else?"

"No, thank you," Sadie told him.

Alice shook her head. "I don't know where he puts it."

When Sadie got back to the Antique Mine, Roz was all alone in the store. She sat at the counter with an old *Godey's Lady's Book* open before her.

"Well, hi, jet-setter. How did it go?"

"Great," Sadie said. "Alice's pie took third in the contest, and Laura's was second."

"Who won?"

"Marisol, with her raspberry tarts."

"Oh, that's nice."

"Yeah. Sara got three ribbons in the gymkhana, including a blue in the Rescue Race."

"Terrific. I'll bet Sara's happy."

"Ecstatic."

"How's Alice taking being beat by your cousin?" Roz asked.

"Okay. I think she had gotten to the why-am-I-even-doing-this point. And the ribbons seemed to mean more to Laura than they did to Alice. Maybe she needed to feel she was truly a part of Silver Peak or something like that." Sadie shrugged. "Anyway, thank you so much for holding down the fort."

"Not many Indians besieging it today," Roz said. "The only things I sold were an old milk can and a mustache cup."

Sadie smiled. "Better than nothing. After all, it's the final and biggest day of the fair. I'm not surprised business is slow on Main Street."

"Did you find out any more about that note?" Roz asked.

"No, but I still think Steve acted funny when he saw it. He said he'd show it to Ainsley, but last time I talked to him, he said he didn't have time."

"I think Steve's okay. He's a little touchy about the tricks he's developing, but I like him." Roz stood and took her purse from under the counter. "Oh, Virginia Radcliff did stop by to ask if you'd refinish a piecrust table for her."

Sadie sighed. "Thanks. I'll call her later. I'll need to finish that blanket chest for Marge first." Working for Marge Ruxton was always a challenge. She was an exacting taskmaster, and her standards seemed to change as they went along. But fixing the hardware on the chest shouldn't take too long, and then she could move on to what sounded like a more interesting project for Virginia.

"You could close the store for the rest of the day," Roz suggested.

"No, I'll keep it open until four. I don't want to disappoint anyone."

Roz leaned on the old desk that made part of the checkout counter. "Have you found out any more about Edwin's pipe?"

"Well, kind of. I did learn that the estate that sold it was from a man who was a descendant of a mountain man, Grizzly Dawson. He supposedly saved the life of a chief's son, and the chief gave him the pipe as a gift. I put in an inquiry to an organization called the Northern Arapaho Council, hoping they can confirm it for me."

"Grizzly Dawson," Roz said, frowning. "Isn't he the one they made a movie about?"

"I'm sure they did. If not, they missed a good bet. But the weird thing is, Ainsley Rodin told Edwin and me the other night that he's also a Grizzly Dawson descendant."

"That *is* weird."

"I didn't know at the time that the pipe was supposedly connected to Dawson." Sadie laughed, pushing the switch on her laptop so it would warm up. "It's probably nothing. This has been a week of odd connections."

"What else?" Roz asked.

"Remember Marvin the Marvel?"

"Yeah."

"Well, it seems George True's father went to the same performance we did. Afterward, he was fascinated with magic tricks. He's the one who had the handcuffs Tulley Morse brought in."

"No."

"Yes."

Roz shook her head. "Well, Tulley hasn't been in, and the handcuffs are still here." She frowned. "Rodin hasn't done any handcuff tricks this week. Maybe he doesn't do escapes. He's showed me a lot of stuff though."

"What kind of stuff?" Sadie asked.

"Well, you know I can't give away his secrets. But I'll tell you, it's amazing how easy it is to distract people so that you can palm a card or a coin or something like that. And how easy it is to pick a pocket."

"Been practicing?"

Roz chortled. "Only on Roscoe. But Rodin does it all the time."

"Picks pockets?"

"For the show. You know. He takes something from anyone who comes near him on stage and makes a joke of returning it. You've seen him do it."

"Oh, sure. He does it almost every night." Sadie stopped and thought about Roz's words. "No. He wouldn't..."

19

"WOULDN'T WHAT?" ROZ ASKED.

"I was just thinking about that first rehearsal, when he had Edwin practice introducing the two of you. I suppose he could have picked Edwin's pocket then."

"Well, sure," Roz said. Her smile faded. "You're not suggesting he actually would?"

"We've been trying to figure out who besides Skip Stewart had access to Edwin's house. He usually locks up, but he'd left the back door open for Skip, and he had Skip lock it when he left."

"You're thinking Ainsley took Edwin's key ring and broke into his house?" Roz's eyebrows almost disappeared in her hairline.

"I'm not saying he did. I'm just saying it's possible."

"But Edwin wasn't missing his keys."

"No, he wasn't." Sadie swiveled back and forth on the stool, thinking. "Rodin could have made an impression. All he needed was a block of clay in his pocket."

"Oh, come on!"

Sadie waved a hand to silence Roz's protest. "Roscoe didn't make any keys last weekend, but the man who owns the hardware in Breckenridge said an older man had a house key made. I was hoping to catch Skip in the act, but I didn't even consider it could have been Mr. Rodin."

"I don't like where you're going with this," Roz said.

"Of course you don't. He's your friend."

"There's more to it than that. More I don't like."

"Oh?" Sadie waited.

Roz cleared her throat. "That first day—Thursday, afternoon—while we practiced the disappearing act for the first time..." Roz's eyes lost their focus and she stared off at an old pie safe Sadie used to display dishes.

"Yes?"

"While I was behind the curtain, I knew he was right on the other side."

"Because he was talking," Sadie said.

"Well, yeah, but...I also heard his keys jingle."

Sadie sat very still. "You heard keys jingling while you were in the disappearing cabinet?"

Roz shook her head vigorously. "No. When I got out of it behind the curtain." She turned to Sadie, a stricken look on her face. "I can't believe he would do that."

"He wouldn't go with us for ice cream after the show Friday night. He had Steve take him home. And he knew Edwin and I were out with the family." Sadie stared bleakly at Roz. Neither one of them said it, but they were both thinking it. Rodin could have had a duplicate key made after the rehearsal and gone to Edwin's house while they were at the Depot the next evening. "He only had to have the key for a minute, Roz. And he got you out of the way, so you couldn't see what he was doing. He turned his back to the grandstand while he spoke to you through the curtain about the trick, but we couldn't see his hands."

Roz shook her head. "I'm not going to believe this. Sadie, it's…it's just…" Her eyes sharpened. "Besides, if anyone brought Roscoe a clay impression of a key to copy, he'd find that very suspicious and call Mac right away. Thieves just don't do that anymore. Not unless they're going to make the key themselves."

"You're probably right," Sadie said. "The guy in Breckenridge didn't seem to think the key he'd made was unusual. Surely he would have mentioned it if he had to construct it from an impression." A sudden thought leaped into her mind. "Was Rodin ever in Putnam's hardware?"

"Sure. Steve needed something to fix one of the tricks— something for the hat illusion, I think. I took him and Ainsley in to meet Roscoe on Friday morning, before we rehearsed. Steve bought some wire."

"Wire. What about Ainsley?"

"He looked around the store and shot the breeze with Roscoe for a few minutes, and then we went over to the fairgrounds." Roz heaved a big sigh. "I should get going. We're meeting at four to go over our list of tricks for tonight. This is our grand finale, you know."

Sadie's computer *ding*ed and she glanced at the screen. "Hold on a minute."

"Why? What's that?"

"A reply from the Arapaho Council." Sadie opened the e-mail and skimmed the reply to her query. "That story is true. The chief gave that pipe in the beaded case to Grizzly Dawson, after he saved his son's life. And Dawson was Ainsley Rodin's ancestor."

She and Roz gazed at each other for a long moment.

"The key thing may not pan out," Sadie said at last, "But I think I have to at least tell Mac about this."

Roz exhaled. "You do what you've gotta do, but I hope your digging backfires and proves Ainsley and Steve weren't involved." She turned and left the store.

———

Sadie pulled into the Remingtons' driveway. Three cars sat in the small parking area. She eased into a slot next to Jane's car and got out of her Tahoe. Hauling in a deep breath, she gazed at the front of the cozy B and B. The two-story, white Victorian was the picture-perfect place to stay in a storybook mountain town. The views from the guest room windows were unbeatable, and the food was fantastic. Why did she get the feeling the house hid a sinister secret?

She hesitated, not sure exactly what she should do. When she had called the sheriff's office, the dispatcher told her that Mac was out on a call, but she would pass a message on to him. Sadie had asked her to tell Mac to meet her here. She had some vague notion that he would be able to catch Rodin before he left for the fairgrounds to meet with Roz—or perhaps to search his room. What Mac did might not matter as much as knowing he would be near the magician as soon as possible.

Of course, the SUV Steve used to chauffeur Rodin around Silver Peak was not in the parking lot. That would have been too easy.

Sadie walked slowly up the steps and rang the bell. After about fifteen seconds, Jane opened the door, her face flushed. She wore jeans and an oversized T-shirt, and her hair was caught back in a ponytail.

"Hi, Sadie. You caught me in my cleaning duds. Can I help you?"

"I wondered if Mr. Rodin was here."

"I'm not sure. If you want to sit down in the living room, I'll ring his room."

"Thanks." Sadie followed her in. Jane went to her desk in the entry and picked up the phone receiver. Sadie strolled into the sunny living room, which was empty, and sat down on the loveseat. From this vantage point, she could still see Jane.

After a pause, Jane put down the receiver and came to the doorway. She opened her mouth to speak just as the doorbell chimed again.

"Oh, sorry," she said, shooting a glance toward the door.

"I can wait," Sadie said.

"Well, he didn't pick up, so I'm assuming he's out."

"Okay."

Jane walked toward the front door, and Sadie stayed where she was. That could be Mac at the door. Even if it wasn't, she decided she ought to wait for him so she could explain the reasons she had summoned him. She couldn't make out the initial exchange at the door, but then Jane's voice became louder.

"Come right in," Jane said to the newcomer.

Sadie heard the door close. She sat forward on the loveseat, anticipating Mac striding in. But the man who came with the hostess to the living room was a stranger. His brown hair was trimmed short, and he had a small mustache. Sadie assumed he was a new customer for Jane.

Sadie shot to her feet as Jane ushered him in.

"I've just rung Mr. Rodin's room, and he didn't answer the phone, but since both you and Mrs. Speers are inquiring for him, perhaps I should go up and knock on his door, just to make sure he's not napping."

"Thank you." The man nodded to Sadie and went to the armchair opposite her.

Sadie resumed her seat. Closer study of the man gave her a start. He looked very much like Ainsley Rodin, only with brown hair and mustache, not Rodin's silver mane and clean-shaven face. Their chins and noses were identical, and the beginning wrinkles at the corners of this man's eyes reminded her strongly of Rodin's.

"I'm Sadie Speers," she said, hoping to gain some information.

He nodded with a slight smile. "Richard Towne."

"I think Jane said you're here to see Mr. Rodin?"

"Yes."

"So am I."

"Are you a friend of Ainsley's?"

"Sort of," Sadie said. "I only met him last week, when he came to perform in our fair."

"I see. Have you been to the show?"

"Every night," Sadie said with a smile. "My best friend is acting as his assistant this week. It's been very entertaining."

Mr. Towne chuckled. "I'm sure. Ainsley has always had a natural flair for it."

Jane returned, her breath a bit short, as if she'd run up and down the stairs. "I'm sorry, but your cousin is definitely out. He may be at the fairgrounds. Would you like directions?"

Sadie tried not to show her surprise. The resemblance should have prepared her for this revelation.

"Is he likely to come back here before the evening performance?" Mr. Towne asked.

"He might. You're welcome to wait," Jane said.

"Thank you."

"Could I bring you some coffee?"

"That would be wonderful," Mr. Towne said. "Thanks!"

Jane nodded and disappeared.

Sadie sat still for a moment, wondering what to do. Mac ought to know about this. She wondered if he had even received her message.

"Did you come to see your cousin perform?" she asked.

"Actually, I'm here on some family business," Mr. Towne replied.

Sadie heard another car drive in and looked out the window. Mac parked his sheriff's car beyond her Tahoe. She was glad he chose that spot, because the shield and lettering on the door was not visible from the window.

She smiled at Mr. Towne. "Excuse me."

"Of course."

She hurried into the entry. Jane was just coming from the kitchen with a coffee mug, spoon, napkin, creamer, and dish of sugar packets on a tray.

"Jane, Mac's here. I'm going out to talk to him," Sadie said softly.

Jane's eyebrows shot up. "I wonder what he wants."

"I asked him to meet me here." Sadie said.

"Okay." Jane blew a wisp of hair out of her eyes. "I may never get those rooms cleaned."

"Don't worry about me and Mac," Sadie said quickly. "We can talk outside. Thanks."

Jane took Mr. Towne's coffee into the living room as Sadie went out the front door. Mac had left his car and walked toward her across the driveway. His uniform was rumpled, and he looked tired, as though he'd already had a long day. "Well, Sadie, what is it?" He didn't say it aloud, but his tone implied that he was a busy man and this had better be good.

She went down the steps and laid a hand on his sleeve. "There's a man in Jane's living room drinking coffee."

"Is that unusual?"

"He's Ainsley Rodin's cousin. He's here looking for Rodin."

Mac's eyes narrowed. "So?"

Sadie huffed out a breath. "He's not the reason I called you to come here, but it could be important. If Rodin doesn't show up here soon, his cousin will probably go out to the fairgrounds to find him."

"Okay. What else?"

Quickly, she told him about the Arapaho pipe's provenance and how she'd had it confirmed that a tribal chief had given it to the mountain man Uriah "Grizzly" Dawson about a hundred and fifty years previously. "And Rodin and the person who put the pipe up for sale are both descendants of Grizzly Dawson."

"So you've made a connection between Rodin and the pipe," Mac said slowly.

"Yes."

"That doesn't mean he stole it. More likely, he was the one who sold it in the first place."

"Or not," Sadie said. "There's more."

"I'm listening."

Sadie walked a little farther from the house and stood between their vehicles with Mac as she went through her reasoning about the keys. She concluded, "So it's possible that Rodin 'borrowed'

Edwin's key ring during the rehearsal, either made an impression or snapped a picture of it, had a duplicate key made that day, and used it to enter his house the next night, when he knew we were all at the Depot after the opening show."

Mac gazed into her eyes for several seconds. Sadie began to wonder if he was going to chew her out for speculating about honest, upstanding people who were bringing a lot of commerce to Silver Peak.

Instead, Mac said carefully, "The key word in all that you said is 'possible.' Not probable."

Sadie gulped. "I know. But…"

"But it's enough for me to go on. I will look into it, Sadie."

"What will you do?"

"Well, I could ask the hardware owner in Breck…"

"I already talked to them," Sadie said. "The only house key they've made lately was for an older man who paid cash. But he didn't say if it was made from either an impression or a photo, so I doubt it was."

"What makes you so sure that's how Rodin would do it?"

"Edwin didn't miss his keys at all. Rodin couldn't have kept them long enough to go have one copied."

"Okay. So the guy who had one made in Breckinridge wasn't Rodin."

"Yeah. That rules out the self-service key machine in Breckinridge too. He would have had to keep Edwin's key several hours. And Roscoe hasn't made any keys lately."

Mac's eyes weren't glazing over yet, so Sadie continued. "Tonight is Rodin's final show. He could leave town as soon as it's over, and you'd lose the opportunity to search his room."

"Search his room?" Mac frowned. "I'd have to get a warrant for that, Sadie. It's Saturday. Do you know where the nearest judge who could issue a search warrant on a Saturday afternoon lives?"

"I have no idea."

"About forty miles away, that's where. Unless I have probable cause—and I said 'probable,' not 'possible'—I can't go into that man's room."

"Not even if Jane lets you?"

"Not while Mr. Rodin is renting it. And even if I could, I wouldn't be able to search his luggage without his own permission or a warrant."

"Oh."

"Yeah, oh." Mac frowned and looked off toward the mountain peaks.

"So I guess I got you out here for nothing," Sadie said.

"I wouldn't say nothing. You might be on to something." He drummed his fingers on the top of his car for a moment.

"By the way, it would be unlikely for him to make a clay impression and ask someone else to make a key from it," Sadie said. "Too suspicious. But I read online that thieves can take a picture of a key and make one just like it with a 3-D printer."

"You think Rodin is carrying a 3-D printer around with him?"

"Well…"

Mac shook his head. "There's a simpler way, but it's low-tech. He or Steve could have filed out a key using a good to-scale photograph."

"Really? I had no idea," Sadie said. "Do you think Rodin has the skills? Steve would, but…"

"Steve Parrish is a very handy guy. I'm not so sure about Rodin." Mac eyed her sharply. "Who consigned the stuff to the auction?"

"I don't know."

"But it had to be someone in that family, right?" Mac said.

"Yeah. I suppose it could be a distant relative."

"Or Rodin. Or this cousin who's sitting in the parlor. Can you find out?"

"I can try," Sadie said. Now that she had the name of one of Rodin's cousins, she might be able to learn some things about their family connections. "I brought my laptop. I think I can pick up Wi-Fi on the Remingtons' network. If not, I'll have to go back to the store."

Mac nodded. "Did the cousin say where he lives?"

"Not that I heard. He gave his name though. It's Richard Towne."

Mac took out his notebook. "But the auction was held in Denver, according to Edwin."

"Yes."

"Okay, I'll make a couple of calls while you check into that." He opened the door of his car, got in, and reached for his radio.

Sadie climbed into her Tahoe and opened her laptop. She hoped she could pick up the pedigree lines she had found earlier and follow their branches.

It was almost six o'clock. Edwin was expecting her to join him before the Skylarks played. She didn't want to be late, but this was more pressing.

The best genealogy site she knew let her view family groups on her screen. She searched first for Ainsley Rodin's family, but nothing turned up on him. That seemed odd until she realized he might have changed his name when he went into show business. She switched to a general search engine for biographical information on the magician. She kicked herself for not doing it before—but then, she hadn't suspected Rodin until today.

There it was. Ainsley Rodin was born David Ainsley Towne. His birth date made her stop and do some figuring. Rodin was seven years younger than she was. His silvery hair had fooled her, and she had assumed he was at least sixty, probably older, but according to this, he was only fifty-five. She studied the accompanying photographs. It was him, all right. So his hair had turned gray prematurely. What else had she gotten wrong?

She remembered the things she had read about Houdini earlier in the week. He had changed his name from Erich Weiss to Harry Houdini. The first name was a corruption of his real name—his family called him "Ehrie." From there to "Harry" was an easy slide. But for his last name, he had chosen a variation of Houdin, a famous French magician of an earlier day.

What if Ainsley had also chosen a name that sounded French as his stage name? There was a famous sculptor named Rodin. What if the magician thought it sounded elegant and exotic?

As her mind whirred through these possibilities, Sadie went back to the genealogy site and waded through the screens. She searched this time for a family named Towne that included males named Richard and David Ainsley.

"Bingo." She wished she could print out a pedigree sheet for both the cousins. Maybe later. For now, she only needed to find information Mac could use. Ainsley's father and Richard's were brothers. A new search with the name of Ainsley's father showed that he had died nearly twenty years ago. Richard's father, on the other hand, had been deceased only about two years. Could the estate from which the Arapaho pipe went to the auction have been his?

She went back one more generation to the first common ancestor, Grandpa Robert Dawson Towne. Was this the family connection to Grizzly Dawson? She kept going. Grandpa Dawson's mother, it seemed, was a granddaughter of the mountain man. The pipe could have been passed down to her. And Grandpa Dawson had died only four months ago, at the age of ninety-six.

Sadie looked over at Mac, who was still sitting in his car and talking on his phone. She took several deep breaths to calm herself and then did a search for the grandfather's obituary. As soon as she saw it, she got out of her vehicle and walked over to Mac's. He released the lock on the passenger side, and she slid into the front seat beside him.

"What have you got?" he asked.

Quickly, she gave Mac the basics of the family connections.

"And Richard Towne was in charge of Grandpa's funeral arrangements," she said, a little breathless. "Mac, I'm betting he was the estate's executor, although the obituary didn't say that."

Mac glanced at his watch. "When does the musical show start?"

"It's supposed to begin at seven—less than an hour from now. Rodin and Roz go on at eight. And they have to get dressed and do their makeup first."

"So he might not come back here first."

As Mac spoke, Sadie caught sight of a silver SUV rolling down Jefferson Avenue.

"That's him," she said.

"All right, you keep quiet and let me handle this," Mac said, eyeing her sternly.

"You got it."

They both got out of the car as Steve Parrish parked the SUV near the front steps. Sadie's heart sank as she saw that he was alone.

Mac walked over to the vehicle before Steve had a chance to get out. Sadie followed him but stayed a few steps behind Mac. Steve's looked toward them, his surprise evident in his expression, and rolled down his window.

"Hello, Sheriff. Can I help you?"

"I'd like to talk to you for a few minutes," Mac said. "It's important."

"Okay. How can I help you?"

"Do you know Richard Towne?"

Steve hesitated and then nodded. "I've met him. He's Ainsley's cousin. Why?"

"He's inside," Mac said. "The three of us are going to have a little chat."

Steve exhaled heavily. "Oh boy. This could mean trouble."

20

"WHY DO YOU SAY THAT?" MAC ASKED.

Steve swallowed hard. "Can I ask what you want to talk about?"

"Why don't you step out of the vehicle, please?"

In Sadie's opinion, Mac was being overly cautious, but she supposed he had to be in his job. She hung back, trying not to insinuate that she was part of the conversation, but Steve shot her a curious glance as he climbed out of the SUV.

"What's going on? Is there a family emergency?"

"Do you know about Ainsley Rodin's grandfather, Mr. Towne?" Mac looked at Sadie. "What was his full name?"

"Robert Dawson Towne," she said.

"Right. Did you know him?" Mac asked.

Steve shook his head. "I knew who he was, but I never met him. He died a short while ago."

"Did Rodin go to his grandfather's funeral?"

"Yeah. He was about to go on tour, and I was getting things ready when we heard his grandfather had died. We flew out two days after the funeral."

"On tour?" Mac asked. "Where?"

"In Europe. We were over there for three months, and we only got back about six weeks ago."

"So..." Mac frowned. "Who was Mr. Towne's executor?"

"That would be Ainsley's cousin, Richard."

"The one who's inside."

Steven shrugged. "You know more than I do on that score, Sheriff."

"Why did you come back here just now?" Mac asked. "Isn't Rodin doing a show soon?"

"Yeah. We just had a light supper, and he had me drop him at the fairgrounds. He asked me to come back here and pick up something from his room." Steve shoved his key ring into his pocket.

"And why did you say it could mean trouble if his cousin is here?"

Steve let out a big sigh. "Ainsley and Richard don't get along so well. As I understand it, they've never seen eye to eye on much."

"And their grandpa's will made it worse?" Mack asked.

Steve hesitated and raised his hands, palms open. "Ainsley didn't talk to me about the details, but I knew he wasn't happy about it. He couldn't cancel his tour though."

"And when you came back from Europe, what happened with him and Richard?"

"I don't know. There was something, but he didn't confide in me."

"Okay," Mac said. "I need to pat you down before we go inside."

"Is that necessary?"

"Until I know what's going on, it is. Put your hands on the roof of the vehicle."

Steve turned around with a resigned expression and let Mac check his clothing for weapons. From one of Steve's jacket pockets, the sheriff pulled a metal cylinder with some kind of lever at one end.

"What's this?" Mac asked.

"It's a coin feeder. It lets the magician feed coins into his hand when he's doing tricks. If he does it right, it looks like they appear out of thin air. In my other pocket, you'll find a dozen quarters. They fit into it."

Mac grunted and completed his search, turning up a wallet, a phone, a compact set of screwdrivers in a plastic case, and the coins Steve had mentioned. Last of all, from Steve's shirt pocket, he took a folded piece of paper. Before he opened it, Sadie recognized the note Roz had found.

"What's this?" Mac asked.

"Sadie found it under the grandstand. Or, I guess Roz found it and gave it to her."

Sadie said, "That's right. We wondered who had lost it, and if it was important. I gave it to Steve."

"And I showed it to Ainsley when we ate a little while ago," Steve added. "He said it wasn't his, but..."

"But what?" Mac eyed him closely.

"The way he reacted when he saw it, I wondered if maybe it was his after all."

"Why would he lie to you?"

Steve was quiet for a moment, then he met Mac's gaze. "I don't know. This thing with Richard..."

"So you think it's from him to his cousin, or from Richard to him?" Mac looked at the note again and read it out loud. "I know you're angry, but this is for the best. Believe me, if I had known your feelings, I would have done things differently."

"I'm thinking maybe Richard wrote it."

"And Ainsley was the angry one?" Mac asked.

"I really don't know. He denied it, and I have no explanation for that."

Mac stood in thought for a moment. "Okay, let's go inside. You stay where I can see you, but let me do the talking."

Steve's shoulders drooped, but he turned and walked toward the front door.

Sadie followed them up the steps as quietly as she could. She was afraid Mac would turn around and tell her to stay outside, but he didn't.

They went into the living room, where Richard Towne was sitting and drinking his coffee. He looked up when he saw them, his eyes lingering for a moment on Mac's uniform, then shifting to Steve.

He stood and extended his hand. "Steve, good to see you."

"Hi, Mr. Towne." Steve shook his head. "This is Sheriff Slattery, and this is Sadie Speers."

"We've met," Sadie said quickly.

"I'd like to talk to you for a moment," Mac said. "Please sit down."

Richard frowned and resumed his seat. "Is anything wrong, Sheriff? I hope nothing's happened to Ainsley."

"He's fine," Mac said, sitting down opposite him. "You're Mr. Rodin's cousin, and you were recently the executor for your grandfather's estate?"

"That's right," Richard said.

"Wasn't it the Arapaho pipe and its beaded case that were auctioned in Denver twelve days ago from your grandfather's estate?"

"Yes, it was," Richard said. "Is that what this is about?"

"Why did you sell it?" Mac asked.

"Because my grandfather left equal shares of the estate to me, Ainsley, my sister, and a mutual cousin, all grandchildren of his. We couldn't all have his house or his antiquities collection, so they had to be sold and the money divided."

"I'm guessing that Ainsley didn't want the things to be sold," Mac said.

"Mostly the pipe you mentioned." Richard let out a sigh. "He wanted to buy it from the estate. He made an offer, and I said I needed to have it appraised first. It might be worth a lot more than what he was willing to pay. And I found out it was. He wouldn't have paid as much as the auction price for it."

"But you listed it in the auction while he was on tour in Europe, didn't you?"

"I had to move things along with the estate. I'd been in contact with Ainsley by e-mail and Skype. He was upset about it and said he shouldn't have to pay the market value. But I reminded him that there were other people involved. He'd basically be shortchanging the other three of us if he got the pipe for less than the fair value."

"So you sold it."

"Yes, but he came home before the auction took place. He could have placed a bid on it if he wanted to."

"This has been a matter of contention between you."

Richard's eyelids lowered, and he nodded.

"So you came here...why? To confront him?"

"The truth, Sheriff?"

"Please," Mac said.

"Okay, when I got the statement from the auctioneer, I saw that the buyer who got the pipe at the auction lived in Silver Peak. No problem. But then, two days later, I learned my cousin had taken on what amounts to a charitable appearance at a small-town fair. Again, no problem—except that the fair was to be held in Silver Peak. Red flags started waving in my brain, I'll tell you."

"Why's that?"

Richard stared at him. "Isn't it obvious? It's too coincidental. Ainsley doesn't do a lot of performances outside his regular shows in Vegas and Los Angeles. Once in a while he goes to New York for a couple of months or does a tour, like he did this summer. But a tiny little mountain town like this? I knew without a doubt he was coming here because the pipe was here."

"But why did you come?"

"He wouldn't answer my calls or texts. I had to know what was going on."

Mac eyed him steadily. "And what did you think was going on?"

"I thought he was probably trying to talk the pipe's new owner into selling it to him."

"So you hadn't heard that the pipe was stolen?"

Richard's eyes widened. "What?" His eyes widened. "No, I hadn't heard that."

———

Sadie parked at the fairgrounds and followed Mac, Steve, and Richard to the grandstand. The curtains were closed, and she could hear the Skylarks warming up for the show.

"He's probably backstage getting ready," Steve said. "This way." He led Richard up the side steps, and Mac and Sadie followed.

In the wings, they found Ainsley and Roz carefully packing props for the magic show into their costumes.

"Make sure you have the feather duster on top of the confetti pack," Ainsley said. "Steve's bringing the..." He broke off as the four newcomers approached. "Steve! And..." He frowned at Richard. "What are you doing here?"

"Hello, Ainsley." Richard walked past Steve and stopped close to them. He smiled at Roz. "Hello. I'm Richard Towne, Ainsley's cousin."

"I'm Roz Putnam. Nice to meet you." Roz's winsome smile evidently won over Richard, as he smiled back.

"Nice to meet you."

"I repeat," Ainsley said tersely. "Why are you here?"

"It seems this is the only way I can get you to talk to me. We need to sort out this business about the Arapaho pipe, Ainsley. I had to sell it. Surely you can understand that."

Ainsley glared at him. "You just couldn't wait a few weeks, could you? You were just plain greedy!"

"Me? You're the one who wanted the lion's share."

"That's not true."

Sadie stepped up behind Mac and Steve, so that she could see the two cousins, almost nose to nose. Roz's jaw dropped and she looked confused.

Mac stepped forward. "Here now, let's all settle down. Is there someplace we can sit down and talk things over?"

"Hello, Sheriff," Ainsley said in a much more affable tone than the one he had used with his cousin.

"Mr. Rodin," Mac said. "Is there a problem here?"

"Just a family matter," Ainsley said. "We can handle it."

"Maybe the sheriff can help us straighten it out," Richard suggested.

"I doubt it."

"Ainsley…" Richard laid a hand on his arm, and the magician whirled toward him, his face contorted in anger.

"Leave me be, Richard." Ainsley pulled on his lapels to straighten his jacket. "Now, if you'll all excuse me, I have a show to do, and I need to prepare."

"Just a minute, Mr. Rodin," Mac said. "I think there's more to this than you're letting on."

"What do you mean?"

"I know this family squabble has to do with your grandfather's estate and the Arapaho pipe your cousin put in the auction."

Ainsley clamped his lips together, and his face turned beet-red. "Sheriff, I go onstage in two hours. Perhaps we can talk after the show, if my cousin is willing to stay around that long."

"No, we need to talk now," Mac said. "If everything checks out all right, you can do the show. But the longer you stall, the less likely that is. Understand?"

Ainsley grunted and looked away.

"Now, your cousin told me that the Arapaho pipe and its beaded case that were auctioned in Denver twelve days ago were from your grandfather's estate. There were four heirs, and he sold some things so that the money could be divided."

Ainsley scowled at Richard. "You could have waited."

"You couldn't have paid the value of that pipe," Richard said.

"How do you know that?" Ainsley snapped.

Mac cleared his throat. "It just so happens that the person who bought that item at the auction lives here in Silver Peak. But you knew that, didn't you, Mr. Rodin?"

"I...I know it now. I heard about Edwin Marshall's trouble. He hasn't made any secret of it."

"But you knew that was the pipe from your grandfather's estate," Mac said. "Why didn't you tell him that?"

"I didn't see any point in it. He'd already lost it. It would only make him feel worse if he knew it had come from my family."

"Where were you last Friday night, after the show?" Mac asked. "Think carefully."

"You mean opening night?"

"Yes."

Ainsley closed his eyes and frowned. "Let's see. That was the night Roz was hurt. She saw Murray Lithgow backstage, and he pushed her. After we closed the act and took our bows, you came backstage, Sheriff, to ask us about that."

"I did. And where did you go after that?"

"*Hmm.*" Ainsley scratched his head, scowling as if remembering that evening was the hardest chore he had ever undertaken.

"I took him back to the B and B," Steve said.

Mac looked blandly at Steve, then back to Ainsley. "Is that correct?"

"Yes, of course. You asked me that once before. Steve drove me back there so I could turn in early. I was very tired, after all the rehearsing and the strain of having my assistant attacked during the show. I believe we had an invitation to go out for refreshments, but I was simply too tired, Sheriff. Didn't think I was up to it."

"And you went straight to bed?" Mac asked.

"I... I think so."

Mac lifted his shoulders in a little shrug. "Funny. I talked to Jerry Remington just a few minutes ago, after I met your cousin at the B and B. He says he took a message to your room about a half hour after you returned that night. Mr. Towne had called and asked for you. But Jerry said that when he switched the call to your room, you didn't pick up."

"I was probably in the shower or asleep."

Mac nodded. "Jerry said he went upstairs and tapped on your door to give you the message, but you didn't answer. He figured you'd gone to bed. But a while later, he passed the door and heard a sound inside, so he knocked again. You opened the door, Mr. Rodin, and you were still wearing your clothes from the show."

Rodin's face had gone a darker shade, so that it was almost purple, but he said nothing.

"So," Mac said, "I'll ask you again, where were you that night?"

Behind Sadie, someone came up the steps. She turned and found Kyle Kenmore, in his uniform, entering.

"Is the sheriff up here?" Kyle asked.

Sadie pointed toward where Mac stood.

"Kenmore," Mac called. "What have you got for me?"

"The warrant you requested, sir." Kyle held out a folded piece of paper.

"Warrant?" Rodin's eyes flared.

"Yes," Mac said with satisfaction. "Thank you, Kenmore. I think that was record time for a weekend request." He opened the paper, scanned it, and turned to Ainsley. "This is a warrant to search your room, luggage, and vehicle."

Ainsley whirled toward him. "Now, just a minute, Sheriff. Surely you don't think I have any contraband in my room."

Mac eyed him calmly. "When I put in the request for the warrant, I also put out some calls about house keys. You see, I believe someone used a key to enter Mayor Marshall's house Friday evening and steal the Arapaho pipe he'd bought a few days previously—the pipe that was part of your grandfather's estate."

"House keys? That's ridiculous," Rodin said.

"Roscoe Putnam is going over the security tape from the time you were in his hardware store. That would be the morning of the show's opening."

"I did go in with Roz and Steve," Rodin said. "Steve needed something for a trick he was building."

"That may be," Mac said, "but I've asked Roscoe to tell me whether you showed an interest in the key-making area, specifically the blank keys."

"Blank keys?" Rodin sputtered. "I didn't have any keys made in his store."

"No, you didn't, but you're a master at pocketing small items," Mac said.

Rodin clamped his jaws together.

"Is your luggage locked?" Mac asked.

"Yes."

"Would you like to give me the keys?" When Rodin frowned, Mac added, "It's that or force the locks, and I don't think you want that."

Edwin came up the steps and looked over the group with interest. "I'm about to introduce the Skylarks. You folks might want to take your discussion somewhere else during the show."

Without warning, Ainsley turned and ran out on to the stage.

"Kyle!" Mac nodded toward the stage, and Kyle dashed out from the wings, in pursuit of Rodin. A second later, a loud crash sounded. Sadie cringed and peered out to see Kyle and the magician in a heap among the parts of the band's drum kit.

21

SPIKE AND THE OTHER MUSICIANS STOOD IN SHOCK, STARING AT the disarray, while Kyle put handcuffs on Rodin. Mac pulled out his phone and punched a few buttons. Edwin and Roz drew closer to Sadie.

"What is going on?" Edwin asked.

"I think the show may start late," Sadie said.

Roz stared at her, shaking her head in disbelief. "This is unreal. Mac thinks Ainsley stole the pipe?"

"I'd say it's more than a thought, Roz. I'm sorry." Sadie patted Roz's arm. "I was hoping I was wrong, but then his cousin came, and it all fell into place." She looked at Edwin. "I'm really, really sorry, but we'd better see if Spike and the guys can put their act back together."

Kyle had pulled Rodin to his feet and was leading him toward the stairs that went down to the ground-level exit.

"I'll ask if I can help them." Edwin hurried over to the band.

"What about *our* show?" Roz asked Sadie. "The magic show?"

Sadie saw tears in her friend's eyes. This meant so much to Roz. Not only that, but it was the last night, and hundreds of people had come to see her and Rodin perform. Her brain was

doing cartwheels as she sought for a happy outcome. "Well…
Maybe you could teach Edwin a trick or two in the next hour."

"Edwin? You want me and Edwin to perform? That's crazy. He
couldn't learn all that stuff in an hour."

"But you could do Rodin's part. You know most of the
tricks."

"No," Roz said. "I don't know all his secrets, and I'm not that
good. Steve doesn't even bring out some of the equipment until
the last minute, so nobody can mess with it. Sadie, we'll have
to refund the people's money. Do you know what that will cost
the fair?"

"Well… maybe Mac will let Rodin go long enough to perform."

After a short pause, Roz said, "I'll do whatever I can, but you
do your part. Make Mac let Ainsley go!"

Sadie swallowed hard. "I'll try."

She hurried into the wings. Steve and Richard stood staring
down the steps. "Where's the sheriff?"

"He left to take Ainsley in."

Sadie ran down the steps. People were filing into their seats
in the grandstand. She spotted Mac's tall form several yards away,
headed toward the parking lot. She ran after him and caught up
to him. Ainsley Rodin trudged between him and Kyle, his hands
cuffed together.

"Mac!"

"What is it, Sadie?" He paused, then turned and nodded to
Kyle. "Take him to the car." Kyle and Rodin moved away.

"Mac, please, can't you let Mr. Rodin go long enough to do the
show? It's the last night, and it means a lot to everyone."

"No."

"But we'll have to refund the tickets if we don't…"

"No."

Sadie sighed. "I guess that's a no."

"Yup." Mac walked away.

She turned and plodded back to the stage. Steve and Richard still stood where she had left them in the wings.

"I'm sorry, Steve," Sadie said.

He shook his head. "I can't believe this is happening."

"So you didn't know anything about it?" she asked.

"Just that he was angry with Richard for consigning some items from the estate before we got home from Europe. The Arapaho pipe was one thing he especially thought should stay in the family."

"Why didn't he go to the auction?" Sadie asked. "He might have been able to buy it back."

"He was tied up. I think he might have put in a phone bid, but it went too high."

"He must have known that Edwin bought it," Sadie said.

Steve nodded slowly. "I think you're right. Or at least that the buyer lived here. I couldn't believe he took this gig—not that it hasn't been fun. I mean, really, I've enjoyed our stay here. It was nice doing a small town for a change. But if he knew where the pipe had gone, that would explain it."

Sadie frowned. "Surely the auctioneer wouldn't have told him who bought the pipe?"

"I wouldn't think so," Steve agreed.

Sadie had hoped to get confidential information from Ron Waverly, without success. The auctioneer was a stickler for protecting his clients.

"He told me," Richard said. "I was the seller. The auction house gave me a list of the buyers and their bids. But I don't remember telling Ainsley anything about the buyer."

"Ainsley was really keen on coming to Silver Peak," Steve said. "He'd gotten the request a day or two before, but he didn't think he wanted to come here, since he'd let his staff take time off. But all of a sudden he changed his mind."

Sadie inhaled slowly, thinking about that. "Was that after the auction?"

"Yeah. And Ainsley is a member of the family that put the estate items in the auction. He's famous too. Don't forget that."

Sadie nodded. "You may have something there. Unfortunately, famous people sometimes get special treatment. And the auctioneer didn't have to actually tell Ainsley who bought the pipe. Just that it went to a small mountain town—Silver Peak. Once he got here, it wasn't hard to learn who had bought it. Edwin didn't make a secret of it."

"I heard about it the day after we came here," Steve admitted. "I didn't hear all the particulars, and I didn't think anything of it. But it all makes sense now. Ainsley changed his mind about coming here because he knew the pipe was here."

Edwin and Roz came in from the stage. "Spike says they can go on in five minutes."

"The drums are okay?" Steve asked.

"There's some minor damage, but they'll get through the set."

Sadie raised her chin as she looked hopefully at Edwin. "So do you think you could do the magic show with Roz?"

"Me? No way. We'll have to cancel it," Edwin said.

"A lot of people will be disappointed. The Fair Committee will have to refund their ticket money. That could mean the difference on seeing a profit or a loss on the fair this year."

Edwin frowned. "What about you, Steve? You know all the tricks. You built most of the equipment."

"Yeah," Roz said eagerly, turning to Steve. "You could do the show."

Sadie sucked in a breath. She knew Steve was disillusioned and depressed. "Of course he could, if he wants to."

Edwin laid a hand on the younger man's shoulder. "Steve, I know this is a bad time, but the fair has a big problem. Could you possibly do Rodin's routine with Roz? It would mean a lot to the audience, and to the Fair Committee."

Steve stared at him for a moment, as if Edwin were out of his mind. "I don't think I'm the best person for that."

"There's no one else," Edwin said. "You're the only one who knows the routine inside out and could go through it with Roz."

"And convince the audience they got their money's worth," Sadie added. "Steve, you made the props. You've practiced those tricks, to make sure they work. I know you've had a shock, but…well, you could do this final thing for Ainsley. He's treated you well, and our whole town would appreciate it so much."

"Well, I have to be here. The sheriff told me not to leave town until we have a long talk. I guess that will be tomorrow morning." Steve sighed and looked at his watch. "What do you think, Roz? We only have an hour."

"I'm game," she said. "And I think it would be great of you to do it."

"I've got to get the Skylarks on stage," Edwin said. "Spike said they can do a couple of extra numbers if it will help. How about it, Steve?"

Steve's mouth quirked in a bitter smile. "Why not? It won't be perfect."

"We won't expect it to be," Sadie said. "Just do your best."

He nodded.

"Thank you," Roz said, her tears spilling over. "Come on, let's go down to the dressing room and practice."

Sadie held out a hand to Richard Towne. "If you'd like to go out front with me, we can get good seats. I'm sure my daughter and grandchildren are saving some in the front row."

"Might as well," Richard said. "The sheriff gave me the same 'don't leave town' speech he gave Steve."

They hurried out to the bleachers. Sure enough, Alice, the kids, and Roscoe were already seated. Sadie briefly introduced Richard and they sat down to watch as Edwin introduced the band. Sadie's mind churned. Somehow she was going to have to explain to Roscoe about the change in the show.

Edwin joined her on the bench, and the band launched into its first number.

"I guess Steve's out of a job now," he whispered to Sadie.

"I guess so," Sadie said, "but he may be able to start the business he's been wanting."

After the third song, Edwin pulled out his cell phone and glanced at the screen. "It's Mac. I'd better take it." He hopped up and walked a short distance away. When he came back, he leaned close to Sadie's ear. "Mac said that if I come by his office tomorrow, I'll be able to pick up the pipe."

"Really?" Sadie almost squealed.

"Yeah. They found it in Rodin's suitcase. A few more hours, and he'd have left town with it."

"Wow." The song ended, and she joined the applause.

"What are you smiling about?" Edwin asked.

"Just glad you're getting your pipe back. And thinking about Mac taking the great Rodin away in handcuffs. Think he got out of them?"

Edwin shot her a quick glance and then smiled. "You're nuts."

———————

At the short intermission in the middle of the music show, Sadie said, "I want to go backstage and see how Roz and Steve are doing. Can you break it to Roscoe that Rodin won't be performing?"

"Sure," Edwin said.

Sadie hurried to the area beneath the stage and found Roz and Steve in the magician's dressing room with an array of props laid out on the makeup table. Roz looked up and saw her in the doorway.

"Hi, Sadie."

"Hi." Sadie stepped inside. "Steve, thank you so much for this. Are you sure you're up to it?"

"No, but I'll give it my best. We don't want to send several hundred fans home disappointed, do we?"

Roz smiled. "That's the heart of a trouper. I assume Edwin will make a brief explanation when he introduces us?" While speaking, Roz handed Steve the magician's cape. Sadie helped Steve put it on.

"I'm sure he will." Sadie knew he would rise to the occasion.

"Great. The hat's all loaded, Steve." Roz handed it to him. "We had planned to do that first, then the melon trick, the scarf illusion, and the floating bottle, only we're using the rabbit this time, so floating rabbit."

"Scratch the melon trick," Steve said. "I can't do that."

"Are you sure?" Roz asked. "That's a big trick. And you already put the dollar in the melon."

Sadie smiled. She would keep quiet about what she had just learned. Or maybe she would discuss it with Edwin later, but no one else.

"I don't think I can pull it off with the audience," Steve said. "I've never done it myself."

"But you've watched Ainsley do it hundreds of times."

Steve put his hand to his forehead and closed his eyes. "Okay." He opened his eyes and looked at Sadie. "Will you raise your hand to help with the trick? I'll pick you for the audience volunteer. I have to have someone who won't give it away if I botch up the trick."

"Sure," Sadie said. Wouldn't Sara be tickled?

"All right." Steve hefted the black top hat, testing its balance, then put it on. He adjusted it slightly.

"How's this?"

"You look great." Roz handed him the baton. "Need anything else?"

"Just my remote mic. Are the props the way I left them?"

"Nothing's been touched. We'll need someone to help bring in the disappearing cabinet for the finale."

"Maybe Edwin can do that," Sadie said. "Would you like him to stay in the wings while you're on, in case you need something?"

"Perfect. You tell him, okay?"

"Sure."

Roz looked up toward the ceiling. Overhead, the Skylarks were singing again.

"Anything special for the intro?" Sadie asked Steve.

He shrugged. "Tell Edwin to…just make the audience not hate me. I used to perform occasionally. I guess he can say something about that, so they don't think I'm a complete novice."

Sadie nodded. "Is it okay to say good luck?"

"I'm not superstitious." Steve managed a crooked smile. "Thanks."

"I'd better get out of here." Sadie gave Roz a quick hug. "See you in a few minutes."

"Right," Roz said heartily. "Don't forget to volunteer."

"I won't."

Steve still looked wan, but Sadie forced herself to turn away. They had to do this on their own. She dashed out to the bleachers. Edwin had moved over on the other side of Roscoe and was talking to him earnestly. Alice and the kids were watching the band. Richard sat staring at the stage, but he didn't look as though he was focused on the music.

Sadie tapped Edwin's shoulder and beckoned him to join her a short distance away. She filled him in on what Steve had said about the introduction and having him stand by backstage.

"No problem," Edwin said. "Come on, that's Spike's finale."

They took their seats and listened to the last song. Sadie was sorry she hadn't given the show proper attention tonight.

"Thank you all. You're a great crowd," Spike said into the microphone. He and the boys left the stage, taking their instruments with them. Two young men dashed onstage to take away the speakers and other equipment the band had used.

"Looks like you're on, Edwin." Sadie squeezed his hand. "Maybe when it's over, we can get Steve and Roz and all go decompress at the Depot."

Edwin strode toward the stairway and a moment later appeared onstage. "Ladies and gentlemen," he said in his fine, crisp tones, "thank you for coming out tonight to support the Silver Peak Fair. This is our closing night, and we have a special treat for you. The Great Ainsley Rodin is indisposed tonight…"

The audience let out a collective groan. Edwin held up both hands. Alice and Theo leaned forward to stare past Sara at Sadie.

"What happened?" Alice mouthed.

"Now, now, don't get upset, folks," Edwin went on, and Sadie waved her hand toward him, hoping the family would turn their attention to the stage. "We have a substitute whom I think you're going to love. He is a master craftsman when it comes to magic tricks and apparatus, and he's a veteran magician in his own right. May I present, with the beautiful Roz Putnam assisting, the mystifying and magical Mr. Steve Parrish!"

The crowd clapped as the curtain rose, but it wasn't the thunderous ovation Ainsley had received night after night.

"I didn't know Mr. Parrish was a magician too," Sara said, joining the applause.

"Oh yes, he's a pro," Sadie said.

Roz strutted onstage, smiling and waving both hands, trailing clouds of chiffon. She turned halfway around and gestured toward the wings. Steve ran out to join her, smiling and waving. He took Roz's hand, and together they took a bow.

The audience settled back with an air of uncertainty. Sadie sent up a silent prayer for Steve and Roz's nerves, and that the crowd would embrace them.

"Good evening, ladies and gentlemen," Steve said, doffing his hat. "It's a pleasure to be here with you this evening."

His smile looked genuine, and Sadie almost believed him.

"For our first trick," Steve said, "we're going to see what the bunny rabbit has stockpiled in my hat. Fall is just around the corner, you know." He reached into the hat and pulled out a winter scarf, gloves, and a diminutive pair of mukluks. He then brought out several more items, too large to fit in the hat, ending with a pair of bear paw snowshoes. Steve frowned at them for a moment. "*Hmm*, I didn't know he was a snowshoe rabbit."

The audience laughed, and Steve set the snowshoes aside. "Time to feed the bunny. I'm sure he's hungry after all that snowshoeing up in the mountaintops. What do we have for him tonight, Roz?"

Roz smiled at him and looked out at the audience. "I was going to bake him a cake."

"In my hat?" Steve asked incredulously.

Sara began to clap and yelled, "Yeah! Go for it!"

Sadie smiled. All week long, she had watched Rodin throw various food items into his top hat to "feed the rabbit." Of course, she and Sara both knew how the trick would end, but it was still fun to watch.

Roz and Steve went all out this time. Roz held up a glass measuring cup full of flour and poured it into the hat. This was followed by baking soda, salt, and sugar.

"Now for the eggs." She cracked two eggs on the edge of the small table where they were working, and the audience groaned as she let the raw eggs fall into the hat. She handed Steve the shells.

"What do I do with these?"

"Just toss them," Roz said.

"Okay." Steve threw them into the hat.

"Not in there," Roz said, as if thoroughly exasperated with him.

"Oh, sorry."

"Never mind," Roz said. She picked up a wooden spoon and began stirring the contents of the hat.

"Don't you need some milk?" Steve fluttered a silk scarf over the table and instantly produced a quart carton of milk.

"Oh, thank you," Roz said. She paused her stirring while he poured a generous amount into her mixture. "That looks about right." She resumed stirring, and after a moment, removed the spoon.

"Ready?" Steve asked.

"Yes." Roz picked up the upside down hat and held it out toward him.

Steve extended the magic wand and tapped the hat's brim. A puff of smoke went up, momentarily obscuring the audience's view of the hat. Steve turned the hat over carefully above the table, and a small, fully decorated cake plopped out on to the surface. Steve pointed at it with his wand and a candle on top sprang into flame.

Steve gave the hat to Roz. She held it while he again swept the wand over it and tapped the edge. Then he reached inside and pulled out the faithful stuffed rabbit Rodin had used earlier in the week.

Everyone laughed and applauded.

Sara leaned toward Sadie. "He did it just as well as Mr. Rodin. No, even better. How do you think he lit the candle?"

"I have no idea," Sadie said.

They moved on to scarves that magically knotted together and unknotted, the stuffed bunny floating through the air, and Sara's beloved melon trick.

"Could I please borrow a dollar from someone in the audience?" Steve asked.

This time, Pastor Don offered a dollar bill and cheerfully wrote his name across it and handed it over to Roz.

"And now may I have a volunteer to hold the dollar for me?" Steve looked out over the crowd.

Sadie stuck her hand up high.

"Grandma!" Sara stared at her in shock. "I thought you didn't want to go onstage."

"It's my last chance," Sadie said, waving her hand in the air.

"Okay, the lady in front," Steve said, pointing to her with a knowing smile.

Sadie hurried up the steps. She caught a glimpse of Edwin lurking in the wings, grinning as she agreed to hold Pastor Don's dollar for Steve.

Going through Rodin's usual routine with hardly a ripple, she experienced what Sara had—watching the magician drape a scarf over her hand, then wave his wand above it. After a poof of color and smoke, Steve snatched away the scarf, and she stared stupidly at her empty hand.

"How did you do that?"

Steve laughed. "You tell me. Is it in your pocket?"

"No."

"Well, then, where did it go?"

Sadie eyed him closely, holding back a smile. "Since I've been here every night this week, I have a sneaking suspicion it's in the watermelon."

Everyone laughed, and Steve turned wide, innocent eyes toward the audience. "There's one in every crowd."

The people roared with laughter.

"And now, Mr....uh..." He turned panicky eyes on Sadie, and she could see a sheen of sweat on his brow. "What's the man's name?"

"Don Sweeting."

"Mr. Sweeting. Would you want to come up here and help us cut the watermelon?" Steve searched the crowd until he saw the tall African-American man leave his seat and make his way to the steps.

"Great. Thanks for helping," Steve said. "Roz, we need the knife."

As Pastor Don gained the stage, Roz took the butcher knife to Steve.

"Okay, let's see what we have here. Sadie, Mr. Sweeting, you can lean right in and watch, but not too close. This thing is sharp."

Steve cut open the melon, retrieved the dollar, and had Don assure the audience that it was his signature on the bill.

"Thank you very much." Steve bowed with a flourish, and everyone applauded loudly as Sadie and Don left the stage.

Other routines followed, including one Sadie had never seen Roz and Rodin perform. Even though he hadn't had a chance to rehearse, Steve pulled off each one flawlessly.

"He's pretty good," Theo said.

"Yes, he is." Sadie had to admire Steve's pluck. From where she sat in the front row, it was impossible to tell that his nerves were being tested tonight.

The show seemed to fly, and soon it was time for the grand finale—the disappearing cabinet. Even though the trick had gone well for the past week, Sadie still held her breath while Roz was out of sight. A glance at Roscoe told her she was not alone.

Steve pulled back the curtain on the cabinet, and the crowd cheered as Roz stepped out wearing a completely different outfit and cradling in her arms a live rabbit. Sadie squinted at the black-and-white spotted bunny.

"Wait a second, isn't that your rabbit?"

Sara, who was whooping and clapping, glanced over at her. "Yep, that's Zebra."

"Zebra?"

"Sort of a joke, Grandma."

"Okay." Sadie resumed her clapping as Roz put the bunny in a box and took Steve's hand for their final bows.

Edwin walked out on to the stage. As Roz and Steve exited stage right, he took the microphone and faced the grandstand.

"Ladies and gentlemen, that concludes our show for tonight. As you know, this is the final night of the fair. Thank you all for supporting the events. The midway will be open until ten o'clock." He paused, then gave an engaging smile. "See you next year."

Mac found the celebrators at the Depot, downing milk shakes and sundaes and telling Steve and Roz what they'd loved most about the show.

"And Mr. Rodin and Steve came by this morning to get Zebra, right before we left for the fairgrounds," Sara said, concluding her explanation of her rabbit's appearance in the show.

"Well, Zebra did a great job," Sadie said.

"Mac, have a seat." Edwin shifted his chair closer to Sadie's to make room for Mac between himself and Steve, who had ordered only coffee.

"How's Ainsley doing?" Steve asked.

Mac sighed. "He's all right. His lawyer came out from Denver. He'd just arrived a few minutes ago, and I left them to talk with a deputy in charge."

Steve nodded and took a sip of his coffee. "I'm glad his lawyer came tonight. Can I see Ainsley when I come to the office tomorrow?"

"If you come early enough," Mac said. "We'll be transferring him to Denver."

The waitress came over carrying a coffeepot and a mug for him. "Get you anything, Sheriff?" she asked as she poured.

"Nope, this is perfect." Mac took a sip of the coffee.

"I can't believe Ainsley actually broke into Edwin's house and stole that pipe," Roz said. Her voice caught and a mist of tears shone in her eyes.

"None of us likes it," Mac said. "It was hidden in his luggage. I'm just glad we caught on before he left town."

Steve lifted his chin and looked bleakly at Mac. "If I'd known, I would have said something. I honestly had no idea."

Roscoe leaned forward. "But how did he do it? I know Sadie asked around about duplicate keys and all that, but really, how did he get in there without Edwin knowing it?"

"Apparently, he borrowed Edwin's key ring during the first rehearsal, when he had Edwin practice the introduction. He took a picture of his house key, then slipped the ring back into Edwin's pocket without his ever knowing it."

"I heard the keys jingle." Roz let out a little moan. "Sadie picked up on it, not me. I still can't believe it."

"I don't get it," Sara said. "How could taking a picture of a key get him into the house?"

"Did he use a 3-D printer to make a new key?" Theo asked.

Mac shook his head. "Nothing that sophisticated. Those fancy printers are very expensive, and it takes quite a while for them to produce an item. No, we found Rodin's laptop in his room. He had deleted the photo of the key from his cell phone, but not before he sent it to his own e-mail. We found it on the laptop. From there, he was able to file out a duplicate key."

Theo stared at him. "Just from looking at a picture of it?"

Mac let out a sigh. "He'd had a lot of experience in making things, right, Steve?"

Steven nodded. "I've been making his tricks for years, but before that, he made the gadgets himself. He's a very clever man."

"And he laid the key beside a dime for scale," Mac added. "Once he got the photo on his computer, he could adjust it until the dime was exactly the right size. Then the key was the right size too, and he could file a blank into the exact shape he needed."

"I'm afraid the blank came from my store," Roscoe said.

"No one on earth is better at making small objects disappear than Ainsley," Steve said.

Alice's jaw dropped. "You mean the magician stole a blank key from Roscoe's store and filed out a duplicate to Edwin's house key?"

"That's exactly what he means," Roscoe said.

Mac nodded. "We'll go over that security footage from your store tomorrow afternoon, Roscoe, but I'm pretty sure that's how he did it." Mac turned to Steve. "I understand you were the only person allowed to handle his luggage. Did you not know he was carrying a small vise and a tool kit? He had several files in his big suitcase."

Steve shook his head. "If you'd have told me that yesterday, I'd have said you were crazy. But if you found it, I guess it must be so."

"Where's Richard Towne now?" Mac asked.

"Jerry and Jane gave him a room for the night," Edwin said. "He went over there after the show."

———

The minute she saw the new issue of *Colorado Mountain Life* in her mailbox, Sadie whipped out her phone to call Alice. Two months had passed since the fair, and school was well under way. Everyone in Silver Peak was battening down for the approaching winter. It was definitely time for a lighthearted family celebration.

"Can you and the kids come over tonight?" Sadie asked.

"I guess so," Alice said. "Can I bring anything?"

"How about ice cream? I think I'm in a pie-baking mood."

"You got the magazine."

Sadie laughed. "Yeah. I'll call Laura."

That evening, all of them plus Edwin gathered in Sadie's kitchen.

"I think it's appropriate that you all eat some of Grandma Wright's famous pie while I read you the article," Sadie said. "Theo, would you fix the hot chocolate please? I'll serve the pie, and Sara can get the ice cream. Alice, you can pour the coffee."

"Where did you get the raspberries for the pies, Grandma?" Sara asked, eyeing the two golden-brown pies sitting on the counter with a rather awed expression.

"I went back to Milo's a few days after the fair ended. Of course, I took Hank with me that time."

"Weren't the berries gone by then?" Theo asked.

"No, I found enough to freeze for this auspicious occasion. And I didn't see any bears."

Edwin chuckled. "What, no trumpet in your back pocket?"

"Hank was sufficient, thank you."

When everyone had their beverage of choice and a dish of pie and ice cream before them, Sadie opened the magazine to the article about the fair and its Colorado Wild Raspberry Baking Contest.

"Mountain dwellers gleaned the succulent fruit from secluded patches of raspberry canes, tucked into hidden niches on the hillsides," she read.

"Wow," Laura said. "That's quite the prose."

Sadie laughed and read on. The writer captured the busy hilarity of the fair and the tension that mounted as the entries were brought in for the contest.

"First place was awarded to Marisol Vidal, a striking young Mexican-American woman whose parents own a popular coffee shop in town." A wonderful picture of Marisol holding her blue ribbon rosette accompanied the text. Her brilliant smile lit up the page. "Ms. Vidal's Raspberry Gem Tarts won the judges' hearts."

Everyone laughed.

"I think that photographer was smitten with her," Alice said.

"Do you blame him?" Sadie went on, "In second place was Laura Finch, also a Silver Peak resident, who is self-employed as a public relations consultant."

"Yay." Sara grinned and clapped quietly, and Laura smiled.

Sadie paused and then read the next paragraph. "Ironically, Ms. Finch's cousin, Alice Macomb, placed third. Both women used the same raspberry pie recipe, handed down to them from their grandmother."

"He's almost right," Alice said, nodding at Laura. "Your grandmother, my great-grandmother."

"Close enough," Edwin said.

"Get this," Sadie said. "The judges declared that the decision was very difficult. Ms. Finch said, 'I'm delighted with my prize, but I almost think Alice deserves it more than I do. She had to face a grizzly bear the day she picked her wild raspberries.'"

"Man, they put the bear in," Theo said.

"I love it." Alice reached over and squeezed Laura's hand. "That was a sweet thing to say. Thank you."

"And last but not least," Sadie said in formal tones, "the recipes for Marisol Vidal's Raspberry Gem Tarts and the Finch-Macomb cousins' Wild Raspberry Pie can be found on page eighty-nine."

"Hooray!" This time, everyone applauded with Sara.

Sadie took her seat and handed the magazine to Edwin. "I'll pass this around, so you can all see the pictures. There's one of the midway and a gorgeous portrait of Marisol, plus a photo of the tarts and one of the line of pies on the judging table, and a cute one of Alice during the judging. Sara, you're in it too. Now, I'm going to eat my pie before the ice cream melts."

"That's a great spread." Edwin passed the magazine to Laura.

"Do you think they'll have it in stores today?" Alice asked. "I want to get about six copies."

"Can I have one to keep, Mom?" Sara asked.

"Sure, if I can get my hands on that many," Alice said.

"I actually got one in the mail today too," Laura said, passing the magazine to Alice. "I think they must have sent one to Marisol as well."

Sadie swallowed her first bite of pie and said, "Why don't you call Maggie Price, Alice? She could tell you what day the Market stocks the new magazines."

"They should have sent you one, Mom," Sara said.

Alice shrugged. "Well, I'm surprised my name is even in it. They only interviewed the first- and second-place winners. My recipe is only there because of a fluke."

Theo shook his head. "I'll bet the reporter wishes you'd won first place. Your bear story would have made a great lead."

Sadie took another bite of pie. Yes, Grandma's recipe was worthy of a prize and a magazine write-up. One more family memory to cherish. Her gaze met Edwin's. He smiled and slid his chair closer to her, so he could put his arm around her.

"Good pie," he said.

"Thanks."

"Great party."

"Oh, now you're buttering me up."

He laughed. "The town council wants me to ask you if you'll be chairman of the fair committee next year."

"Oh no. Roz did a great job."

"She's retiring herself," Edwin said. "She suggested you."

Sadie shook her head. "I repeat: No, but thank you. I always seem to have enough to do when the fair rolls around, without trying to run things. I'm sure someone very competent will step forward. Anne Hastings, for instance."

"I figured you'd decline," Edwin said with a sigh. "Anne is next on my list."

Sadie smiled and reached for her coffee mug. She looked around again at her loved ones and sent up a silent prayer of thanks.

About the Author

CAROLE JEFFERSON IS THE PEN NAME FOR A TEAM OF WRITERS who have come together to create the series Mysteries of Silver Peak. *Sleight of Hand* was written by Susan Page Davis. Susan is the author of more than sixty novels and novellas in the historical romance, mystery, and suspense genres. She is the mother of six and grandmother of ten. A Maine native, she now lives in western Kentucky with her husband, Jim. Visit her Web site at susanpagedavis.com.

The Watcher

SADIE SPEERS PULLED UP IN FRONT OF THE HOUSE AND TURNED off the engine. She didn't need to check the address. She'd had her eye on this house for years. The four-story Victorian, perched on the top of one of Silver Peak's steepest hills, was built in the Queen Anne style, dripping with gingerbread trim and lacy, ornately-carved woodwork and topped with a cupola. Sadie loved old houses, and this was one of the finest specimens in town, built, like most of the houses on Jefferson Street, in the heyday of the town's mining boom. Sadie's boyfriend, Edwin, lived in an elegant old Victorian directly across the street, and Sadie had seen this house many times and been curious about it. She'd never been inside though, and she was thrilled that Mabel Fleagle had asked her to come by today.

Sadie stepped out of the car and made her way up the cracked cement walkway that bisected a patch of overgrown crabgrass.

Little tufts of green sprung up between the bits of pavement. It smelled fresh after last night's spring storm, and the whole world seemed bright and green.

Mabel and her husband, Ardis, a contractor Sadie knew from his work restoring the Silver Peak Opera House, and many other small and large construction projects in Silver Peak, had recently bought the old Victorian and were fixing it up. Mabel had come into the Antique Mine, Sadie's antique shop, a few days back looking for furniture for the entryway, and Sadie had steered her toward a burled oak hall tree, a beautiful piece with a beveled mirror and hand-carved coat hooks, but Mabel hadn't been certain it would look right. Mabel had asked Sadie to come take a look at the space and give her expert opinion, and Sadie had been thrilled to do so, mostly so she could see the inside of such a stately home.

Movement on the covered front porch caught her eye as she started up the steps.

"Oh. Ardis." She was surprised to see him in the shadows of the porch. He was standing in front of the door, looking down at a piece of paper, an envelope clutched in one hand. A stack of magazines and bills had been tossed on the cushion of the wicker chair next to the front door.

"Hi, Sadie." Ardis looked up from the paper. He hesitated for a second, and then he gave her a smile, but it didn't reach his eyes. He wore a flannel shirt over his T-shirt and jeans, and everything was dusted with a fine layer of plaster powder. "Didn't mean to startle you." He was a small man, but strong, with thick dark hair and big glasses, but his shoulders were stooped, and he seemed somehow deflated. He stepped back and lowered the piece of paper he held in his hand.

"It's not a problem. I just didn't expect to see you there," Sadie said, joining him on the porch. The wooden planks needed a good sanding and coat of paint, but they seemed to be solidly built of good strong maple. She hesitated. She didn't want to be nosy, but something wasn't right. "Is everything okay?"

Ardis had glanced back down at the paper in his hands, and looked up again at her. He seemed confused by her question somehow.

"I'm sorry, Sadie," he said. "Please come on in. Mabel is waiting for you." He stepped back and gestured toward the front door.

"You sure you're okay?" Sadie asked. If there was anything she could do to help, she wanted to offer.

Ardis hesitated. He glanced back down at the paper in his hand, a single sheet of letter-size paper that had been folded into thirds, and then up at Sadie again.

"Everything is fine, I guess. It's just…" He held up the paper. "We just got this weird note in the mail, and it's throwing me off a little. It's from someone who claims to be watching the house."

"What?" Sadie wasn't sure what she'd been expecting, but it wasn't that. "Watching the house?"

"Here." He held out the paper to her, and she took it from his hands. "You're into mysteries, right? Take a look."

Sadie reached for the paper and looked down. It was a letter, printed on standard printer paper.

Dear Fleagles,

I am so glad you are all getting settled into your new home. Does Bitty like her room? It's always been one of my favorites. And Tyler's room has such a nice view of the street. You can see everything that goes on from there. It's so nice to have young blood in the house again. Have you found what's hidden in the basement yet? I think you'll be surprised.

The Watcher

Sadie read the note once, and then read through it again, trying to understand what she was reading.

"Oh my goodness," she said. "What is this? Who is this from?"

Ardis shrugged. "I wish I knew. This is the third letter like this we've gotten, signed by someone who calls himself The Watcher. But this is the first one that mentions the kids."

Sadie's stomach lurched. This was creepy enough, but to find out that there had been more letters like this?

"Are the others along the same lines?"

Ardis nodded. "Whoever it is says his family has been watching the house for generations, and now it's his turn. And from the stuff he's writing in the notes, it seems like he really is watching it."

"Oh my." Sadie was repeating herself, but she couldn't think of what else to say. This was disturbing. "When did they start?"

"The first one arrived just after we moved in, a little over two weeks ago. The second one came last week." He shook his head. "We thought the first one was a joke. A terrible, tasteless joke. When the second one came, we were a little concerned, but now, this…"

Sadie understood completely. This went beyond jokes. Someone knew his children's names and where their bedrooms were. This was criminal territory.

"Have you reported it to the police?" She held out the letter, and he took it back.

"No." He folded the letter up again and slipped it back inside the envelope, which Sadie could see was a standard white business envelope with no return address. "Again, we thought the other letters were nothing to worry about. But now…"

"I think you should," Sadie said. "This is really taking things too far."

"I think I should too," Ardis said.

"Who would do something like that?" Sadie asked. She'd seen some strange things in her life, but this was new. Something seriously unsettling was going on.

"I have no idea," Ardis said, shaking his head.

Ardis led Sadie inside the house and told his wife Mabel about the latest letter, and she was as shaken as he was. She agreed that the police had to be notified, and while Ardis called the sheriff's office, Mabel and Sadie measured the spot in the entryway for the hall tree. Sadie agreed that the piece at the shop was the perfect size, and would complement the antique mirror Mabel had hung on the opposite wall perfectly.

"It really is a lovely house," Sadie said, eyeing the staircase that led off the gracious main center hall to the second floor. The floors needed to be refinished, and the walls were scuffed and marred, and everything was coated in a fine layer of plaster dust, but she could see from here that the "bones" of the house were good.

"Would you like to see the rest of it?" Mabel asked.

Sadie hesitated. She would have liked nothing more than to take a tour of the historic home, but she knew now was probably not the best time.

"You've got your hands full at the moment," Sadie said, hitching her bag up on her shoulder. "I would love to take a peek at some point, but…"

"Honestly, I would appreciate the distraction," Mabel said. She brushed back a lock of hair that had escaped from her ponytail. "Otherwise I'll just sit here worrying until the police come, and probably afterward as well. If you're interested, I'd be happy to take you on a tour." Mabel was tall and willowy, and she had a confident, commanding presence. Sadie knew she'd been a horse trainer before she and Ardis had had children, but these days she had her hands full managing three kids. Sadie had no doubt her experience breaking unruly horses had come in handy trying to wrangle her brood.

"If you're sure…" Sadie hesitated.

"Of course I am."

Sadie looked at Mabel's no-nonsense jeans and plain white long-sleeved shirt and realized that Mabel probably didn't say too many things she didn't mean.

"Come on. What used to be the formal parlor is right through this doorway," Mabel said, gesturing at a room at the front of the house. The room was gracious and well-proportioned, and when the plaster molding around the ceiling fixture was repaired, it would be a lovely room.

"It used to have some rather unfortunate wood paneling, but we took that all down and brightened things up."

Sadie nodded. The walls were painted a warm grayish beige, and it looked modern and clean, though the room itself was historic.

"I like that marble fireplace," Sadie said. Mabel nodded and led her into the formal dining room, with another beautifully carved mantle currently coated in a thick layer of peeling paint, and then to a more relaxed family room.

"We're going to open up this wall," Mabel said, gesturing to the wall the back of the room, "and combine it with the kitchen to create an open flow."

Sadie nodded. With the wall gone, there would be a more modern feel to the rooms, and she thought it would be lovely. This kitchen itself was small and outdated, but Mabel explained that they intended to update the cabinets and appliances and put in an island and some high stools. She then led Sadie through an old-fashioned larder and down a set of rickety stairs, where Mabel showed her a built-in wine cellar and storage areas. It had the dank smell typical of basements, but it was vast, and Sadie got a sense of how large this home really was.

"What's that?" Sadie asked, gesturing at a line of numbers etched into the wood on the beam above the built-in wine racks. From here it looked like a 20, a 23, and another 20—or maybe a 28? It was hard to tell.

Mabel shrugged. "Who knows? There are numbers like this carved a few places throughout the house, but your guess is as good as mine as to why they're there. That's part of the charm of old houses for me. So many people through the years have left their mark."

They went back up to the main hallway, and Mabel led her up the stairway to the second floor. A few of the boards were loose and a couple of the balusters were missing, but the staircase was built out of mahogany and was carved with intricate swirls and chains of flowers.

"Do you know when the house was built?" Sadie asked, running her hand along the banister. With a little sanding and some stain, it would be as good as new.

"1882," Mabel said. "It was built by John Franklin."

"The railroad owner?" Sadie had taught history at the high school before she'd retired to open up her shop, and she'd come across the name John Franklin in some local history books. John Franklin had been one of the men responsible for bringing the railroad to Silver Peak, opening up the local mines and the surrounding area to development. He was usually thought of as something of a robber baron, a titan of industry, which Sadie knew was not meant to be entirely flattering. Mabel nodded as she stepped into the hallway of the second floor. Well, that explained the grandeur of the house and the expensive details that even decades of neglect couldn't obscure.

"The house actually has a really interesting history," Mabel said. She showed Sadie a bathroom in need of serious updating, but containing a gorgeous claw-foot tub—and the master bedroom. It had another marble fireplace and a nice view through big windows. "Legend has it that he died in this house."

"He was poisoned, right?" Sadie remembered this story.

"Exactly." Mabel nodded. "And they never found out who did it."

Below them, Sadie could hear the front door open, and then heavy footsteps in the entryway. A moment later, she heard the deep resonant voice she recognized as belonging to Sheriff Mac Slattery. The police had arrived to investigate the letters.

"So your house has an unsolved murder." That wasn't something you expected to find house shopping. "Do you know where in the house he died?" *What if he'd died right where they were standing?*

"I found some old newspaper accounts about it, and they say he was found in his study, though no one seems to know exactly where in the house that was. Apparently the house has gone through several big renovations over the years, and rooms were reconfigured, so no one seems quite sure."

"That's probably for the best," Sadie said, though a piece of her couldn't resist wondering. "It would be hard to sleep if you knew it had happened in your bedroom."

Mabel nodded. "Who knows if it's even true, but that's what they told us. We thought it was a fun piece of trivia, that it added character to the place."

She looked like there was more to say, and Sadie waited for her to go on. She had a distressed look on her face. When she didn't continue, Sadie prompted, "Is everything okay?"

"I was thinking about the first mysterious letter we got," Mabel said. "The one that arrived two days after we moved in."

"It said something about John Franklin." She shook her head. "I'm trying to remember what it said exactly. Something about how The Watcher's ancestors have been watching the house since John Franklin's day. I'm trying to remember the exact wording, but it suggested that if we knew who killed John Franklin, we'd know who he was."

Sadie couldn't help it. She wondered if it was true. If she could help Ardis and Mabel figure out who had poisoned John Franklin all those years ago, would that end their Watcher problem now?

But how in the world would she figure out a mystery no one had solved in more than 150 years?

A Note from the Editors

WE HOPE YOU ENJOYED MYSTERIES OF SILVER PEAK, PUBLISHED by the Books and Inspirational Media Division of Guideposts, a nonprofit organization that touches millions of lives every day through products and services that inspire, encourage, help you grow in your faith, and celebrate God's love.

Thank you for making a difference with your purchase of this book, which helps fund our many outreach programs to military personnel, prisons, hospitals, nursing homes, and educational institutions.

We also create many useful and uplifting online resources. Visit Guideposts.org to read true stories of hope and inspiration, access OurPrayer network, sign up for free newsletters, download free e-books, join our Facebook community, and follow our stimulating blogs.

To learn about other Guideposts publications, including the best-selling devotional *Daily Guideposts*, go to Guideposts.org/Shop, call (800) 932-2145, or write to Guideposts, PO Box 5815, Harlan, Iowa 51593.